ALLURE OF THE VAMPIRE KING

BLOOD FIRE SAGA BOOK 1

BELLA KLAUS

Copyright © 2020 by BELLA Klaus.

All rights reserved. This book or any portion thereof may not be reproduced or used in any manner whatsoever without the express written permission of the publisher.

www.BellaKlaus.com

CHAPTER ONE

*T*here were two types of vampires in this world, preternaturals and supernaturals. Right now, I couldn't work out which of the two followed me through the dark.

I pulled up the collar of my leather jacket and strode down the path, cringing at the smoky magic hovering behind me like a wraith. It didn't matter which kind had tracked me down to Grosvenor Square in London—I had hoped to never see a vampire again.

Supernatural vampires were alive and only required the smallest amount of blood for sustenance, while the preternaturals were undead and needed blood to avoid reverting into unmoving corpses.

While a preternatural vampire could drain your

blood and leave you an exsanguinated corpse, a supernatural vampire could break your heart.

My gaze darted across the lawn and into the trees that bordered the garden square. He could be anywhere, waiting for his opportunity to pounce. I could sense most magical beings, but I didn't wield an ounce of power, which was unfortunate because immense speed and strength would be useful for getting me out of my current predicament.

Echoing footsteps synchronized with mine, and a ripple of anxiety ran down my back. It was an October morning, hours before sunrise. I'd been foolish—I realized that, now. Three years of never seeing or sensing a vampire, and I'd almost forgotten that the creatures ever ventured into the human world. But the hackles rising on my back could only mean one thing:

He was getting close.

I quickened my pace through the paths, my gaze darting side to side, both hands clutching the Dharma salt I kept in my pockets—a habit Aunt Arianna instilled in me at a young age.

My aunt was a witch, as was everyone else in my coven who lived in the supernatural city of Logris. Me? I was a Neutral—a powerless mortal who moved out to start a new life in London. I was also the magicless mortal about to become a vampire's snack.

Shadows lengthened across the lawn that made up most of Grosvenor Square, intersecting the path ahead. Maybe it was a supernatural vampire, the harmless kind. Sunrise was less than an hour away—a preternatural wouldn't risk getting caught out in the middle of daylight. But why would a supernatural stalk a human?

My breaths became shallow, and my pulse roared between my ears. Thirty more feet. Thirty more feet and I would leave this empty square and enter the relative safety of the streets.

At this time of the morning, postmen made deliveries, security staff in the surrounding embassies changed shifts, and people traveled into work around the streets. All I needed were a few more steps, and I'd be free of this stalker.

Pulling out fistfuls of salt from my pocket, I broke into a jog. The vampiric presence at my back kept at the same distance. If it was a preternatural vampire, it would snatch me out of the square and soar into the sky. At least that's what I thought they did.

Nobody I knew had ever encountered an undead creature. According to what they taught us at the Academy, they were extinct.

If I reached the crystal shop without getting clawed or bitten or eaten, I promised myself never to venture outside in the dark. At least not without an appropriate magical repellent or an Uber.

A yellow DHL van slowed through the trees and parked outside the entrance. As the driver opened the door and walked around to the trunk, I broke into a sprint and bolted out into the street.

He staggered back and clutched his chest. "Blimey, you gave me a fright."

"Sorry." A nervous laugh bubbled up to the back of my throat.

As I walked around the van and crossed to the other side of the street, the presence behind me stopped moving, as though observing me from within the park. I didn't dare to turn around and look.

Releasing the salt from my right hand, I rifled through the pocket of my leather jacket for my keys.

Salt crystals stuck to my damp palms. I ignored them and jogged the fifty feet along the square, passing the Crystal Shop's side display, rounded the corner of Upper Brook Street, and reached the entrance.

At six-fifty-five, Upper Brook Street was a hive of activity with people streaming into the Starbucks at the end of the block and to the Pret a Manger sandwich bar across the road.

While none of the humans fetching their morning coffee could help me fend off any kind of vampire, they carried enough recording devices to deter any otherworldly attacker.

The Crystal Shop was a glass-fronted store with its insignia emblazoned in calligraphic script. Large amethyst and citrine geodes stood in the display among rose-quartz spheres and delicate-looking pieces fashioned into protective bracelets and amulets.

As I hurried into its doorway, the keys slipped from my trembling fingers and fell onto the doorstep with a clank.

The presence within the park shifted, making my skin tighten into goosebumps. Cold terror barreled through my insides, and a curtain of red hair fell across my face. I dropped down to my knees, snatched the keys off the ground, and jammed the key in the lock.

Somehow, I managed to unlock the door, nearly crying with relief at the warm, frankincense-and-myrrh-scented air wafting through the shop's interior. After staggering inside, I locked the door and glanced through the glass display across the road into the empty park.

Even if whoever had stalked me was gone, it was too early to feel safe. Preternatural vampires needed invitations to enter people's dwellings, but the rules about stores where the owner lived upstairs were shaky.

Just in case its preternatural magic deemed the crystal shop a public space, I rushed to the counter and picked up a two-foot-tall pillar of Dharma salt.

Most human crystal stores sold Himalayan salt, a rose-pink substance they used in cooking, to make lamps, and in spa treatments. Dharma salt came from a monastery in the same mountain region, but the monks who mined it were mages who blessed the crystals with the power to absorb evil.

If a preternatural vampire tried to cross the threshold, the salt would suck out its corrupted magic, leaving it an unmoving corpse.

At least that was the theory. Nobody in recent history was powerful or crazy enough to create a mindless blood-drinking monster with an insatiable thirst.

Supernatural vampires were bad enough. I squeezed my eyes shut and exhaled a long breath. How many times had I told myself not to think of vampires? Especially one in particular whose very name made my veins sear with anger.

I stormed across the shop floor, picking up a pamphlet that had drifted down from a stand. Even if supernatural vampires didn't leave people bloodless husks, they certainly left them loveless.

"Mera?" Istabelle's muffled voice drifted down from the upstairs apartment.

"It's only me," I shouted back. "Did you sense the presence in the square?"

"What?"

I walked around the counter and stood at the door separating the shop from the hallway that led to Istabelle's home. "Something followed me across Grosvenor Square."

"What?" she repeated.

"Never mind," I shouted in a louder voice. "Where's the delivery?"

"It's coming at eleven."

"Right," I muttered. Last night as I was cleaning up, Istabelle had told me the delivery man was on his way.

Exhaling my exasperation in a long sigh, I leaned against the counter and glanced around the shop's interior. The only reason I'd come early was to unpack the important shipment in time for opening hours.

Apart from being a little sketchy on details, Istabelle Bonham-Sackville was a great boss. After the grand disaster that had caused me to leave Logris, I'd become an embarrassment to my coven and a cautionary tale to others on the dangers of loving above one's station.

Istabelle hadn't cared that I'd made myself a public spectacle. She understood what it was like to be born without magic and live among supernatural beings.

I exhaled a sharp breath through my nostrils. We weren't completely magicless, it was just that our power was neutral—completely unusable, which meant we appeared on the outside as humans, regardless of our actual supernatural race. Istabelle had even taken me as her apprentice and taught me crystal and herb healing.

Aunt Arianna said she was at least a century old,

but Istabelle looked no older than sixty and traveled the world searching for magical objects. Her ability to sense power meant that she could also harness magical stones for basic protection and healing.

Istabelle even found me an apartment around the corner from the shop—something out of the reach of a twenty-four-year-old with zero family wealth.

Sure, it was tiny and consisted of one room, but it was in the heart of Mayfair and within walking distance of Hyde Park, Bond Street, and a whole host of other London attractions.

By now, the sun had risen, and pedestrians streamed down Upper Brook Street on their way to work. After lighting the incense sticks, I unlocked the cash register, replenished the smudge sticks, dusted the dream-catchers, and reached under the counter for the key to the basement, where Istabelle kept the grimoires and other ancient books. With two-and-a-half hours until opening time and no deliveries to unpack, that left plenty of time to catch up with my reading.

I turned toward the basement door, and a frantic banging on the glass sent my heart tightening with panic.

If that was my stalker... Shaking off those thoughts and putting my faith in the Dharma salt, I peered over my shoulder.

Beatrice stood in the doorway, her mahogany hair blown in all directions by the wind. Like me, she stood five-five, but unlike me, she had gorgeous, tanned skin and the curves to fill out a Dolce and Gabbana suit. I wasn't so well-endowed, with nervous energy that kept me thin.

I jogged across the shop floor, darting around the stand of postcards and pamphlets. Beatrice was my best friend in London and knew nothing of the Supernatural World. We'd met in my first month here at a speed-dating Meetup and ended up finding each other more interesting than the men.

Beatrice beckoned at me to hurry. I glanced down at my watch and frowned. Seven-thirty? She worked for an international tax consultancy around the corner and didn't start work until nine.

I unlocked the door and pulled it open, letting in a rush of cold air. Beatrice barrelled into the shop with a chuckle, and bumped her stilettos into the Dharma salt pillar I'd left at the entrance.

"What are you doing in Central London so early?" I asked.

"Oh. My. Aftershocks." She raised her arms, wiggling her fingers in a jazz-hands movement.

I took in her flushed cheeks, sparkling brown eyes, rumpled shirt, and creased skirt. She'd worn that navy blue suit yesterday, and her hair looked like someone had backcombed it with large fingers.

"Did you work all night again?" I asked.

"I had a date with the most amazing man in Berkeley Square." Beatrice stepped back and beamed.

"Can I nip into your flat and change into a fresh suit?"

"Sure. But what happened last night?" Beatrice kept a few outfits at my place, which made going out after work easier. I reached into my jacket pocket and pulled out the keys.

"Thanks, love." Beatrice plucked the keys from my hand and launched into her story.

She'd been swiping through one of those dating apps and got matched with a Swiss Banker called Christian. After swapping some pictures and chatting through the afternoon, he asked her out for coffee, which led to dinner at Hakkasan, an exclusive Chinese restaurant five minutes away.

My brows drew together. "How did Christian get reservations at such short notice?"

Beatrice waved my question away and went on to describe a steamy evening that made my eyes bulge and my cheeks turn hot.

It wasn't like I was a virgin or a prude. I'd been with one person—once, and it had been the happiest and most pleasurable experience of my life. What happened hours after would forever make me link love to heartbreak.

My spirits plummeted, and I could no longer focus on Beatrice's exciting tale of leather paddles and cuffs. The buzzing of her phone cut through my morbid thoughts, and she stopped talking to reach into the pocket of her laptop bag.

"Is that Christian?" I asked.

Beatrice glanced down at the screen of her smartphone and grinned. "Aw… He misses me already." She texted something back and wrapped an arm around my shoulders. "Meet for lunch?"

"Okay."

"My treat!" With a happy chuckle, she jogged through the shop, opened the door, and disappeared around the corner to cut across Grosvenor Square.

I scratched my head, marveling at Beatrice's adventurous spirit. The woman was an accountant, but there was nothing prudent about her personality.

Beatrice said that life was short and the time she had to enjoy her youth was even shorter. Because of this, she seized every opportunity for happiness, no matter how brief or if it would end in disappointment or heartbreak.

My shoulders sagged, and I clicked the latch. I wish I could be free like Beatrice, but every time a man showed even the slightest bit of interest in me, my mind conjured up images of how things could go wrong. And thoughts like that sent me into a spiral of despair.

I clutched the amethyst pendant that was supposed to stop negative thoughts and felt for a pulse of power. Empty. No wonder I'd fallen into thinking about what had happened in Logris.

"Time to hit the books," I muttered to myself. Next Monday, Istabelle would test me on the properties of somniferous herbs—plants like valerian root, lavender, and chamomile, which helped people sleep.

If I couldn't answer her questions on their magical properties, she would be disappointed, and I couldn't let her down after everything she'd done for me these three years.

As far as subterranean libraries went, Istabelle's was pretty cozy. A little larger than my studio apartment, its walls consisted of mahogany shelves that extended from the white-tiled floors to its twelve-foot-high ceiling.

A pair of bright table lamps provided atmospheric light and were perched on a wooden desk that stood in the middle of the room. On either side of the workspace was a pair of the most comfortable battered leather armchairs.

As I reached the bottom of the mahogany spiral staircase, I inhaled the crisp scent of preserving crystals. Some of the items she kept down here were priceless, although I never got the chance to see them. Istabelle hadn't yet given me access to the storeroom she secured beyond a hidden entrance in the shelves.

My fingers grazed the herbal compendiums, but the memory of this morning's stalking had me drifting to the other side of the room, where Istabelle kept tomes about supernatural beings and a few ancient diaries she had amassed from probate sales.

Why would a vampire follow me across the

square? After my final humiliating night in Logris, I was a joke within the supernatural community. None of them would waste their time tracking me to London just to watch me and do nothing.

One of the leather tomes along the left of the library caught my eye: THE IMMORTAL VAMPIRE by Magnus Eaglecrest. I tried pulling it off the shelf, but it wouldn't budge until I gave it a hard tug. Feeling the strain of its weight against my biceps, I clenched my teeth and placed it on the table.

If this was a vampire movie, it would have landed with a thud and a cloud of dust, but I cleaned twice a week and replenished the library's preserving crystals monthly.

After settling into the buttery-soft armchair, I flipped over the first few pages of thick parchment that felt as heavy as leather.

Like most creatures of the Supernatural World, the vampire may live forever until killed. After thousands of years of living, some vampires tire of existence and allow their souls to ascend the mortal plane. To return, the vampire must undergo three challenges.

This was all very interesting, but not the information I needed. I turned several more pages, only stopping when my eye caught the following text.

Should the supernatural vampire succumb to the wielder of flame, his soul will remain in his corpse. Upon death, his heart will putrefy, and he will rise as a preternatural vampire—a being of unbridled evil.

To prevent this terrible occurrence, the vampire corpse must be tethered to stone, its heart removed and preserved to prevent putrefaction.

I flipped ahead, muttering under my breath, "How do I protect myself from vampires?"

Back at the academy, we learned that all vampires found Dharma salt repellent, but only the preternatural kind found it deadly. Perhaps it was related to the putrefying heart.

Sunlight, silver, and natural fire repelled the undead, preternaturals, but the supernaturals remained immune to such weapons. I skimmed through the entire book, looking for anything else, and ended up engrossed in the author's study on vampire reproduction habits. Only one in a thousand vampire females were capable of giving birth.

On the rare occasions they produced a pure-blooded child, the offspring would become extremely powerful and be immediately elevated to the status of a king.

Vampire King.

A shudder seized my spine, and I clenched my teeth, kicking myself for not replacing the amethyst crystal around my neck. The mere mention of that loathsome title stirred memories in me I needed to suppress.

"Mera, dear?" Istabelle's voice filled the library. "Time to open the shop."

"Sorry. I lost track of time." I rose from the armchair and headed up the spiral staircase.

Istabelle stood in the middle of the shop floor, clad in a fitted silk dress of flamingo pink. A thick belt in the same fabric cinched her in at the waist and a quadruple string of pearls broke up the bright color.

Today, she wore a pair of ivory combs in her white, cotton-candy hair, pulling the mass of undefined curls back behind her ears.

"Go on, then." She swept her arm to the door, where a blond man hopped from foot to foot on the doorstep.

Even with his head down, I could tell by the willowy frame and honey blond highlights that this was Jonathan.

My lips tightened.

The man wasn't unattractive, and he seemed sort-of okay. I only wished he would stop using his weekly sound bath sessions to ask me out on dates.

Most clients lay in the treatment rooms with their eyes closed, enjoying the feel of the black tourmaline crystals soaking up negative energy from their chakras, but not Jonathan.

He watched me the entire time I walked around the treatment table, striking Tibetan singing bowls with the mallet. Jonathan talked over their healing chimes, asking me if I wanted to go down the road for coffee, across the road for a sandwich, round the corner for lunch, dinner, whatever.

Each time I said no, hoping he would give up because he clearly wasn't interested in a sound bath, but each time, he insisted on booking another session. The rent on a store in central London was exorbitant, and we couldn't refuse business.

I sent Istabelle a pained glance, but she swept across the shop floor and rounded the counter. My gaze flicked back to the glass door, where Jonathan now stood with a raised hand and a tiny smile.

"Sorry for the late opening." I opened the door, letting in a gust of drizzly wind.

He wiped his feet on the doormat. "It's about this morning's sound bath."

My heart filled with hope. "Do you need to cancel?"

"Can I postpone it until the afternoon? I have a stock take at work and—"

"No problem," I said with a tight smile. "Is three okay with you?"

He gave me a jaunty salute. "It's a date."

Before I could contradict Jonathan, a man in a FedEx uniform slipped through the front door, holding a small package. "Delivery for the Crystal Shop?"

I eyed the inch-thick envelope-sized box. "I'll sign for it."

Jonathan said something about seeing me later. I gave him an absent nod and signed the delivery man's electronic touchscreen with a stylus. After handing me the package, he left, and I brought it to the counter.

If this was the delivery Istabelle was expecting, it certainly didn't require anyone to come in early. I weighed it in my hand, feeling no more than half a pound, and turned it around. It felt nothing like the usual packages we received via courier, but it was addressed to the business, rather than Istabelle herself.

I walked to the door that led up to her apartment and knocked. "Istabelle? Special delivery."

"What's inside?" she shouted back.

"Hold on." I opened a drawer beneath the desk and fumbled for a box cutter. After slicing through the tape holding the cardboard together, I eased out its flaps, revealing an unmarked velvet box. As soon as I touched the box, it thrummed with power.

My throat dried. Whatever was inside felt rare and expensive—not meant for the hands of an apprentice. I turned to the door and shouted, "Something extremely powerful."

"Open it." Istabelle said.

I raised a shoulder. Perhaps I'd underestimated her willingness to trust me with priceless objects.

Inside the box lay a bracelet made of faceted citrine hearts, each about an inch in diameter and held together with a chain so delicate it resembled a single strand of hair.

A breath caught in the back of my throat. Citrine was a common enough gemstone that we recommended for those wanting to boost their happiness and wealth but something like this had the juice to make millionaires.

To my naked eye, each heart was flawless, with a triple-A gemstone-grade clarity that reminded me of pale fire.

"Did you order a citrine bracelet?" I asked.

"No."

My brows drew together. Who in the Natural World would send such an item to a shop that sold crystals? Based on its power alone, it was worth nearly everything we had on the shelves, including the three-foot-tall geodes.

Istabelle didn't ask any more questions about the bracelet, so I reached for the lid, ready to place it in the safe.

As soon as my fingers touched the velvet, the bracelet snaked up my hand and locked itself around my wrist.

I sucked in a breath through my teeth. The wretched thing wasn't just an inert magical item, someone had enchanted it to capture one of our wrists.

The question was, why?

CHAPTER TWO

I stared down at the bracelet glittering on my arm, turning it stone by stone for signs of a clasp. The annoying thing was seamless, appearing bound by magic.

"Istabelle," I shouted. "Please, come down."

The older woman didn't answer, and I hoped she wasn't on the phone to Australia or somewhere like that, arranging another long-distance purchase.

My boss sourced magical stones from all over the world, coming in varying levels of power, but this was the first item we'd received that had ever done something sentient.

I reached into the counter drawer, picked up a pair of wire cutters, and slipped them between two of the heart-shaped stones.

The door opened, and a customer staggered in, clutching her belly. She was thin, wearing a pinstriped pencil suit, indicating that she probably worked in one of the offices nearby. Ropes of greasy blonde hair hung over her pale face, which looked at odds with her smart attire and laptop-sized Louis Vuitton bag.

I shoved the cutters back into the drawer and straightened. "Welcome to the Crystal Shop," I said in my best shopkeeper voice. "How may I help—"

"Do you have something for upset stomachs?" She held on to a shelf displaying crystal balls, barely able to stand.

"Are you alright?" I walked around the counter, crossed the shop floor, and stared down at the woman's source of pain.

I couldn't see magic—only feel it—but the energy radiating from her torso was rough and jagged, reminding me of daggers too blunt and rusty to cut. They weren't just jutting out of her but moving.

My gaze snapped to the woman's face, which was contorted with pain. This was a psychic attack.

There was an ethic for healing. If I saw something was wrong with a person, I couldn't just fix it without their knowledge or consent.

Istabelle taught me that it would be a violation. I had to ask her if she needed help, if she wasn't a client, bring it up in conversation, and then offer.

Psychic attacks at this level weren't deliberate. There wasn't usually a human sitting somewhere with a voodoo doll, sending negative vibes.

A person working in a hostile office where they were the target of malevolent thoughts could find themselves feeling the negativity in their physical body. Attacks like this occurred when the thoughts coalesced into shards of energy too powerful to be ignored.

The woman stared up at me, her eyes wide. "Do you have a natural remedy for stomach aches?"

I guided her to the corner, where two small armchairs were arranged around the shelves of esoteric books. "Take a seat, and I'll bring over a few items."

Sometimes, all a crystal required was to be in the presence of the person who needed them to work. Without touching her or placing my hands on her body, I could already tell that her biggest problem was psychic protection and not an upset stomach.

I walked across the room to the trays where we kept the protective crystals and stopped at the ones already polished into pendants.

My fingers lingered over the display. Onyx, obsidian, and black tourmaline. All three had similar properties in that they protected the user from negative energy. While the first two tended to absorb the energy, black tourmaline transmuted it into positive. My instincts guided me to the black tourmaline.

I turned around to take another look at the woman, whose features relaxed. Without thinking too much about it, I let my gaze snap to the basket of smooth pendants and selected one nearly the size of my palm.

"How about this?" I walked back to the woman and placed the pendant over her solar plexus chakra.

Chakras were the body's energy centers. According to what Istabelle taught me, we had seven, and the solar plexus dealt with weight, self-esteem, and boundaries. It was also the area that most commonly received psychic attacks.

The woman inhaled a deep breath and sighed. "That's so much better than the antacids they sold me at the chemist. I'll have to thank my sister for recommending your shop. How much is it?"

Warmth filled my chest. The best part of this job was seeing the difference these crystals could make in a customer's wellbeing.

We'd have to find a chain long enough for the pendant to hang close to the solar plexus, and a session or two with the sound bath would break up those energy forms. If she was willing, I could teach her ways to protect herself from all the attacks.

"A crystal this size is 29.99," I replied with a smile.

She reared back, her nose wrinkling. "For a poxy stone?"

My lips formed a tight line. How could I tell her that this particular stone had magical properties that would not only absorb the negativity thrown her way but transform it into something positive?

Comments like that would lead to a barrage of

questions demanding proof of magical ability, threatening the exposure of the Supernatural World.

"This particular piece of black tourmaline was sourced from Asia," I replied.

"Black tourmaline, huh?" She pulled out her smartphone and fired up her eBay app.

After tapping in the name, she huffed. "It says here I can get a large piece for seven pounds, including shipping."

I raised a shoulder and walked back to the counter, with the crystal in my palm. Istabelle taught me never to argue with customers over our prices. If they couldn't see or feel the value of our products, well, that was their decision.

The few supernatural customers who came here never balked because they knew what they were buying. Some humans were open to new age and natural healing, but this lady seemed to place more value in material things like her designer accessories than in her health.

She stood and snatched a copy of The Crystal Bible off the shelf. "I can get this cheaper on Amazon, too."

"Alright." I pulled out a drawer where we placed crystals that needed cleansing.

Since the black tourmaline pendant had relieved the woman's pain, we couldn't sell it to anyone else without removing any traces of her or her attackers' energies.

With a huff, she threw the book down on the chair and stomped out of the store, bringing in a blast of cool air from outside.

I rested my hands on the counter, watching her stride across the road. With each step she took toward the other side, her posture curled in on itself. Now that she'd left the store's protective environment, her pain had returned.

The door leading to the apartment opened, and Istabelle poked out her fluffy head. "You called?"

I showed her my wrist. "The delivery just attached itself to me. Can you help me get it off?"

Istabelle's gray brows drew together. "I didn't order firestone."

My gaze dropped to the transparent heart-shaped crystals. "I thought this was citrine."

She shook her head. "Firestone only takes the appearance of triple-A-grade citrine," she said in lecture mode. "The difference is its temperature. While citrine is warm, firestone has an absence of heat until activated."

"How do you activate firestone?" The words slipped from my lips before I could stop them.

What I really wanted to know was how to take off the bracelet, who sent it, and why in the Natural World it had decided to attach itself to me.

Istabelle launched into an explanation of the stone's immense capacity to store and discharge fire-based energy. There were few magical volcanoes around the world, such as the one beneath the Aegean Sea.

Magical miners used the stones to gather and store fire for warfare. Firestone was one of the reasons why the supernatural communities around the world seldom went to war. Each held an arsenal of stored energy powerful enough to destroy entire cities.

But the real question was why someone had turned this stone into jewelry and sent it here.

Istabelle picked up the cardboard box and frowned. "There's no postmark on the packaging." Her gaze wandered to the velvet case. "And that has a magic muffling enchantment."

I chewed my lip. "What are you saying?"

"Whoever sent this knew you were sensitive to magic and wanted you in particular to open it."

My heart sank. Nobody from Logris, except Aunt Arianna and a few close relatives, knew I was here. My birthday was close, but they always sent gifts to my apartment, not the shop.

Istabelle opened the drawer, slipped on goggles and a pair of gloves, and pulled out a pair of diamond shears. My stomach trembled at the thought that she'd ignored the wire cutters and gone straight for the item that could cut through magic.

"Turn your head, dear," she said.

I did as she said, feeling the shears slip beneath

the tiny string holding together the crystals. She snipped and hissed out a breath.

"What's happened?" I glanced down at the bracelet, which still lay in place around my wrist. "What happened to the wire?"

She dangled it between her fingers. "Unfortunately, the stones have bonded to your skin. This level of magic is beyond our capabilities. I'm afraid you'll need to see a practitioner in Logris."

My heart skipped several beats. Not just because I had the magical equivalent of a bomb casing wrapped around the wrist of my right arm. The thought of returning to Logris filled me with nauseous anxiety. It was where so many had witnessed that night of heartbreak and humiliation.

I shook my head. "There's got to be somewhere else."

Istabelle placed a hand on my shoulder. "You'll have to face them sometime. We may not be magical, but we live long lives and the more time you spend out of your community, the more you'll age."

"Maybe I don't want to live beyond a hundred years."

"Perhaps not, but you can't wait around to see what that firestone might do."

She was right, but I wasn't ready to face anyone from my old city. I exhaled a long sigh, trying to expel the boulders of dread weighing down my belly. "Do you have any books about firestone downstairs?"

"There are several, but I recommend you see a professional immediately."

"I'll..." My throat dried. The last thing I wanted to do was return to Logris. By now, everyone would have learned about my awful exit. "I'll think about it."

Istabelle stepped back, offering me a patient smile. "Whatever you say. I'll come down later to relieve you for lunch."

For the next few hours, I couldn't stop thinking about the firestone hearts around my wrist. They weren't a bracelet because nothing was holding them together. I slid my fingers beneath the stone, but it was like trying to separate my fingernails. The stones felt like they'd become part of my body.

In between unpacking a delivery of new books and serving customers, I tried everything I could think of to dislodge the stones. Onyx, which was supposed to remove negative attachments, didn't have any effect and neither did any of the flower remedy samples we kept around the shop for psychic protection.

The morning raced by, and Istabelle returned to the shop floor at twelve to replenish our display of rose quartz hearts. Rose quartz was our biggest seller. It radiated a gentle, unconditional love, strengthened the heart chakra, and boosted happiness.

I wore it continuously during my first year working at the Crystal shop, drawing on its strength to help me overcome my past. Some women bought it by the pouchful because it helped the wearer attract love while enhancing self-esteem.

At twelve-thirty, Beatrice strode into the store, her chocolate-brown eyes sparkling with happiness and a chignon with loose tendrils of hair framing her heart-shaped face. She wore a navy blue dress tailored to skim her curvaceous figure.

This was one person who certainly didn't need rose quartz, as she had no trouble attracting men.

She flashed Istabelle a dazzling smile. "Hello Mrs. Bonham-Sackville, I'm here to whisk Mera away for a long lunch."

"Take as much time as you need." Istabelle waved me away.

I wasn't sure if she was talking about lunch or making a decision to see a healer in Logris about my firestone problem. Either way, I zipped around the counter and hurried to my friend.

"Thanks." After shouldering on my leather jacket, I looped my arm through Beatrice's, and strode out into Upper Brook Street and rounded the corner to Grosvenor Square.

Beatrice glanced over her shoulder. "I booked us a table at Gordon Ramsay's Bar—"

"Sorry, Bea," I said with a groan. "Can we eat at mine? I'm having a bit of a problem."

Her steps faltered. "What's wrong?"

I pulled up my sleeve. "This bracelet won't come off."

"Try warm water and lots of soap." She reached into the pocket of her jacket and extracted her smartphone. "Let me cancel the reservation and get us something out of Deliveroo. Is Thai okay?"

I inhaled a deep breath, my heart melting with gratitude. Beatrice and I were so different. While she was an extraverted tax specialist who loved taking risks, I was an introverted shop assistant who liked to play things safe.

Maybe it was because of our differences that we got along. She was generous, exciting, and always willing to show me new things and places around London. I thought she liked my stabilizing influence, and knew she loved being my guinea pig for herbs and crystals and healing techniques. Whatever it was between us, we worked to create a balanced friendship.

We were about to cross the road to cut through Grosvenor Square, but I steered her alongside the Georgian houses that bordered the square, saying I wanted to take the long route.

Each of the buildings bordering the huge garden was pretty much the same: seven-stories tall, brick townhouses that contained offices, embassies, and those wealthy enough to afford an apartment in Mayfair.

Istabelle was fortunate enough to have purchased

an entire floor between World Wars One and Two and had paid off the mortgage decades ago. I still couldn't believe my luck.

"Christian's been texting all morning," Beatrice said with a sigh.

"Christian Gray?" I gave her a playful bump on the shoulder.

She chuckled. "He may as well have been last night."

A giggle bubbled up in the back of my throat. "No mere man could be that good."

"He's better," she said with a grin. "No hang-ups, no contracts, just a night of pure pleasure."

I thought Beatrice would divulge why he was better than the Fifty Shades hero and talk about his toned pecs, six-pack abs, and other salacious delights. Instead, she described how handsome he looked across the table in the restaurant, his impeccable manners, dress sense, and witty conversation.

My brows drew into a frown. Beatrice was the Queen of Juicy Details. I lived for her stories because of how she would bring them to life, making me feel like I was the one enjoying her exciting adventures.

All this talk of his personality made me think he'd already burrowed under her skin and was making his way to her heart.

As we reached the end of the road and rounded the corner, I asked, "Are you planning on seeing him again?"

"We're meeting again," she said with a happy sigh. "He's been sending me texts the entire morning and wants me to go to his work's Halloween bash next weekend."

Beatrice had had several casual relationships of varying lengths and with some of the most exciting-sounding men in London. There was the independent filmmaker we met at the iMax cinema cafe, who had approached us with his photographer friend, the footballer who took her to New York for Valentine's day, and the bass guitarist who was now on tour with Elton John.

She always played it cool, never getting attached, but this was the first time she'd ever agreed to see one so soon after the first date.

I bit down on my lip, listening to her rave about Christian, wondering if it was wise to jump into things with a guy so quickly.

My only relationship, we took things slowly and even then—I shook off those thoughts. That man didn't belong anywhere in my head.

As we reached my building on the corner, something small and warm brushed against my leg. I glanced down to find Macavity trotting toward the communal front door with his tail in the air.

Macavity's fur was a perfect leopard skin, with circular and U-shaped black spots filled with brown. He had either run away from home or was cheating on me with his true owner.

He certainly wasn't a stray because Bengal cats like him could cost up to five thousand pounds in London. Also, he wore a collar around his neck engraved with his name. This cat was exceptionally gorgeous, and for some reason, he chose to spend his time with me.

I placed the key in the front door, and Macavity bolted down the black-and-white-tiled hallway and up the marble stairs.

Beatrice chuckled. "Somehow, he always manages to beat the elevator."

While we walked down the end of the hall and waited for it to arrive, Beatrice fired up her Deliveroo app and checked on the delivery. According to the GPS display, the driver had already picked up the meal and was ten minutes away.

My apartment was one of several studios that took up the attic space of our Georgian building. Istabelle called it compact and bijou, but I called it home.

The first time I stepped into the apartment, I fell in love with the quartet of tall windows overlooking the leafy square. Daylight flooded the studio's ivory walls, making it look larger than its twenty-by-thirty-foot size.

On the right was my sofa bed, which still lay in its unfolded state with two dressers on either side that doubled as coffee tables.

On the left, a huge unit of closets took up the

entire wall, arranged around a dressing table alcove where I'd placed a flatscreen TV and DVD player. There was even enough space for a tiny glass-top table with two dining chairs.

Beatrice headed for the kitchen at the back wall, which was a row of slate-gray units with a built-in oven, microwave, and fridge. She picked up the kettle and filled it up at the sink.

"Green tea?" She opened the top cupboard and rifled through my shelf of herbal brew.

"Actually, I'm going to try out your suggestion. Back in a second." I padded to the right of the studio and into the bathroom.

It was more of a wet room than anything else, with a sunflower showerhead at the very end of the narrow room, a mirror unit, and a generous sink considering its size.

Macavity already sat perched on the counter by the sink, lounging on his haunches as though readying himself for a show.

"Hungry?" I asked.

He glanced down at the crystals encasing my wrist.

"Yeah." I turned on the tap, dispensed a generous dollop of liquid soap, and then murmured what happened to Macavity under the sound of the running water.

Beatrice was a great friend, but I couldn't confide in her about the Supernatural World. Besides, the conversation never came up. She knew I grew up on the other side of the River Thames, which was sort-of true because Logris was all the way in South London.

The supernaturals who established it in the seventeenth century carved out a chunk of Richmond Park and sectioned it into areas for vampires, witches, shifters, and elemental mages. Angels, demons and faeries also occupied the space, but they mostly lived in different realms.

Beatrice also knew I'd had my heart broken by an older man, but that was the most I could tell her without arousing suspicion.

The water warmed my skin, and I ran my soapy fingers over the stones embedded in my flesh. They seemed darker than they had been in the shop, and cloudier, as though their clarity had downgraded from triple-A to A.

"It's not working," I muttered.

Macavity tilted his head to the side. "Meow?"

"Soap and water mixed together can dislodge tight jewelry," I said. "Humans use it—"

The cat recoiled as though I was suggesting I give him a bath.

"Alright, I'll shut up, then."

Macavity gave me an approving nod.

After rinsing off the soap, I opened the mirror cabinet and extracted a glass jar of Dharma salt. If it was powerful enough to suck out corrupted magic from a preternatural vampire, it would surely remove the curse keeping those wretched stones attached to my skin.

After scooping up a generous amount with my fingers, I set to work trying to ease the melting salt beneath the crystals. The firestone darkened even further to a deep orange and then to a henna brown.

"Bloody hell," I snarled.

Macavity jumped down from the counter, bolted to the door, and tapped on it in a demand to be let out.

With a frustrated breath, I trudged across the bathroom and opened the door. It looked like I was on my own.

When I glanced down at my wrist, there was no sign of the bracelet. In its place was a tattooed ring of hearts.

CHAPTER THREE

A week later, I was still saddled with the tattoo, and nothing could get rid of it. Istabelle couldn't fathom how firestone could have transformed itself from crystal to ink, and she concluded that it must have dissolved with the Dharma salt.

That sounded a little bogus, but I had to admit that I hadn't kept my eyes on the bracelet the entire time it had been on my wrist.

I left messages on Aunt Arianna's phone, asking her if she knew anything about firestone. As a witch, she might know more about the crystal's properties, but I didn't hear back from my aunt and decided that reaching her so close to Samhain would be futile.

Samhain was one of the nine significant festivals in a witch's calendar. Each year, the coven spent weeks preparing for the great Sabbat. This particular one was about communing with the dead, as the veil between our world and the afterlife was at its thinnest.

I'd missed the last few, but every night on the thirty-first of October, I would think about the mother I'd never met and wonder if she would return to us as a spirit or reincarnate. This year, I just wanted the Sabbat to be over, so Aunt Arianna could help me figure out what was happening with this firestone.

I sat at the glass dining table with a bowl of hot chocolate I'd made from melting down an entire bar of Green & Black's dark chocolate with eighty-five percent cocoa solids.

The rich scent of cocoa beans and vanilla filled my nostrils, and I dipped a freshly baked croissant into the delicious drink. Maybe calling it hot chocolate was a stretch, seeing as it was thicker than cream, as dark as coffee, and contained just enough milk to make it liquid.

Macavity perched on the other side of the table, engrossed with his plate of tuna.

My phone rang, and I put Beatrice on speakerphone.

"Mera." What she said was a garbled sob of words tumbling into each other to form a continuous wail.

A fist of shock hit me in the gut, and I dropped my croissant into the hot chocolate. Beatrice sounded hurt—more than hurt. She sounded worse than she did when her dad had died.

"Slow down." I picked up the phone and placed it to my ear. "What's happened?"

"Christian," she cried. "He's ghosted me."

I locked gazes with Macavity, not sure what on earth this meant. The cat blinked, his green irises narrowing.

"Start from the beginning," I said. "Where are you?"

She hiccuped. "Home."

I pulled back the phone and checked the time. Eight-thirty. If Beatrice wasn't on the train, whatever happened had to be bad. "What did Christian say?"

"I went to his flat, thinking we would go out for dinner," she said through sobs. "He let me in, saying he'd already eaten."

My brow furrowed. "Okay, so you got a takeaway?"

She made a spluttering sound. "He told me to order something for myself and didn't even offer me his Deliveroo app!"

I chewed the inside of my cheek, wondering why a guy would invite a girl to his home and make her buy her own food. "What happened next?"

"I couldn't just get something for myself, so I ordered for both of us. He wolfed his down in front of the TV and didn't even offer to pay his share."

"He sounds like a dick." I stuck my finger in the warm chocolate and placed it in my mouth, barely tasting its rich flavour.

"The worst part was that after we had sex missionary style, he turned away and asked me to leave."

All the chocolate lodged in my windpipe, and I lurched forward, croaking worse than a psychotic toad. "What?"

"His eyes were so cold," she said, her voice trembling. "At first, I thought something was troubling him, and I asked if he was alright."

My fists thumped at my chest, King-Kong style. "What did he say?"

Beatrice let out a shuddering sob. "That not everything was about me."

A bitter taste formed in the back of my throat, and I stared down at Macavity, whose face remained buried in his plate of tuna.

What Beatrice described reminded me a little of my own experience, although my relationship unfolded over years and culminated in cold eyes and a frosty dismissal.

"Christian sounds fickle." I cleared my throat. "Sorry you had to go through that."

"He didn't even walk me out to my Uber," she said.

I shook my head, my heart sinking at the notion that that men everywhere were the same. In the past three years of living vicariously through Beatrice, I'd thought that human men were kinder than supernatural males since neither party was magical or could treat the other as lesser because of a lack of status.

It looked like things were the same everywhere.

"Have you spoken to him since?" I asked.

"I texted to ask how his meeting went. Just to give him the benefit of the doubt." She paused to blow her nose.

Holding my breath, I waited for her to continue. This had to be where he either called or texted back to say it was over.

"Do you know what he said?" Beatrice asked.

"No?"

"That one date doesn't make a relationship, and I should stop bothering him."

I stared down at the phone. "What?"

She laughed. "Psycho, right?"

"At least you got to see his awful personality before you could fall in love." I cringed as I said the words. They seemed so clinical and callous given that Beatrice was still crying about Christian, but I meant what I'd said.

She'd been seeing this guy for less than a week, and he'd pursued her every day with a fervor that had swept her off her feet. My relationship had extended for years. Years of courtship, years of getting to know each other, and years of sweet promises.

He had promised me everything—marriage, children, his crown, and even given me a ring he claimed had belonged to his mother.

For the time we'd been together, his personality had intertwined with mine because we'd met while I was young and still impressionable. We even shared similar tastes in food and coffee and wine because he was the one who introduced me to fine cuisine.

Hearing Beatrice explain how Christian denied they'd even had a relationship was an echo from my past. Christian had pursued Beatrice and made plans for Halloween and Christmas.

He'd even invited her to his apartment, just like how that vampire had bought me the gown, dressed me in jewels, only so I could look like an overdressed clown and get rejected in front of Logris high society.

"How could I have been so stupid?" she asked.

I exhaled a long breath. "Did he give you any indication he was lying?"

"No."

"From everything you told me, he was pursuing you," I said. "He sounds like a man with a sadistic streak and a short attention span."

She sniffed. "On some level, I knew he was too good to be true. A sexy banker who wasn't boring?"

"Some people would say that about tax accountants," I said.

Beatrice chuckled. "I probably dodged a bullet. Imagine getting a shitty text like that after being with him for months."

My chest tightened, and I lowered my gaze to the

bowl of hot chocolate. There was no need for me to picture a situation like that because I'd lived it. Lived it for the past three years, endured the betrayal, recurring memories, and bouts of fury that arouse from those harsh words. If it hadn't been for Istabelle, I might never have survived it.

"That would be devastating." I picked up the croissant, letting a trail of chocolate seep back into the bowl.

Just as I was about to place it in my mouth, Macavity raced across the table, snatched the pastry, and jumped down to the wood floor.

I glowered at his retreating back as he darted into the bathroom. What the hell was his problem?

"Why don't we meet for lunch?" I said. "While the food's cooking, I can perform a sound bath and wash that man out of your aura."

Beatrice let out a pleasured groan. "That sounds heavenly. Can we move it to dinner instead? I don't want to sleep alone tonight."

I inhaled a deep breath, my spirits lifting with the hope that this time next month, Beatrice would have written Christian off as a loser who couldn't be honest about his intentions. "Sure."

"Thanks, Mera," she murmured. "I really needed that. The next time someone acts so keen, I'll slow things down and take time to get to know them."

My face broke out into a grin. "Brilliant."

Beatrice sighed. "I wish I could be as strong as you."

After she said goodbye and hung up, I couldn't help but think she was wrong. True strength was about taking chances, even though the price of that might be getting hurt.

Beatrice embodied that sense of courage. Me? I was too busy trying not to dwell on past hurts to give myself the opportunity for new love.

I dipped my finger in the hot chocolate and took a long suck of the sweet, velvety liquid. It was rich and sensual and bittersweet, reminding me of romance.

The next time we went out together and were approached by two men, I would make an effort to be friendlier to the other guy. Maybe the way to get over a broken heart was to move on and rebuild it with exciting experiences instead of living through someone else.

By loving with all her heart and never holding back, and by learning lessons along the way, Beatrice was giving herself the best chance of finding happiness and love.

∽

Despite the rousing speech I gave myself over breakfast, I opened up the shop, my stomach queasy with the stirrings of dread. Jonathan had a sound bath booked just before lunch, and he would almost certainly ask me out.

This new Mera I resolved to be—the one who took up opportunities for relationships—it didn't extend to Jonathan, right? I had a feeling that one date with the guy would lead to constant requests for more.

I stepped into the store and unlocked the cash register, only for a delivery man to arrive shortly after with a large box. The description on the packing slip said it was quartz crystals, but I wasn't about to take any chances.

This time, I slipped on a white coat, a pair of goggles, and magic-proof gloves. If any enchanted objects were lurking within the depths of this delivery, I'd be ready for it with a pair of diamond shears.

I scored through the tape enclosing the large package with a box cutter, and pulled back the cardboard flaps, exposing clusters of clear quartz.

Each lay nestled within thick cardboard dividers, their prisms radiating a healing power. Quartz was the master crystal, the stone that amplified meditation, enhanced the abilities of other crystals, and boosted the powers of witches who used their magic to heal.

For people like Istabelle and me who had no magical power of our own, quartz helped to focus our ability to sense the power in others.

Someone tapped on the window. I glanced up to

find a pair of girls standing outside peering through the display. I smiled at them and waved them inside.

They were in their late teens, dressed in thick coats and jeans, looking as fresh-faced as I did when I first fell for he-who-I-would-never-name.

"I heard you can do love spells," said the taller of the pair, a redhead with hair a few shades lighter than mine.

"We can put together a few crystals to help you attract the love of your life," I replied with a smile. "Is that what you're looking for?"

She shook her head and nudged her friend, a plump mousy-haired girl, who nudged her back. "We've got a lock of a guy's hair. Could you do something with it?"

I replaced the flaps on the box and pulled off my goggles. Every so often, a customer came in looking for potions or hexes or some other kind of spell.

While humans might be able to offer such services to each other, the Supernatural Council forbade us from selling magical constructs—real or fake—to humans.

It didn't matter that we couldn't perform such enchantments. The fact that we knew the Supernatural World existed meant that none of our actions, either by word or deed, could inform humans that magic was real.

"Sorry, girls," I said. "That sort of thing isn't what we do."

Their faces fell, and the redhead stuffed her hands into her pockets. "Is there something I can put in his drink, then?"

I counted to three before answering—only because of this morning's conversation with Beatrice, who had entered into what she had hoped was a relationship under false pretenses.

If Christian had told her outright that he wanted a week of sex with no attachments, Beatrice would probably have swiped past him on the dating app.

"What would you say if I told you a man wanted me to sell him something to put in a girl's drink, so she would fall in love with him?" I asked.

They exchanged horrified glances. "You can't do that to another woman."

"Exactly." I clasped my hands behind my back, hoping the pair would put what they wanted to do in context.

Love spells did exist, as did substances that could increase a person's sexual desire, but the Supernatural Council frowned on interfering with the free will of others, and the penalty for that was death.

The only beings who could get away with driving people into a frenzy of lust were demons like incubi and succubi, as they fed on sexual energy. Vampires, to a lesser extent, were immune from that edict because their saliva contained traces of a venom called thrall that drove weaker supernaturals wild with lust.

Jonathan walked into the store two hours early for his appointment and clad in a camel-colored duffle coat the exact style of Paddington Bear's. He strolled to the book corner with his hands behind his back and perused the titles.

I snatched my gaze away from him and turned back to the girls. "Can I tempt you with some rose quartz hearts?" I swept my arm to the left, where we kept the rose quartz. "We also have them in balls and wands and obelisks."

The redhead shook her head but walked in the direction of the quartz crystals. "Thanks, anyway."

I watched her leave, hoping she would change her mind about forcing the poor guy to fall in love.

"Hi, Mera." Jonathan raised his palm.

"What can I help you with today?" I asked.

He glanced down at the floor, then back into my eyes, and smiled. His pale blue eyes flickered down to my lips, making me stiffen.

Something about him was off, but I couldn't explain what. He didn't contain an inkling of magic, but the way he stared at me sometimes seemed to look beneath the surface and into my soul.

It was like he had a magnet inside him that forced him to continue coming for a sound bath he didn't want and ask for a date he knew I would refuse.

"Jonathan?" I asked.

He licked his pale lips. They were thin, much like his long nose and the rest of his face. If I had to describe him as a cartoon character, he would be Shaggy from Scooby-Doo. Not unattractive, but not the guy who incited a girl's lust.

"I was wondering if you'd like to—"

"Mr. Drake," Istabelle's voice rang out through the shop. "Are you bothering my lovely apprentice again?"

Pink—not red—bloomed across Jonathan's cheeks. That wasn't to say he was cold-blooded, but nothing about him, from the shade of his blond hair to the permanently forlorn expression, implied he had any heat.

"Mrs. Bonham-Sackville," he stuttered. "I'm not… I would never… I have the utmost respect for Miss Griffin and wouldn't dare to—"

Istabelle raised her palm and smiled. "You have an appointment later today, yes?"

"Eleven-thirty, yes," he replied.

"Do you need to reschedule?"

Jonathan flinched. "What?"

"I'm trying to ascertain if your employer has scheduled another stocktake," Istabelle said in a louder voice.

The two girls from earlier giggled. I glanced from Jonathan to Istabelle, wondering why she'd chosen today to confront him. He had come here last week to reschedule. Did she suspect that this was his new ploy to come into the store and see more of me?

Jonathan stammered out something indecipherable, ending with, "See you in a bit, then."

He scampered to the door, eased it open, and snuck out like a ghost.

As soon as he disappeared into Upper Brook Street, I turned to Istabelle with my brows furrowed. "What was that about?"

"I was in treatment room number two during your last session. He's not interested in sound baths, is he?"

"How did you—"

"Who on earth would disrupt the healing vibrations with constant chatter?" She shook her head and chuckled. "A word of advice, my dear. Unwanted suitors can block the heart chakra just as much as devastating heartbreaks. If you want to attract new love in your life, throw away the old."

I sucked in a deep breath through my teeth. It was as though Istabelle had read my intentions for the morning and was parroting them back at me. Perhaps she could sense my resolve to do better in my energy.

"You're right," I said. "Would it be okay to refuse to perform sessions with him?"

Istabelle smiled, her gray eyes shining with pride. "I've been waiting for you to ask. One of these days, you'll learn—"

Her face froze as though she'd seen something startling through the window.

That was about when I felt the curl of smoky magic around my senses. Unlike last week, when that magic had felt like a noose around my neck, this smoke was nearly four times as powerful and felt more sensual than a caress.

As I turned, I caught sight of the two girls standing by the quartz crystals. The one facing the window also froze and grabbed her friend's arm. Curiosity stirred through my insides, and I spun toward the window.

Standing outside was a man about six-foot-two, with a strong build and broad shoulders. He wore a blue suit so dark that it appeared nearly black, with a navy shirt that curled around his prominent pectoral muscles.

The man seemed preoccupied with a tall amethyst geode that obscured his face and the top half of his athletic body, but the gaps in the display gave me a tantalizing glimpse of a corded neck, thick biceps, and muscled legs beneath slim-fitting pants.

The long-dead butterflies in my stomach fluttered back to life. I couldn't see his face, but even after three years, nobody could mistake that exact shade of bronze skin. A reddish-brown that looked like it had been warmed in the fires of sin.

I shook my head from side to side. It couldn't be him. It could be any one of his four brothers—Constantine, Sylvester, Ferdinand, or Lazarus, or any of the vampire nobles he was related to by blood.

After what he said to me that evening on the palace steps, he would never track me down to an obscure crystal shop in London.

He stepped away from behind the geode, and his violet eyes looked into mine with an intensity that hit me harder than a slap.

Valentine Bloody Sargon was about to walk into my life.

The Vampire King who had broken my heart.

CHAPTER FOUR

I leaned back on the counter, trying to catch my breath as Valentine opened the door and sauntered inside. Those wretched eyes of his glinted like he was looking at his next meal.

My insides trembled. Neutrals like me were supposed to have the most delicious blood.

It was like being caught in the gaze of a panther or some other apex predator with the gait and grace of a dangerous feline.

My heart pounded hard enough to burst, making my ribs reverberate with every frantic beat. Valentine didn't walk—he stalked. Right now, I was his prey.

Tall, dark, muscular, and sleek—he looked the same as he did in my dreams. Dreams that I would try to suppress with amethyst geodes and Native American snares. Dreams that would make me awaken with a quickening heart. Dreams that would haunt me through the days and half the night.

I'd resigned myself to Valentine Sargon being a ghost of loves past, a specter that I could escape if only I strengthened my mind and rebuilt my shattered heart.

Yet when he walked into the store, seeming to fill the air with his intoxicating, masculine scent, he was as real as the worst waking nightmare.

Istabelle swooped past in a puff of lavender perfume. "Welcome to my crystal shop. How may I be of service?"

"Good morning, Mrs. Bonham-Sackville," Valentine said in a deep voice that resonated with every nerve, including the sensitive bundle between my legs that had awoken the moment he walked into the store.

Heat surged through my veins, coalescing in a traitorous part of me that pounded in time with my fluttering heart. I breathed hard, trying to force the sensations somewhere else, but it was impossible to concentrate with him taking up all the space.

His dark gaze lingered on mine, and the corners of his lips curved upward. "May I speak with your assistant?"

I sucked in a breath through my teeth, and the pounding of my heart quickened to the beat of a battle drum. How did he know Istabelle's name? Had he known all this time where I'd gone or just recently tracked me down to the Crystal Shop?

"Mrs. Bonham-Sackville's assistant is busy," I snapped, making the girls in the corner clap their hands to their chests and gasp.

Valentine turned to them and grinned, revealing perfect white teeth. I knew exactly how those girls were feeling—awed at the sight of such a breathtaking male. He was the reason why I found even the most attractive human men so unexciting.

Vampires weren't just physically perfect, they exuded a raw sensuality that bewitched all reason and ensnared a person's heart. But they were vain, loathsome creatures who basked in the power they held over others and had no qualms about toying with people's emotion the way a cat would toy with a floundering bird.

The girls huddled together and giggled, not seeming aware of how dangerous the beautiful predator was in their midst.

I pressed my lips into a tight line. Valentine was probably soaking up their adoration the way he had basked in mine when I was too young and inexperienced to know better.

"Go home," he said in a hypnotic voice that sent a palpitation of desire through my heart.

I clenched my teeth, holding back a torrent of rage. Rage at myself for reacting to Valentine and rage at him for using his infernal wiles.

As though in a trance, the pair put the rose quartz crystals back in the baskets and drifted to the exit. A large man wearing black opened the shop's door, letting them out, and blocked the shop like a sentinel.

"Mesmerism on humans?" I snarled. "Disturbing a place of business with your guards? Whatever will the Supernatural Council say?"

Valentine turned his violet gaze back to mine. "Morata."

I flinched. "You have no right to call me that."

Morata was short for Inamorata—what he called me during what I thought was our courtship. It meant lover in Italian and was the title of a Dean Martin song he loved to play whenever we danced.

My heart raced like a feral beast caged within my ribs. I tore my gaze away from the monster's eyes and focused on the beauty spot on his left cheekbone. He had a bloody nerve to even stand within ten miles of me after what he did, let alone dredge up that term of endearment.

"Your Majesty." Istabelle dipped into a deep curtsey. "Allow me to give you a tour of my humble establishment."

Valentine's gaze left mine, and he offered Istabelle a gracious smile. With those violet eyes no longer attempting to hold me captive, I could finally exhale. Istabelle knew how much heartbreak I'd suffered in the first year of my apprenticeship—she'd helped me through the worst of it with healing sessions.

She'd never mentioned being acquainted with the King of the Vampires, and she would have hinted something over the years if they were in communication. This was probably her way of buying me time so I could calm myself before confronting Valentine.

I walked around the counter, tamping down my suspicions. Valentine must have found me through one of the many enforcers who monitored the Natural World for illegal supernatural activity. They weren't friends or acquaintances or anything else.

Istabelle was over a century old, and Valentine had ruled the vampires for five hundred years. Of course, she'd recognize him. Valentine was a member of the Supernatural Council and one of the seven most powerful magical beings who ruled Logris.

He was also very hard to forget.

Istabelle guided him to the front of the store, where she kept the most beautiful crystals set into precious metals to form jewelry. I tore my gaze away from them and focused on the box of quartz clusters still lying on the counter.

Sweat dampened my hands and beaded on my brow. My every instinct screamed at me to bolt through the door, jump on the back of a red double-decker, and disappear, but it wouldn't work.

Running would only trigger Valentine's hunting instincts, then I'd be trapped. Trapped in those strong, muscular arms, trapped in that mesmerizing gaze, trapped into doing whatever he desired.

I slipped my trembling fingers into the magic-proof gloves, put on my goggles, and opened up the box.

Instead of being the serene representatives of purity, the quartz clusters seemed too angular, too sharp, too kaleidoscopic.

Staring at them too long could pull me into meditation or an unwanted memory. Touching them—even with gloves—amplified the pain and resentment and humiliation that still lingered in my soul from how things ended with Valentine. I closed the flaps and eavesdropped on their murmured conversation.

Istabelle held a huge block of gray moonstone, a crystal we sometimes recommended for those with lingering grief.

I swallowed hard, hoping she was just talking about crystals in general and not reporting my progress to him in code.

With the cold, cruel words he had hurled at me across the steps of his palace, Valentine made it abundantly clear that he wanted me out of Logris and out of his life. Why would he follow up on me?

They moved on to the selection of herbs next, and Istabelle chatted to him about her selection of herbal teas. By now, the pounding of my heart had faded to a dull ache, and my insides burned with curiosity.

Valentine glanced at me over his broad shoulder, making my pulse quicken. The corner of his mouth curled into a smile, and my veins filled with angry, prickly heat.

He'd heard my heart with his enhanced vampire ears and probably thought I was excited. Hadn't it occurred to him that pulses also rose due to fight or flight?

"Thank you, Mrs. Bonham-Sackville." Valentine took Istabelle's hand and brought it to his lips.

Istabelle lowered her lashes, and a faint blush darkened her pale features. I couldn't blame the woman.

Valentine had an advantage over even the most beautiful of vampires. His power and charm and title were enough to stir anyone to passion, but all he stirred in me was fury.

"Would you like to see our book corner?" she asked.

"Perhaps later," he said with a smile that had her swaying on her feet.

"Then I will take my leave." Istabelle retreated to the far end of the shop, placing a trembling hand on her flushed cheek.

Valentine inclined his head and turned to me with an arrogant smirk. "You seem distracted. I thought you would have finished unpacking your delivery by now."

"It's hard to concentrate with an unholy presence in the shop," I snapped. "What do you want?"

His brows rose. "Is that any way to speak to a customer?"

"Don't tell me you traveled all the way from Logris to buy a crystal."

"Perhaps not."

"Then what are you doing here?"

Valentine swept his arm toward the exit, where a limousine awaited on the curb. "We need to talk."

I turned to the box of quartz clusters, pulled back the flap, and pulled one out onto the counter. With the adrenaline searing through my veins, the stone had zero effect.

For the next few minutes, I busied myself unpacking and dusting off the clusters. Perhaps if I ignored Valentine, he'd slink out of the shop and back to where he came from.

"Mera." His chastising voice cut through my attempt at distraction. Even though he'd uttered just one word, he'd left the rest unsaid. Valentine would not be ignored.

"What do you want to talk about?" I snapped.

"Come with me, and I'll explain everything."

I brushed stray bits of cardboard off my protective white coat. "I'm not in the habit of going places with strange vampires."

A growl reverberated across the shop, sending the fine hairs on the back of my neck standing to attention. My heart revved like a motorcycle and a thrill of terror mingled with fury and excitement. Who did this man think he was?

I bared my teeth and hissed. "Don't think that snarling like an animal will get me to obey your every command. In the human world, we use our words."

His features evened out into the annoying expression of calm he often used with servants who had made a mistake. "Then perhaps a considerate apprentice could consider the impact our conflict is having on your master."

My gaze flicked to Istabelle, who leaned against a crystal display, clutching her chest.

All the color had leached from her face, and her features fell slack. Her fear was proof enough that she hadn't been in contact with Valentine and didn't know that he kept a tight rein over his temper.

I turned back to Valentine, my eyes narrowing. "Perhaps a considerate member of the Supernatural Council could consider the impact his animalistic urges are having on others?"

His eyes narrowed. "Mera—"

"Get out." I pointed to the door.

Impatience flickered across his features. As he bared his teeth, the tips of his incisors lengthened.

"I will not ask you again," he said in a do-as-His-Majesty-says-or-else snarl.

My pulse quickened. This was the voice he used before flicking his wrist and sending someone flying across the room. Valentine wouldn't hurt two defenseless women—at least not physically—but I couldn't let pride and stubbornness result in the old lady falling into a faint.

Pulling back my shoulders, I made a disdainful noise in the back of my throat, acting like vampire kings came to the crystal shop to harass me all the time.

"Very well. If stepping outside will make you leave, I suppose I'll have to oblige." I walked around the counter and across the shop floor toward Valentine, who offered me a tight smile.

He strode ahead of me and held the door open. The man guarding the shop lumbered aside to let us out, and I stepped out into the cool morning.

A driver in a black uniform stood by the limousine and gave Valentine a low bow.

I pressed my lips into a thin line and scowled. Scoundrels who treated people like shit didn't deserve respect.

A black cab drove past, its diesel engine clicking and coughing out smoke. On the other side of the road, a Royal Mail van paused outside the little Tesco Metro supermarket.

I let my gaze skip to the store on its right. At this time of the day, the Pret a Manger opposite was only half full. Two suited men sat outside beneath the cafe's burgundy awning, both smoking cigarettes. I longed to be inside the store, drinking a cup of coffee, with Valentine a distant memory.

"You're still wearing your safety spectacles," Valentine said.

"Goggles." I turned back to him and met his eyes. In the direct sunlight, they were a deep blue that bordered on a dark turquoise with not a hint of the red that made them look violet.

Goosebumps prickled across my skin. I used to love those eyes. Now, I despised them.

"Pardon?" Valentine frowned.

I shifted my gaze to the beauty mark on his cheekbone. "They're not spectacles."

Valentine smiled, as though he found my attempt at petulance endearing. The sight of him looking at me with any expression other than an apology sent a flare of anger through my insides.

"Won't you take them off?" he said.

Something inside me cracked. It was bad enough that he'd dared to show his face, bad enough that he'd demanded that I leave the shop, but I wasn't going to tolerate his attempts at making idle chit-chat.

"What the hell do you want from me?" I yelled loud enough for the passersby to gape. "You breeze back after three years, disrupt my place of business, and intimidate my boss. Say what you want to say and bugger off."

Valentine flinched. It was the tiniest of movements that lasted only a blink of an eye, but I'd grown up around vampires and every other sort of supernatural creature and so I knew that figments of the imagination were often what they appeared. Then he smoothed out his features into a mask of calm.

"It's complicated." He swept his arm toward the open limousine door.

"Mera?" asked a male voice from behind.

I turned to meet Jonathan's hopeful blue eyes. He stood with his hands in the pockets of his duffle coat and his narrow shoulders hunched.

"Hi, Mera." His thin lips curled into a tiny smile. "I came early for our session—"

"What session?" Valentine snapped.

Ignoring him, I glanced down at my watch. Eleven-ten. For once in my miserable existence, I wished Jonathan had arrived much earlier.

Right now, walking around a prone man who wouldn't stop talking about himself and asking me for dates was far preferable to getting into the back of a limo with a treacherous vampire king.

Valentine placed a possessive hand on my shoulder and pulled me into his larger body so I stood with my back flush against his chest. He overwhelmed me with his size and his strength and his scent. Sandalwood and sensuality swirling around me like smoke.

Every muscle in my body relaxed at his touch, bringing back the old feelings of being loved and protected and treated like I would become his.

I had all been a lie. A twisted sick lie executed by a man so rich and powerful and bored of life that he needed to pluck innocent girls from obscurity and Tears stung to my eyes and bile stung to the back of my throat as I fought to control my traitorous body.

Valentine meant nothing to me apart from a time in my life I was trying to forget.

The warmth of his palm seeped through my white coat and into my flesh, reminding me of younger, brighter days when I could have interpreted the gesture as protective. Now, it was nothing short of an intrusion.

Shrugging him off, I turned back to Jonathan. "Could you go inside and wait, please? I'll be with you in a few minutes."

Jonathan's gaze wandered over my shoulder to where Valentine was probably glaring at him to get lost. "Is this man bothering you?"

"Yes." I shook my head. "He's no-one. Just a messenger from home."

Jonathan's frown deepened. "Would you like me to escort you back into the shop or anywhere else?"

A warning growl vibrated against my back. If I didn't get rid of Jonathan now, Valentine would resort to something forceful.

Pulling my lips into what I hoped was an I'm-not-being-kidnapped smile, I swept my arm toward the shop. "I'll join you in ten minutes. Please wait for me inside."

Jonathan glanced from me to Valentine and back to me again. "Are you sure?"

"How many times does the lady need to tell you to leave?" Valentine snarled.

"Alright." His Adam's apple bobbed up and down, and he stared at Valentine as though committing his face to memory. "Ten minutes."

With his hand on the small of my back, Valentine guided me into the waiting limousine. Without realizing why, I found myself stepping through the door.

Its interior was white, with an L-shaped leather seat, tinted windows, and a fully-stocked bar with crystal decanters already filled with liquid. I lowered myself into the seat and blinked. What the bloody hell just happened?

"Who was that man?" Valentine entered after me, not having the decency to sit a seat apart. His muscular thigh pressed against my leg, the way it used to do when we were supposedly courting.

Heat pulsed between my legs, reminding me of how he used to kiss me in limousines like this, making me beg for more. I scooted away from his encroachment and toward the door, but the central locking clicked, and the limo pulled out into the road.

My eyes bulged, and I spun around to meet the arrogant git's triumphant features. "Did you just use your magic on me?"

"Who was he?"

"Answer my question," I snapped.

The corner of his lip curled into a half-smile. "It was for your own good. Now, you answer my question."

"What business is that of yours?" I narrowed my eyes.

"Tell me." He scooted around, trying to meet my gaze.

"You had something to say, remember? Spit it out so I can leave."

"Mera," he barked.

I flinched. Even though I'd experienced the harsher side to Valentine's personality just once, most of my memories of him were of a kind and patient man.

My throat dried from breathing so hard. I itched to demand why he'd kept up the deception of loving me for so long, only to cast me aside the moment I'd given him what he wanted. Surely no girl's virginity was worth that much effort.

I ground my teeth. The last time I had been vulnerable to Valentine, that had resulted in the public shattering of my reputation and pride. I wasn't about to expose myself to a second helping of his cruelty and let him stomp on my heart.

"Who was he?" Valentine asked again with an edge of power in his voice.

"He's a client, alright?" I said through clenched teeth. "And I'm only answering you because I want to get this conversation over with, so I can return to the shop."

Valentine's eyes hardened. "Not today."

The limousine continued down Upper Brook Street toward Park Lane, where we would soon approach Hyde Park. This was kidnapping, plain and simple, and my fury kicked up another notch. I twisted around in my seat and bared my teeth.

"I thought you just wanted to talk," I said.

"We will." He sat back, a look of satisfaction returning his features. Daylight filtered through the tinted windows, giving his skin a golden tinge and bringing out the blueish highlights in his black hair.

Some people might have described the effect as hypnotic. To me, he was the supernatural equivalent of a carnivorous plant.

I turned my gaze to the crystal tumblers sitting within holders at the bar. "Are you going to lie about this being a short conversation, too?"

"You're the one who said it would be brief," he replied. "What I need to explain to you will take time."

I ground my teeth. The bloody bastard was correct. "There's such a thing called lying by omission."

Valentine chuckled. He probably thought he was several steps ahead of me. Maybe he was, considering he'd been born a century before William I had conquered England. The vampire had had centuries of practice honing the art of seduction and probably thought that toying with the hearts of magicless girls was an art form or a sport.

"Were you stalking me last week?" I asked.

He grabbed my hand. "Are they following you already?"

I twisted around in my seat and met his solemn gaze. "You know what's happening?"

Valentine inhaled a deep breath, his eyes seeming to drink me in. "I didn't think it would be possible, but you've grown even more beautiful in the years we've spent apart."

Somewhere deep behind the mental barriers, the black tourmaline I wore around my neck, and the Dharma salt I always carried in my pockets, my heart wanted to melt. But that was just the effects of his words. Words like that could make a girl throw her senses out of the window, desperate to hear more from those beautiful, lying lips.

Not me. I was no longer that girl.

"Are you responsible for the firestone bracelet?" I murmured.

He lowered his lashes, his gaze drifting to my right hand. Valentine's large fingers caressed my skin, sending pleasure skittering up my arm and straight into my heart.

A breath caught in the back of my throat, and my traitorous eyes fluttered shut. It felt like an eternity since I'd allowed any man to touch me except for a perfunctory shake of the hand. The mere touch of Valentine's skin against mine made my pulse flutter.

I hated this man, yet his touch brought back the memories of our last day together and how he had kissed every inch of my skin, teased me to submission, and lavished me with words of adoration as we had made love. Right now, I felt like his bloody instrument. My body was playing along with Valentine, even though my mind screamed at it to stop reacting.

He pulled back the sleeve of my white coat, and the pad of his thumb brushed over my pulse point. "The enchantment worked perfectly."

My eyes snapped open, and all traces of pleasure vanished in an instant. "You sent the firestone bracelet."

"No," he replied with a furrowed brow.

"But you know who did?" I screamed.

Valentine didn't answer.

"Did you hire a witch to enchant the stones to sink into my skin?" I held my tattooed wrist in front of his face.

"Inamorata," he said.

"Don't Inamorata me," I snapped. "Answer my damned questions."

Valentine exhaled a long breath. "Mera, your life is in danger."

CHAPTER FIVE

I twisted around in the limousine's leather seat and glowered into Valentine's dark eyes. What kind of game was he playing? Last week, I felt the presence of a vampire following me through Grosvenor Square—one of Valentine's bloody subjects.

He admitted to knowing about the firestone, even though he claimed he hadn't sent it. Every piece in this incomplete supernatural puzzle added up to a bored Vampire King looking to spark things up with an old flame.

"Is this a bet?" I asked.

His brows furrowed. "Did you hear what I said?"

"I suppose this is the point where I stare into your eyes and beg you for help?"

I retreated back along the leather seat, trying to put as much distance as possible between myself and the manipulative vampire. I wasn't in any danger whatsoever. That vampire who had followed me through the park had probably come from Valentine.

"Tell me why you're really here," I snapped.

"We think you're being watched," he said.

"By?" I folded my arms across my chest. "And is this the royal 'we' or do you have an accomplice?"

His nostrils flared, a sign that I was wearing out his patience. I clenched my teeth. If Mr. Tall, Dark, and Brooding Vampire King wanted a sycophant, he was fishing in an empty pool. The only thing he would get from me was belligerence until he started sharing some facts.

"Well?" I asked.

"It's best for your safety that you change location—"

"No," I shrieked.

He reared back. "Mera."

"Prove it."

The limousine turned right at the traffic lights between Park Street and Upper Brook Street and paused in the traffic. To our left was the leafy expanse of Hyde Park.

At this time of the year, most of the leaves had changed into the glorious oranges and yellows and crimsons I associated with autumn in Britain, but the lush colors were shades of dark blue through the limousine's tinted windows.

My fingers twitched toward the door. If I'd been

in a limo with any other man, I'd have taken the opportunity to leave, but Valentine loved to hunt, and I wasn't in the mood to play Jerry to his Tom. Besides, Valentine had already predicted I might bolt, hence the central locking.

As the vehicle continued alongside the park, Valentine said, "You want me to find your assassin?"

My skin tightened with annoyance. The way he said the words made me sound like I was too stupid to live and wasn't prepared to take precautions until someone had made an attempt on my life.

The girl who had once believed in him had been stupid, gullible, and naive, but even she had grown up and wouldn't put her trust in Valentine's cold cruel heart.

I met his curious gaze with a hard glare. "I've lived in Mayfair for three years, and the only supernaturals we've seen have been customers."

"Except for the person who stalked you through Grosvenor Square," he replied.

"A vampire who was probably working for you," I said.

Valentine turned his gaze away from mine, and a muscle in his jaw flexed. Clearly, our reunion wasn't going as he'd planned.

I stared out of the window into Hyde Park, wishing I was alone and taking a stroll in the fresh air. Anything was better than sitting next to a man who hadn't acknowledged having sliced through my heart with his cutting words.

It wasn't like I was being stubborn. That vampire stalker only appeared once and could have followed me into the shop or attacked me on the doorstep when I'd dropped the keys. Instead, he remained on the other side of the road and never returned.

There was no reason to uproot myself and move away from my apprenticeship with Istabelle and my friendship with Beatrice. Especially not on the say-so of the vampire who had already proven himself a liar.

"Your ten minutes are over," I said without looking into his face. "Take me back to the shop."

"I can't do that," he murmured.

Anger flared in my chest. Who did he think he was, the police? "Why not?"

"I can't in good conscience leave you here to be hunted."

"This conversation is going around in circles, and I have a session with a client," I said. "Why would I believe a word of what you say when you won't give me any details?"

Valentine's hand slid atop mine, the skin of his palm as smooth as velvet. Desire trickled down my spine and heat spread across my skin. Despite three years of trying to forget the man, deep down, a traitorous part of my body still yearned for his touch.

Before that desire could reach Valentine's

enhanced sense of smell, I flinched away, pulling back my arm.

"Don't touch me." I raised my hand and struck at his face.

Valentine caught me by the wrist, a growl reverberating in the back of his throat. "Will you behave yourself and listen to what I have to say?"

My breath quickened, and heat rose to my cheeks. It had been a mistake to go for the slap. His reflexes were much faster than mine, and I'd just given him another chance to touch me.

Valentine's eyes darkened, and red flecks appeared across his irises, indicating a heightened emotion or the need to feed. With a rolling growl that made my insides shudder, he asked, "Well?"

The pounding of my pulse filled my ears, and every ounce of moisture evaporated from my throat. "Let me out."

"In the middle of Park Lane?" he asked with a smile.

"I'll walk the rest of the way back to work." I pulled at the hand restraining my wrist, but he was too strong, too persistent, too determined to carry out this abduction.

For what felt like the hundredth time since he'd haunted the crystal shop, I asked myself why. Why someone could shatter a girl's heart and return on the day she decided to move on. Why he had chosen me as a target for his sick games. Why he wouldn't believe me when I demanded that he leave me alone.

Breathing hard, I lowered my lashes, careful not to spend too long in his gaze. Vampires could enter the mind of a weak supernatural, and the only defense from this was avoidance.

After what felt like an eternity, he released my arm. "Are you hungry?"

It was like igniting a match. Didn't this bloodsucking wanker just tell me there was an assassin after my hide? Or had that been a sick attempt to make conversation?

"Why aren't you listening to a word I say?" I asked from between clenched teeth.

"Mera," he said my name like a sigh. "I know you're disappointed with—"

"Don't," I snapped. If he dared to describe our last encounter as disappointing, I would throw my Dharma salt into his eyes.

Valentine frowned. "What's wrong?"

"Don't presume you know anything about me."

He tilted his head to the side and studied my features like I was a point of endless fascination. It was the sort of look a person gave a malfunctioning computer when trying to work out which button would activate a reset.

"You're always stressed when you're hungry," he said, sounding nostalgic.

"I'm agitated because unlike some people, I

follow through with my commitments," I snapped. "Now, will you please let me out so I can tend to my client?"

The twinkle in his eyes and the tiny smirk on his full lips told me he didn't believe a word about my wanting to tend to Jonathan.

What annoyed me most was that he ignored the barb I'd directed at him about commitments. Being a vampire royal sure made a person think they were beyond reproach.

Valentine patted my hand. "We can discuss everything over a quiet meal."

His idea of a quiet meal turned out to involve dining in the Dorchester Hotel, which the limo approached by driving the three-mile perimeter of Hyde Park in busy lunchtime traffic. By the time we reached our destination, my stomach growled, making Valentine shoot me I-told-you-so smirks.

They wouldn't have been so aggravating if Macavity hadn't stolen my last croissant this morning. Aunt Arianna's homemade chocolates should have arrived by now, but either she'd forgotten to send them or they were delayed in the post.

Valentine stepped out of the limo first, letting in a gust of cold air. "Shall we?"

"What do you want?" I squeezed my eyes shut and clenched my teeth.

Every dream I'd had about Valentine had either ended in an orgasm or waking drenched in perspiration with slick folds and a heart pounding in time with the pulse between my legs.

If I maintained my dream weavers, I could keep him out of my thoughts, but one slip-up, and this dinner would give my mind fodder for even more vivid dreams.

"Come." Valentine reached into the limousine and took my hand, the touch sending sparks across my skin.

I stepped into the restaurant with Valentine, cringing at being miserably underdressed in jeans and a sweater and woefully inappropriate on his arm. Two huge vampires trailed after us, looking like they could smash the place up with their fists. Dotted around the place were suited people whose supernatural energies radiated off them like sirens. I clenched my teeth. Of course Valentine would have planted his people here. He never left anything to chance.

Looking at us together, anyone would think I was his intern and not his ex. Thankfully, someone had checked my white coat, and I'd already stuffed the gloves in my pocket.

The waiter guided us through a foyer of green lights trailing down the walls like ivy, into the restaurant's luxurious interior. Every wall was paneled with mahogany with deep green carpets that reminded me of freshly-mown grass. Elegantly dressed people sat around round tables, enjoying beautifully presented food on large, white plates.

My throat thickened, and I fought back memories of bursting into tears of happiness before he undressed me on the rug and pleasured me with a tenderness that made my toes curl, my heart ache, and my lips murmur his name over and over until the words became a moan. Afterward, he whisked me into his bedroom and we spent the rest of the afternoon making love.

My heart pounded. A rush of heat filled my veins and surged to my cheeks. What the hell was this—his attempt at rekindling old mockeries?

I raised my head and met eyes that stared at me through a haze of affection I now recognized to be false. If he wanted a public scene, it wasn't going to happen. The girl who broadcasted her emotions to a baying audience died that night in Logris.

The waiter poured a small sample into Valentine's glass, allowing him the first taste. When Valentine inclined his head, the waiter turned to me with the bottle.

I shook my head. "None for me, thank you."

Valentine waved the waiter away.

As soon as the man disappeared behind the shimmering curtain, I asked, "What's this really about?"

"Eat something first," Valentine said. "You look like you haven't slept well in days."

I pointed at the tattoo on my wrist. "It's been difficult to focus on relaxing with a magical anomaly etched into my body. Tell me something, or I'll leave."

"It's firestone."

"Obviously," I snapped. "Why are you part of a plot to infect me with an object used to store a dangerous and explosive power?"

His brows rose. "I'm impressed you identified it."

Actually, that had been Istabelle, but I wasn't about to admit that to Valentine and have him change the subject.

He stared at me, looking for the reaction I used to give him in response to compliments: heated cheeks, lowered eyelashes, and a stuttered denial. That wasn't going to happen.

The waiter returned with a bowl of bread rolls, butter, and quails' eggs served in teaspoons. I continued glaring at Valentine until he spoke.

"Your aunt, Arianna, came to the palace last month."

My lips parted. I'd spoken to her two weeks ago, and she hadn't once mentioned having contacted Valentine. "Is she alright?"

"Someone told her a mage had been asking about you, and she wanted to know if the inquiry came from the Supernatural Council."

I held my breath. There were seven monarchs in the Supernatural Council, each representing one of the seven supernatural races—vampires, shifters and weres, demons, angels, faeries, witches, and elemental mages.

There was no reason why any of them might have

an interest in me. Not even the Witch Queen knew of my existence, and I came from a long line of her subjects.

"Why did she come to you and not our queen?" I asked.

Valentine frowned. "Isn't the answer obvious?"

"No," I snapped.

After Valentine had dumped me, I had returned to Aunt Arianna in tears. She had thrown her arms around me, saying it was better to know a vampire's heart before I'd made the mistake of becoming enthralled by him—or worse, pregnant with his vampire offspring.

He dismissed my words, seeming as though he didn't want to bother giving me an explanation. "A group of enforcers broke into your cottage early this morning."

I clapped a hand over my mouth. "Is Aunt Arianna—"

"She was out on a Samhain retreat," he replied.

The longest breath of relief escaped my lungs, and I slumped into my seat.

"Grosvenor Square is no longer safe." Valentine leaned across the table and offered me his hand. "We've prepared a warded safe house in London. You can move in there with me—"

I pulled my hands into my lap. "Not as your mistress!"

He paused. "No."

My wretched heart had the gall to sink. I don't know why because I was perfectly content without Valentine and ready for a relationship with someone else. I neither wanted him nor needed him, but something about what he said set off a tiny alarm.

"Is the Supernatural Council investigating me?" I asked.

Another pause. "They shouldn't be."

They wouldn't have any reason to track me because I hadn't done anything wrong except be duped by one of their own. And I'd left, not lowering myself to raise a fuss.

Whoever had been asking after me couldn't have been an old friend from the academy. Neutrals were rare and often overlooked. Besides, if their intentions were innocent, they would have asked Aunt Arianna directly for my contact information.

The waiter arrived with our starters of tuna tartare, served with sliced radishes, avocados, and a ginger sauce. I took a bite of the fish and nearly hummed out loud as it melted in my mouth. There was nothing better in the world than sushi.

"How's the food?" Valentine asked.

"It would taste better if I knew what you were hiding."

He exhaled an impatient sigh. "I'll take you to the safe house after lunch. If it's not to your liking, you can choose somewhere else."

I sat back and shot him my most venomous

glower. "There's no reason anyone would come after me, since I haven't said or done anything wrong."

He was about to answer when the waiter brought our main course, a Wagyu sirloin that was so tender it disintegrated in my mouth. The buttery meat combined savory with sweetness and was served with charred broccoli, garlic mashed potatoes, and roasted cauliflower.

Valentine didn't bring up the subject of my supposed danger, and I took that to mean he'd given up on trying to convince me to go to this mystery safe house for reasons he was unable or unwilling to divulge.

Dessert was my absolute favorite—a chocolate and hazelnut bomb that imploded the moment I doused it with warm chocolate sauce. Valentine ordered a hazelnut gelato, which he pushed across the table, and chuckled when I set upon it like a ravenous cat.

Perhaps sweet things were my weakness, but it would never be my heart.

As we enjoyed the most delicious blend of Black Ivory espresso, he leaned across the table and frowned. "What kind of services do you offer in the crystal shop?"

"None, right now, since you pulled me out of work," I snapped.

His brows rose. "Mera?"

I knew it was childish, but I wanted him to feel

what it was like to squirm. "Oh, you know…" I took another sip, letting the bitter taste roll over my tongue. "A bit of this, a bit of that. Anything to keep the customer happy."

"And this Jonathan fellow is a regular?" he asked.

I nodded but didn't elaborate. Even I couldn't muster up words convincing enough about Jonathan to portray him as anything but mildly annoying and overly clingy.

The phone in my pocket buzzed, making me flinch.

Valentine raised a brow. "Answer it."

"I'll listen to the voicemail later."

His features tightened, and a petty flare of triumph warmed my chest. If he was looking to overhear my conversation with whoever had just called, I was onto him.

We sat in silence, staring at each other from across the table. Valentine's looks were everything—sleek, black hair with highlights that changed color according to the surroundings, a strong brow and sharp cheekbones.

I avoided his eyes because a girl could get lost in those orbs for hours, and dropped my gaze to his full, curving lips and dimpled chin.

After having a guy like that, it was no wonder I couldn't muster up an interest in human men. Valentine looked like the god of scoundrels and seduction had carved him out of bronze and breathed him into life.

"Will you at least consider a bodyguard?" he asked.

"Like the man who stood outside the shop?"

Valentine inclined his head.

"Do I have any choice?"

He flashed me a grin of dazzling eyes and impossibly white teeth that made my heart flip.

Tamping down my reaction, I twisted my features into a scowl. "What's the point of asking me?"

Valentine raised a shoulder. "At least the next time a vampire follows you across the square, you can be assured he's looking out for your safety."

I paused, examining his face for clues of duplicity, but Valentine had always been such a convincing liar. My lips tightened. It wasn't as though I had any choice in the matter. Valentine would send whoever he wanted to follow me wherever I went. He was probably only asking me as part of an elaborate plan.

"Fine," I said with a sigh, "But this vampire of yours had better not get in my way."

The corners of his lips curved into a smile. I narrowed my eyes, wondering what the hell Valentine was scheming.

CHAPTER SIX

After excusing myself to go to the bathroom, I took the long route around the hotel, feeling out for signs of Valentine's guards. They'd all lined the main pathway from the entrance to the restaurant, so I found myself able to take a side exit undetected.

I stepped out of the hotel, grimacing at the line of people waiting for black cabs. By the time Valentine realized I had ditched him, I'd still be out here, a standing target.

On the other side of the busy highway was Hyde Park in all its leafy glory. Right now, I could disappear into those trees, but it would mean crossing that busy road. Cold wind swirled through my hair, beckoning me to get moving or it would freeze my ass. The crystal shop was only a ten-minute walk away and would be shorter if I cut through the back streets.

Instead of turning right into Park Lane and enjoying the sights of the park, I took the nearest street and hurried down the side of the hotel. Valentine was probably rising from his fancy booth, wondering what was taking me so long. Too bad I'd be back home before he realized I'd had enough of his edicts and half-truths.

Wrapping my arms around my chest, I hit the paving stones at double time. The white coat was still in the cloakroom where the waiter had checked it, and I hadn't been about to alert Valentine of my leaving by trying to get it back.

I left that lunch more confused than ever, still not knowing if this supposed danger hanging over my head was an elaborate hoax. It helped me understand one thing: Valentine Sargon was as slippery as he was untrustworthy.

As I turned left into South Audley street, which had the narrowest sidewalk I'd seen in the whole of Great Britain, I wondered if Valentine had any faerie blood.

Faeries were also unfeasibly beautiful creatures renowned for their ability to seduce. Like vampires, they needed supernatural beings of low magical power to reproduce, but that didn't mean they respected us or humans.

While supernatural vampires treated human

blood as a delicacy, the delicacy of choice for faeries was human misery. Anyone unfortunate enough to strike a bargain with a faerie often found that it backfired, so they not only didn't get what they'd bargained for but ended up in a form of eternal slavery.

As I turned into South Grosvenor Street, a long, black vehicle filled the periphery of my vision. I quickened my pace, even though it was impossible to out-walk, outrun, or out-anything a limousine.

Behind it, someone honked their horn, followed by the driver's shout to stop curb crawling, followed by the whirr of an electric window.

My breath quickened. Valentine was going to say something. He could have stepped out and walked at my side. It was an overcast day, and sunlight didn't bother him as much as it did other vampires, but he peered out through the limousine's window, saying nothing as he watched me trudge through the backstreets of Mayfair.

I shook my head. Strip away the handsome exterior, extensive wealth, and cultured conversation, and he was just another entitled asshole who used his silver tongue to get what he wanted out of a girl before casting her aside.

It was four by the time I reached the tree-lined garden of Grosvenor Square, and I was sick of the limousine, the angry drivers behind it, and Valentine's silent presence.

Guessing that he already knew where I lived, I pulled out my key and stopped outside my building, opened its front door, and stepped into the warm hallway. As soon as it clicked shut behind me, I rested my back against its wood and exhaled a long breath.

I survived. I survived the return of Valentine without once feeling a pang of love or longing or lust. I stared into those violet eyes, seeing nothing but a supernatural beauty honed by magic to ensnare its prey.

Warm triumph filled my chest, and I bounded across the black-and-white-tiled hallway, taking the marble stairs two at a time.

This was it. The beginning of the rest of my life. A life I was free to live as a human. My thighs ached from the seven-story climb. When I reached the attic, my breath came in rapid pants, feeling like I'd had a great workout. In a way, I had. I'd worked Valentine out of my system.

I unlocked my apartment door, and a bolt of warm fur streaked out into the hallway with a *mraaw!*

"Macavity?" I twisted around, watching the leopard skin cat bolt down the hallway and down the stairs. "What's wrong with you?"

When I checked my phone, it was a voicemail from Beatrice, saying she was bored at work and asking if we could meet earlier. I texted back, telling her I couldn't wait, and she texted back to say she would meet me at Souk.

Souk was a bar that served Moroccan food and the most delicious cocktails. Most people went to check out the Middle Eastern decor and stayed to smoke the hookahs, elaborate tobacco pipes that allowed you to smoke a range of exotic blends through long tubes.

The bar attracted a young, artistic crowd—the complete opposite to Christian—and I couldn't wait. After changing into a pair of dark jeans and a tank top, I sauntered into the bathroom and stared into the mirror.

The girl looking back seemed to glow. I drew close to the reflection, examining my features. Gone were the faint circles under my eyes and the dull grey in my blue irises. Instead, my eyes shone with the fire of determination. Determination to start my life anew and commit Valentine to a distant memory. Even my skin glowed with challenge.

Stepping back from the mirror, I grinned and applied a coat of mascara and lip gloss. This was how I used to look when basking in the light of Valentine's love. Now that he was out of my system, I could bask in the light of my own happiness.

Valentine's limo wasn't anywhere on Grosvenor Square, even though I felt the distant presence of a brooding vampire.

I walked down Duke Street and continued down Oxford Street, which was heaving with shoppers. Outside Selfridges, I caught the 390 bus, which took me down to John Lewis—also on Oxford Street—and walked the back roads of Soho until I reached Souk.

London was a mass of contradictions, crowded landmarks and highways crammed with tourists and shoppers and workers, then as soon as you ducked into the backstreets, it was the epitome of peace.

Souk's exterior consisted of a burgundy sign and awning that shaded its tinted-glass front. Six-foot-tall menus stood before the window, and behind them, glowing red lights hung down from the ceiling like they were floating in midair. It was four-thirty, which meant happy hour had already started.

I stepped into its warm interior, letting the mingled scents of tobacco smoke and herbs engulf my senses. The strains of exotic string music played over the speakers with a techno beat, soft enough to allow the patrons to hear themselves talk.

I glanced around red walls decorated with gilded paintings of smoking celebrities, including one of the Mona Lisa smirking around a pipe. Along the edges of the bar, they'd arranged low cushioned seats around circular tables topped with carved leather.

At this time of the afternoon, the place was only half-full, with mostly students nursing half-priced drinks. A quartet of girls sat at the closest booth around a glass hookah, watching their friend suck tobacco out of a long pipe. Pale liquid bubbled at the base of the pipe as she blew out white streams of smoke from her lips.

It wasn't something I had ever wanted to sample. At least not outside the supervision of Istabelle, who made a tobacco-free blend that could help a person achieve altered states. All I'd seen when I inhaled her herbs were flames, which I thought reflected hell.

Beatrice rose from a bank of seats behind the circular bar and waved.

I raised my hand, headed toward the bar, and ordered an extra-large jug of marrakechia. It was Souk's version of a sangria but made with red wine, pomegranate seeds, cardamom, Grand Marnier and triple sec.

Unlike most places where it was a red wine watered down with lemonade and chunks of fruit, Souk's sangria was more like spiced wine.

After paying for the drinks, I brought the jug and two glasses over to my friend's seat. Instead of the usual suit, she wore a double-breasted, tailored dress that skimmed her curves, making her look like she was dressed for a hot date.

Beatrice's mahogany hair flowed over her shoulders in loose waves, and her deep-red burgundy lipstick was striking against her dark skin. Despite the glamor, I still saw the pain in her red-rimmed eyes.

Her pretty face broke out in a grin, and she bounced on her cushion. "I stopped by the shop this lunchtime with a hot chocolate. Do you know what I heard?"

I set down the jug and glass on the table and lowered myself into the seat. "Sorry I wasn't around."

She batted my arm. "Why didn't you tell me you knew devastatingly handsome supermodel types who bundled girls into limos?"

My eyes narrowed. "Istabelle told you that?"

"No, Jonathan." She rolled her eyes. "Would you believe he was sitting in the book corner, waiting for you to arrive? As soon as I stepped in, he barraged me with questions about your mystery man."

I pressed my lips together, suppressing a frisson of annoyance. What was it with this guy? Istabelle would have offered to take over my sound bath session, the same way I stood in for her when she was running late.

Picking up the jug, I poured her a generous portion, slowing the stream so only a few pieces of fruit and cloves and cardamom plopped out into the glass.

"Sorry for the interrogation," I said with a groan. "Would you like me to order you something to eat at the bar?"

She waved away the apology and picked up her drink. "Absolutely not. You're going to tell me about this man and why you've kept him a secret. Does he have a friend? A distraction like him might help me get over that two-faced wanker."

I huffed a laugh and poured myself a glass of

sangria. Christian was a mere annoyance compared to the years-long mind games of Valentine Sargon.

"Who was he?" she asked. "The ex you never talk about?"

My gaze met hers, and I caught the expression. It was the kind of hunger for vicarious excitement I used to feel for her juicy details. I wouldn't push if she wasn't ready to talk about Christian.

"It was him," I murmured. "That first year we met, I was too much of an emotional mess to tell you what happened between us."

She brought the glass to her lips and hummed. "That's why I didn't press, and when you seemed better, I didn't want to bring up the subject and drag you down."

I turned to my friend and met her warm brown eyes. They didn't sparkle as they usually did, and I hoped the pain of Christian's betrayal wouldn't linger. "If it wasn't for you and Istabelle, I'm not sure I could have emerged from how that relationship ended."

Beatrice leaned toward me, her lips parted with a question.

Inhaling a deep breath, I scrambled for a way to skirt around the most salient points, such as our true age difference, and the fact that he was royalty and a vampire.

"He was older…" I lowered my gaze to the table. "My boss, I suppose."

Beatrice whistled. "Sexy?"

"To an eighteen-year-old with no experience of life." I raised a shoulder. "He really made an effort to dazzle me, which wasn't difficult, considering I'd never had any luxuries."

My throat dried. Maybe I wasn't so over Valentine as I'd thought. He'd swept me into a whirlwind of sweet words, fun dates, fancy dinners, and passionate kisses, culminating in a marriage proposal.

"He gave me an engagement ring, and I gave him my virginity." I gulped. "Shortly after, he denied that we'd ever even had a relationship."

"Bastard." She squeezed her eyes shut and exhaled a long breath. "What is it with men and their conquests?"

"Maybe they miss the days of hunting woolly mammoths and instead hunt women?" I asked.

Her eyes opened, and she flashed me a broad smile. "You could be right about that. Perhaps the way to get rid of that Jonathan stalker is to say yes."

I wrinkled my nose. "Somehow, I think my hunter theory only works on the alpha types."

We both took long sips of our marrakechia. The spices hit me first, followed by a whiff of fresh pomegranate. Beneath the heady flavors was a fruity merlot—on the opposite spectrum to the dense, savory Châteauneuf-du-Pape I drank with Valentine.

Beatrice waggled her brows. "So… what did he want?"

I shook my head. "Who knows? The man was so cryptic, it almost sounded like another game."

"Will you play along?" she asked from behind her glass.

I reared back and stared at my friend as she swirled her drink. "Whatever for?"

Beatrice raised a shoulder. "Fancy dinners, nights out on the town, dirty weekends, and a few generous gifts?"

"Trust me. Now that I'm free of his influence, the last thing I want is to become ensnared."

She twisted around in her seat, staring at me through shining eyes. "That's what I love most about you. Your strength."

I snorted. "This time next month, you'll have dismissed Christian to a wankstain in history. That's what it means to be strong."

Beatrice's shoulders sagged, and the smile in her eyes dimmed. She set down her glass, picked up the menu, and sighed.

Guilt tightened my chest, and I drew in a sharp breath. I wrapped an arm around her shoulders, not knowing if I had been dismissive toward the depth of her feelings for Christian.

Over the three years I'd known her, she'd had relationships that lasted from days to weeks, most of them ending with dismissals and a few ending with tears.

Beatrice was the most resilient person I'd ever

met. Each time a relationship ended, she had dusted herself off and declared herself ready for the next adventure, so why would things be so different with Christian?

I licked my lips. "Sorry if that sounded flippant—"

"It didn't," she said. "I'm more upset about letting myself get duped."

"Life can be so crap." I leaned into her side and blew out a long breath. "It's hard to tell yourself that things are going too quickly when there's an excited man who keeps calling."

Beatrice nodded. "From now on, I'll play hard to get."

"And miss out on the fun?" I asked.

The corner of her mouth curled into a smile. "Alright. I'll play not so easy to get."

"It's a pity we have to play these games at all." I peered over her shoulder at the menu. "What do you want to eat?"

"Ugh," she said.

"What's wrong?"

"When you weren't in the crystal shop, I left to go back to work, but Jonathan followed."

My brows rose. "What?"

"I know," she said with a groan. "I even ducked into Starbucks to escape his incessant whining and ordered a huge panini, hoping he wouldn't wait around for the baristas to grill it."

My brows drew together. Something in her

pained expression told me her plan to avoid him had backfired.

"Do you know he plonked himself opposite me, sipping from a thermos flask and demanding to know your intentions toward the mystery man?"

"Bloody hell," I muttered.

"At one point, I nearly choked on my panini."

I pursed my lips. Up until Valentine showed up at the shop, Jonathan had only been a minor annoyance. The next time I saw him, it would be to cut ties and ask him not to keep bothering me for dates.

We ordered our favorites starters—stuffed olives, kofta kebabs made of minced lamb infused with a delicious array of herbs, maakouda, a spicy potato pancake that came with a yoghurt dip, and caramelized onion hummus with slices of toasted pitta bread. The waitress brought a sweet mint tea, served in a glass.

By the end of happy hour, most of the students had left, replaced by a mixed crowd of office workers and casually-dressed people looking like they would move on to one of Soho's many nightclubs. Beatrice bought herself a hookah blend of passion and hops, which emitted a yellowish smoke that mingled with the other scents drifting around the bar.

Loud chatter filled the space and the DJ increased the volume, playing an Arabic song overlaid with the voice of a man rapping in French. As Beatrice's eyelids drooped, we moved on to nous-nous coffee, a half-milk, half espresso-blend stronger than any latte.

I was about to ask for the check when a waitress placed a bucket of champagne on our table. It was a 2008 Dom Pérignon. In a place like this, it probably cost five hundred pounds.

"Excuse me?" I met the woman's dark eyes. "We didn't order champagne."

The waitress pointed toward the bar. "It's from the gentleman over there."

My pulse quickened to the beat of the drums playing over the speaker. Alcohol had dulled my senses, and I couldn't feel an approaching vampire. Had Valentine followed me here?

I peered over the waitress's shoulder for signs of the dark-haired menace. Instead, a middle-aged man with salt and pepper hair standing close turned to us and tipped an imaginary hat.

Disappointment pulled my heart into my stomach. Maybe it was because I hadn't allowed myself the chance to tell Valentine how I really felt. It certainly wasn't out of wanting to see the vampire king.

I snatched my gaze away from Mr. Tall, Dark, and Peppery to meet Beatrice's narrowed eyes.

"Thanks, but no thanks," she said over the volume of the Moroccan rap.

The waitress bent toward us. "Mr. Masood is a regular here. He buys drinks for girls all the time and never expects anything in return. He always tips me well for delivering a bottle."

I exchanged a glance with Beatrice. This scenario sounded as fishy as the tuna tartare I'd had for lunch. Guys who sent over champagne usually wanted to saunter over to ask how we were enjoying the drinks, making girls feel obliged to offer them their company in exchange for their generosity. This one showed no sign that he wanted to join us.

Taking a deep breath, I concentrated on the bottle. It was fine, but power radiated from the champagne flutes the waitress set on the table.

"How much does he usually tip?" I asked.

Her brows drew together. "A tenner. Why?"

I slipped a hand in my pocket and opened my purse, but the waitress shook her head, seeming to understand what I was trying to do.

"Did any of the girls who accepted his drinks ever return to the bar?" I asked.

Her eyes widened. "What are you talking about?"

"Just be careful with that guy," I muttered. "Could you bring the payment machine, please? We're leaving."

She offered me a slow nod, and hurried in the direction of the bar.

Beatrice leaned into me and frowned. "What was that all about?"

"Time to go home. There's a hunter on the prowl."

I pulled out my smartphone, fired up the Uber app and called for a car.

Someone five minutes away accepted my request, and I slipped my phone in my pocket and waited for it to buzz with the driver's arrival. When the waitress returned with the card scanner, I paid her and rose off the low seat, making sure to accidentally knock the glasses on the floor. They didn't smash as I'd hoped but rolled under the table.

As we walked through the busy bar, the man's gaze followed us through the crowd. It was time to make an anonymous report to the Supernatural Council's enforcers, or tell Valentine that there was a supernatural in Soho, preying on girls.

CHAPTER SEVEN

As we stepped out of the bar and bundled into the Uber, hints of unstable crackling energy lashed at my back. It was the sort of rage I'd only experienced from a were creature or a shifter.

I peered through the tinted window in Souk's door, waiting for it to slam open with a half-transformed Mr. Masood, but a large group of men approached the guards stationed outside, who refused to let them in.

I turned my attention to the backseat, where Beatrice sat beside me with her head bowed, seeming too tired to ask questions. If this had been a bar in Logris, Mr. Masood would have chased after us, raging that we had wasted his costly champagne.

Beatrice bowed her head and dozed off in the back of the car, making me wonder if she had gotten any sleep the night before. From the way her voice had cracked in the morning, it sounded as though she'd spent the entire night trying to decipher Christian's dismissive behavior.

After crossing Oxford Street, which was still busy with double-decker busses and late-night shoppers, the Uber took the backroads and deposited us outside my building in Grosvenor Square. I nudged Beatrice awake and brought her inside to stay the night. Since she kept so many items in my closet, she barely needed to go home during the week.

The next morning, I awoke to the door clicking shut, followed by the nutty scent of freshly-brewed coffee. I sat up on the sofa bed to find Beatrice sauntering inside with a huge paper bag. She was already clad in a black suit and my hot pink tank top that looked a thousand times better against her tanned skin.

"You went out?" I croaked.

She shook her head and smirked. "I told the Deliveroo driver not to ring and met him downstairs."

Beatrice walked to the table and set out plate-sized paper cartons, transparent cups of orange juice, insulated coffee cups, and some mystery items in white paper bags. Because of her long commute, she usually woke earlier than me and must have used that time to arrange this wonderful surprise.

"Thank you." I placed a hand over my mouth to stifle a yawn. "How are you feeling today?"

She turned to me and paused, her eyes rolling to the ceiling. "Silly."

"Why?"

"At our age, we should know there's no such thing as love at first sight."

"True." I slid off the bed and padded across the studio's wooden floor. "But it's hard to fight infatuation."

After extracting some disposable knives and forks, she lowered herself into the seat. "Combined with the most mind-blowing sex."

"Yeah," I said with a sigh.

Beatrice turned to me and frowned. "You still remember—"

"It's hard to forget sometimes." Not that I had anything to compare it to, but that first and only time with Valentine was also the first time he'd consented to bite me.

My throat dried, and a tiny flutter of desire pulsed between my legs. Vampire saliva had the power to make a girl beg, but vampire bites were as addictive as crack cocaine. They had ten times the explosive power of a good orgasm and the vampire's saliva lingered in the bloodstream long enough to wreak havoc on the victim's dopamine receptors.

At least that was how Istabelle had described it during a desperate patch when I had been tempted to return to Logris. I'd been suffering the most horrific withdrawal and hadn't even known until she pointed it out. After realizing how deeply sex with Valentine had affected my body, I became determined to endure an intensive detox, no matter how much it would hurt.

I took my seat, watching my best friend crack open the packages and peer at their contents.

"Gosh, I love living in Central London," I said, licking my lips.

"You're so lucky." She placed a polystyrene box in front of me. "But I suppose Wimbledon isn't that bad. We also get all the restaurants down there or via an app."

"If a person could afford it, they'd never need to cook." I opened up the container to find poached eggs in hollandaise sauce with grilled tomatoes, portobello mushrooms, sliced avocados, and potato rosti, an upscale version of hash browns.

Beatrice hummed her agreement, opening her portion of bacon, sausage, and black pudding, which I found too heavy for a weekday breakfast.

"Thanks for this." I sliced through the grilled tomatoes, watching its contents spill into the container.

"It's me who should be thanking you," she murmured. "How many times have you given me a place to stay when I've been too distraught or knackered to go home?"

I shook my head and smiled. It was a miracle enough that I managed to score this amazing little studio. Istabelle paid me enough to feed and clothe myself and I made decent tips from healing. Without Beatrice's sparking personality and her international tax consultant salary, my social life wouldn't be so glamorous.

"Baked beans?" She raised a polystyrene tub.

"Yes, please."

She pulled off its lid and poured half its contents into my container. "How could I have been so..." She shook her head. "So—"

"Don't punish yourself for trying to find happiness," I murmured.

She turned her sad brown eyes to me and frowned. "He was just too good to be true."

I exhaled a long breath and dipped a piece of mushroom into the yolk. What was it the humans said? "It was something to chalk up to experience."

"Yeah." She tore off a piece of sausage with her teeth.

My mind rolled back to how I'd felt seeing Valentine outside the store. Resentment, apprehension, and hope?

"What are you going to do about your ex?" she asked through her mouthful.

"Ignore him." I bit down hard on a crunchy piece of potato and scowled into my breakfast.

Beatrice paused, waiting for me to elaborate.

I shook my head. There was no going back to him after such a cruel breakup. "Did you know he had the nerve to look confused when I didn't fall at his feet?"

"Typical." She pulled off the lid of her orange juice and took a large gulp.

Valentine reminded me of a movie I once watched—Dangerous Liaisons, starring Glenn Close and John Malkovich as a pair of jaded aristocrats who toyed with others for amusement.

One of their victims was a pious woman played by Michelle Pfeiffer, who John Malkovich had taken great efforts to seduce and then dump at the request of Glenn Close's character. After he'd completely destroyed Michelle Pfeiffer, he proudly announced that winning her back would be his greatest triumph.

I shook off those thoughts. Valentine probably didn't want me back—not even as a joke. Maybe he came to warn me about the Masood character prowling Central London for girls.

I took a long sip of my orange juice, letting the sweet liquid slide down my throat. Maybe I was wasting too much energy and thought on a man I wouldn't see again for another three years.

After breakfast, Beatrice left to catch up with the work she'd missed the day before, and I hauled myself into the shower and prepared for a day at the crystal shop.

Jonathan was waiting in the doorway with his shoulders around his ears and his hands stuffed into his camel-colored Paddington Bear coat.

My heart sank. "What are you doing here?"

"You didn't turn up for our eleven-thirty session." Jonathan kicked a penny into the side of the shop.

My insides cringed. "Sorry about that, but I won't be able to see you anymore."

His gaze rose to meet my eyes, and he rocked forward, looming in on me like a specter. "Why? Because of that man?"

I shook my head. "You seem to want something from me I can't give you."

Jonathan's mouth fell open, and his eyes went round with faux shock. "Sound healing?"

Irritation fizzled across my skin. I'd spent enough time reading the Cosmopolitan website to know when I was being gaslighted. And I could count on every finger and every toe the behaviors Jonathan displayed that indicated he wanted our association to extend beyond professional.

Pursing my lips, I exhaled an annoyed breath. What was the point of arguing with him when he would argue back to extend the conversation and change my mind?

Instead of playing his game, I answered his question directly. "I can't give you sound healing, either."

He continued standing in the doorway, blinking rapidly as though trying to dislodge something in his eye.

A taxi stopped behind us, its diesel engine rattling. Someone opened the door and slammed it shut, and the taxi moved away. Jonathan's eyes slid in the direction of the retreating vehicle.

"Who was that man you were with yesterday?" he asked.

"Please leave," I said.

He raised his chin and scowled. "Mera, it's a simple question."

"And none of your business." I curled my hands into fists. "For the second time, leave."

Jonathan's Adam's apple bobbed up and down. He licked his lips, seeming to want to say something but shook his head instead. "Give me a call if you change your mind. Do you want my number?"

"Mrs. Bonham-Sackville will have it somewhere in her archives, and I won't change my mind." I stepped aside, giving him ample space to leave.

Jonathan's breathing quickened, making his thin chest rise and fall. I was about to threaten to call the police when he stepped out of the shop's entranceway and stared down at me like a man committing a face to memory.

My insides writhed at the scrutiny, and I forced myself not to flinch. When he finally turned to walk down Upper Brook Street, I finally emptied my lungs with a sigh of relief.

That didn't mean I would turn my back on Jonathan. Even though he'd never once raised his voice or indicated he would turn violent, the man's behavior was becoming unsettling.

Jonathan continued down the road with his head bowed and his long feet scuffing the paving stones. I took a step back, wondering what had become of my promised vampire guard, and bumped into a large figure.

My breath caught. "Sorry."

I whirled around to see a stern-looking man with slicked-back hair and charcoal-gray eyes. He glowered down at me and bared crooked oversized teeth.

"Watch where you're going, girl," he snapped.

"You, too," I said.

He paused and glared at me from over his shoulder. "Pardon?"

The challenge in his voice made my hackles rise. I pulled back my shoulders and raised my chin. "You were walking behind me when I stepped backward. That meant you must have seen me coming, right?"

The man flinched and hurried down the road. Now it was my turn to glower at his back. I'd only taken one step back and that was toward the Crystal shop. Why hadn't he walked around me or sidestepped?

I shook my head, letting him also disappear down the road. Maybe it was Samhain that messed with everyone's minds or Mercury being in retrograde or the Ides of October. Maybe it was just me, attracting the wrong kind of attention.

I stepped into the doorway, unlocked the shop, and made sure to lock it. Istabelle emerged from behind the counter, making my heart leapfrog into my throat. I staggered back with my hand on my chest. "Bloody hell."

"Sorry for frightening you, dear." She placed her palms on the counter. "I simply couldn't sleep, knowing you'd disappeared with King Valentine."

A tight band of guilt wound around my chest and settled at the base of my throat. I'd been so preoccupied with the return of Valentine and with Beatrice's heartbreak over Christian that I hadn't considered what my boss might be thinking.

Isabelle was the only person in the world—natural or supernatural—who knew the effect Valentine had had on my body and soul. Istabelle had bloody healed me. Of course she would worry.

I crossed the shop floor, inhaling a long, deep breath and forcing it out of my lungs. "It should be me apologizing."

"What did His Majesty want?" she asked, her voice breathy with concern.

"He says I'm in danger."

Istabelle reared back. "Whatever from?"

I spread my arms wide in a shrug. "There's a lot he wouldn't say, but I met a shifter in a bar who sent over a bucket of champagne with enchanted glasses."

"What kind of shifter?"

"I couldn't tell," I said with a frown.

She raised a hand. "Of course. At your age, I found it hard enough to distinguish between supernaturals. You've done extremely well to identify his species."

The tightening of my chest loosened a little, and I told Istabelle everything I'd learned about Mr. Masood.

"Did you know why I didn't feel his magic until after I'd left the bar?"

"That was probably his rage," she said. "Sensing intense emotions in supernaturals is part of being sensitive to magic. It made his power bleed through."

My brows furrowed. "Bleed through what?"

"Have you heard of the Cleopatra stone?" she asked.

I shook my head.

"You've heard of chrysopoeia, correct?" Without giving me a chance to reply, she continued. "Back when alchemists tried to transmute lead into gold, they developed a more noble substance than anything that occurred in nature."

"The Cleopatra stone?" I asked.

She shook her head. "It's not a single object but a manufactured substance that cloaks power while allowing its wielder to use their magic."

I bit down on my lip, picturing the man from last night standing with a huge lump of rock in his pocket. "You think Masood was wearing it?"

Istabelle nodded. "How else could he have entered an establishment and observed you for long enough to select you as his target?"

"Me?" I placed a hand on my chest.

"Do you know how rare we are?" she said.

I raised a shoulder. About one percent of supernaturals were born without magic, but while I was growing up, I'd only heard taunts from people my age that I wouldn't amount to anything other than a blood cow or a surrogate for a wealthy vampire.

"There's a reason why the King of the Vampires sought you for a mate," she murmured.

"Because a supernatural is guaranteed strong offspring with a magicless supernatural," I parroted.

"Don't underestimate that power." She shot me an admonishing glower. "Take the morning off to learn everything you can about Cleopatra stone and how to overcome its ability to cloak magic."

"What will we do about Masood?" I asked.

"I'll get in touch with the enforcers." She swept her arm toward the door that led to the basement library.

~

After work that day, Macavity and I sat at the little dinner table. He ate a piece of fresh salmon I'd gotten half-price at Tesco, and I'd baked the other piece and served it with coleslaw and potato salad the store had also knocked down because of its expiry date.

That was the benefit to working opposite a supermarket and knowing which times of the day the staff discounted the soon-to-be-out-of-date food.

"Want to know what I learned at work today?" I asked the Bengal cat.

His right ear twitched, his way of telling me he was still listening but wasn't interested enough to make eye contact.

"Only a few alchemists managed to create the philosopher's stone, and one of them was called Cleopatra the Great."

Macavity paused to spare me a glance.

"Not the Egyptian queen," I said. "She was a lady who developed a special item that could mask magic. People call it Cleopatra stone."

Macavity raised his head from the plate and sat on his haunches, which was unusual for a cat who hadn't finished eating his fish.

I set down my knife and fork, wondering if he was being more attentive because it was Samhain or if he was about to cough up a hairball.

"Alright," I said, giving him the benefit of the doubt. "Cleopatra stone hides the magic of supernaturals, and it's used by elite members of the Council's enforcers for covert missions."

His eyes narrowed.

I tilted my head to the side. Did he think I was making it up? When Macavity didn't utter a meow of protest, I continued. "But it only works to a certain point. When their emotions run high or its user is in danger, they can overpower the stone and expose their hiding place."

Macavity jumped down from the table and scampered to the door.

My shoulders sagged. So much for believing the cat was actually listening. He probably just stopped eating to get a bit of fresh air.

I opened the apartment door, expecting him to run off into the hallway and down the stairs, but he only moved his front paws through the doorway, tilted his head, and meowed.

"What's wrong?" I crouched down to his level, holding the door for balance.

Macavity turned around and trotted back to the dining table.

I stared out into the apartment building's communal areas, wondering what the cat wanted to tell me. Nobody was outside, in the hallway, or on the stairs, so I guess he just changed his mind about wanting a walk.

When I turned back to check on Macavity, he stood on the table with his front paws on my plate, gulping down my cooked salmon like a demon.

"You little—" I clenched my teeth.

Why was I pissed off with a cat who had already proven himself a food thief? I slammed the door and stalked over to the refrigerator, where I'd left the rest of the potato salad and coleslaw.

"That's the last time I'll ever fall for that trick," I muttered.

Macavity ignored my rant and continued eating my salmon before moving back to his plate. What was wrong with the bloody cat? He was already cheating with me with whoever gave him that name tag. The creature was also a wretched flirt who would take snacks from anyone who thought he was cute.

I tore open a pack of cooked chicken I'd planned on using to make sandwiches for tomorrow's lunch and added a few pieces to my new meal.

The worst part about having a posh cat was his expensive tastes. Macavity wouldn't eat kibble or even gourmet cat food. Whoever really owned him had fed him on a diet of meat and fish, meaning that the cat didn't recognize anything else as food.

Macavity's paws hit the wooden floorboards, indicating he'd already finished the best parts of my former meal. Moments later, something warm and furry rubbed against my leg.

"Bugger off," I muttered.

He pulled himself up the cupboard with his front paws so he stood like Puss in Boots. "Meow?" he asked, curling his tail like a question mark. "Meow!"

"You didn't finish your actual dinner," I said with some bite. "Go away."

Macavity shook his head, letting out a series of plaintive yowls.

I glowered down at the green-eyed menace. "No."

He sat on his haunches and placed his front paws together, looking like he was praying.

"Alright then." I cringed as I said the words. How could I let a cat boss me around in my own home? "If you're still hungry after finishing your salmon, I'll give you a bit of chicken."

Macavity bolted across the room, leaped onto the chair, then onto the table, and ate his salmon at a more sedate pace.

What a devious little cat.

I had a few minutes to finish my new meal before Macavity could harass me for more food, so I took the sofa instead of the table. The cat raised his head and stared at me through narrowed eyes, seeming to have worked out that I didn't trust him around my meals.

No longer in the mood to tell Macavity about my day, I picked up the remote and fired up our favorite movie, Dirty Dancing.

It wasn't like I saw myself as the main character, plucked out of obscurity by an unfeasibly handsome man with a body that could twist a girl into knots. Dirty Dancing was just a guilty pleasure with an amazing soundtrack and great dance moves.

When Macavity was in a good mood, he'd even allow me to lift him over my head and he'd stretch out his front and back legs.

The Ronettes finished singing *Be My Baby*, and

Macavity jumped down from the table. I glanced at the plates, finding them both devoid of salmon.

"Where do you put all that food?" I shook my head, wondering if I should get him checked out for worms.

Macavity stalked toward me, licking his chops. As he walked across a beam of moonlight streaming in through a chink in the curtains, the cat froze.

"What's wrong with you now?" I stuffed a large forkful of chicken and potato salad in my mouth.

The cat hissed, jumped back and bolted for the door.

I rose to my feet, leaving my meal on the sofa. "I swear, if this is another trick—"

Macavity fell onto his side, jerking and shuddering and yowling as though scalded. Cold shock barreled through my gut and spread across my insides. I'd finally overfed him and now he was having a fit. My numb fingers scrambled for my smartphone, but I'd left it on the table by the half-eaten plate.

"Please don't die." I dashed across the room and picked up the phone.

A low growl reverberated across the room, sounding like it had come from something larger than a domestic cat. Macavity twisted and turned on the wooden floorboards, now twice his normal size and increasing with every passing second.

Panic exploded across my chest, bringing with it

enough adrenaline to leap over the convulsing cat and wrench open the door. I'd never seen what happened to a were during the full moon. Their bites were infectious with absolutely no cure.

I bolted down the hallway and tumbled down the stairs with my pulse pounding between my ears, urging me to hurry out of there before I got infected or torn to shreds.

As far as I knew, no were-creatures ever spent their lives as cats outside the full moon, but I wasn't about to wait around for Macavity to finish his transformation.

CHAPTER EIGHT

I dashed down the marble stairs, holding on to the iron banister for balance. The cold barely registered on my bare feet because Macavity's low growl sent a fresh spike of cold panic through my veins.

The staircase curled down toward the ground floor, now seeming an endless labyrinth of concentric circles. What the hell was I doing? I should have taken the bloody elevator. Should have locked myself in the bathroom and climbed out onto the roof.

At any moment, Macavity would finish his transformation, and the ever-ravenous cat would pounce.

My bare feet stumbled and slapped on the stairs, stinging my soles with every step. I didn't have my phone, my keys, my pajama bottoms.

Just as I rounded the corner and dashed through the landing of the fourth or fifth floor, a dark figure stepped out from the shadows. It was the man from earlier, who bumped into me on the street. I sprinted toward him, caught in his staring black eyes.

The man bared his teeth and snarled, raising his hands above his head. Normally, I'd find a sight like him menacing, but I had minutes—if not seconds—before Macavity caught up with me and attacked. His gaze dropped to my bottom half and he gaped. Hadn't he ever seen a half-naked girl running for her life?

"Get out of my way," I bellowed.

His lip curled, looking like he was about to say something threatening when Macavity roared.

A heavy thud reverberated through the hallway, making my heart want to leap out of my chest. The bloody cat had finished transforming and was now trying to break down the door.

The man's gaze turned upward. "What in the name of Tartarus—"

"Run." I barreled past, letting the loud snarls speak for themselves.

"Wait," he growled.

Something cool and slimy looped around my wrist, and pulled me into a body that radiated cold power. The man's arms wrapped around my waist, and more of that slime snaked around my neck, cutting off my air.

I screamed, and a flare of yellow light filled the hallway, making him release me with a moan.

An explosion of crashing wood echoed down the stairwell, wiping away speculations on what just happened. Macavity had broken through my apartment door and was probably ready for fresh meat.

Creepy guys with shadowy powers didn't matter. If I didn't put as much distance as possible between me and the transformed cat, I'd either be dead or joining him next month under the full moon.

As though propelled by an invisible force, I glided down the stairs, now taking them three or four at a time. Macavity made a low rumble that filled my veins with ice. Finally, I reached the bottom of the stairs, dashed down the black-and-white-tiled hallway to the front door, and escaped into the night.

Cold wind swirled around my body, chilling the sweat clinging to my bare flesh. The front door slammed behind me, but it was too early to cry out my relief. If Macavity could break out of my apartment, he might be able to break out of the building.

Strong hands caught me around the arms, pulling me into a broad chest. A burst of terror squeezed my heart, tearing a scream from my trembling lips.

"Morata," murmured a familiar voice.

My head snapped up, and I stared into Valentine's worried eyes. "There's a cat—" A breath caught in the back of my throat as the full extent of what I'd just escaped seized my muscles in a full-body tremor. "Werecat."

A guttural roar echoed from behind the door,

sounding deep within the hallway. Valentine ushered me away from the building, through the cars parked around the square, and across the road to where the trees bordered the fenced garden.

My flesh crawled at the prospect of being close to a predator's hiding place, but it was nothing compared to the way my heart pounded at the prospect of a gigantic werecat.

Valentine pressed a key into my hand. "Take this and get into my car."

"We should leave together," I stuttered.

"Someone is out to either kill or capture you." He closed my fingers around the key. "If I don't eliminate them now, you'll be running until they succeed."

Valentine released my shoulders and stalked across the road. He turned around and met my gaze with flashing red eyes.

"Go," he barked.

Flinching at the ferocity of his command, I stared down at the key. It was one of those fobs with a button and a logo and no actual metal to stick into a keyhole. I pointed it further down the road and pressed what I hoped was a command to open the door. The indicator lights of a black Lamborghini flashed on and off, so I jogged to the car and slipped into the cool leather seat.

The sliders on the dashboard were a cross between a recording studio's MIDI controllers and something out of Star Trek. I couldn't tell if they were for controlling the car or controlling the stereo.

Valentine had taught me to drive in Aunt Arianna's Volkswagen Polo. I had no idea how to work this over-engineered dickmobile. I fumbled around the steering wheel for an ignition and snarled. The Lamborghini didn't even have a key.

"Bloody hell," I muttered under my breath and peered into the side mirror, watching Valentine at the building's front door.

One of its panels exploded, and a massive paw swiped at the vampire's face. I clapped both hands over my mouth to suppress a yelp. In the dim light, I couldn't see what Macavity had turned into, but I was guessing it was the size of a tiger or a lion.

My fingers trembled across the dashboard, pressing switch after switch until they stumbled over a red button, and the engine roared to life. Now to pull out of the parking space and get the vehicle moving. I took another glance out of the rearview mirror to find a beast as large as a liger leaping toward Valentine.

"What?" I cried.

The streetlights illuminated an orange form with a dense pattern of black spots, looking like a larger, more muscular version of Macavity's domestic cat form. Except that now, the creature was frozen in midair.

Valentine twisted his raised hand and spun the

huge cat in the air. With a roar, the monster tried swiping at Valentine's face, but he was too fast. Every muscle in my body froze. What the hell was that vampire doing to the big cat?

I couldn't even call that thing a leopard because they were supposed to be no longer than five-three. This thing seemed longer than Valentine's six-two frame and was supernatural, meaning it could match the strength of a vampire.

A cry caught in my throat, and I clutched at my chest. Valentine didn't move things often with his mind. What if his control slipped? He'd get mauled. And all I could do was sit like a damsel in a distressed t-shirt in a soon-to-be-opened-like-a-can-of-corned-beef sports car.

The next time I dared to look out of the window, Valentine floated an unmoving Macavity through the front doors. My throat dried. He'd won?

I turned off the car and opened the door, trying to piece the events of the evening together. Macavity, the ravenous stray cat who had slept on my bed for several full moons, had chosen tonight to transform. Why? Because it was also Samhain?

Cool wind blew down the square, and shadows cast by the nearby trees shifted. I stared into the garden for signs of movement or for the feel of the unstable, angry energy of Mr. Masood, but the only supernaturals I could feel came from my building. Just the sharp, feral magic of a newly transformed

Macavity and the seductive, smoky power of a vampire.

I bit down on my lip. Werewolves and werecats were difficult to kill. As a vampire king, Valentine had to know this. Perhaps he was keeping Macavity hostage until the full moon ended for an interrogation. I had to find out what was happening upstairs and tell him not to waste his time. Macavity would only transform back into a cat.

My building's front door was a mass of broken pieces, hanging off a single hinge. I eased my way through the gap in the doorframe, crept over splintered wood, and continued to the stairs.

"Miss Griffin?" trilled a haughty voice from behind.

My heart stuttered. I whirled around with my hand on my chest to lock gazes with Mrs. Howard, the old lady who lived downstairs. She wore a brown, fur-lined housecoat that looked like something out of the 1950's.

"Yes?" I replied.

"Will you tell whoever keeps playing their DVDs to be more considerate to their neighbors? I heard that racket through my doors."

She stared at me through glazed eyes, indicating she'd recently been mesmerized and likely ordered to tell everyone that the noise they heard was just a movie.

"Alright, Mrs. Howard. I'll do that," I murmured.

"And tell that gentleman I met in the hallway that dogs, no matter their pedigree, are not permitted in this building!"

"Right." I bounded up the stairs in case Valentine had ordered the old lady to say something else.

Not everyone in our building lived here full-time. Many were politicians and high-level executives who rented a pied-à-terre to cut down on a daily commute and returned to their country homes on the weekend. For example, the man downstairs flew in from Scotland so he could represent his constituency in the Houses of Parliament.

Thankfully, it was a Friday night, and the few of us who stayed the weekends were probably out having fun. I continued up the staircase, passing flickering wall lights that Macavity had probably smashed on the way down. On the third floor, something warm dripped onto my fingers.

I snatched my hand away from the banister and glanced up. Dark liquid drizzled from the fourth floor, looking disconcertingly like blood. My heart spasmed, and shards of terror splintered my insides.

This had to be Macavity's doing. Supernatural vampires didn't thirst for the liquid and only required a trace amount to maintain their iron levels.

My pulse pounded between my ears and an iron ball of dread rolled around my belly as I made my slow ascent up the stairs. Who had Macavity attacked and were they still alive? I swallowed several times around a dry throat, hoping that the blood just came from a flesh wound.

A ragged breath escaped my lips. I wished I'd listened to Valentine and driven across the river to Beatrice's or even around the corner and stayed the night on one of the shop's treatment tables. It was too late now. Now, I would have to witness the extent of Macavity's rampage and possibly his death.

I reached the fourth-floor landing and rounded the corner to find three fingers lying in a pool of blood. A single black shoe lay a few feet away from the dark liquid, but apart from that, there was nothing—no footsteps or smudges or smears— nothing to indicate that the person had survived and had managed to escape.

Shuddering at the thought of walking through someone's blood, I backed down the stairs and took the elevator up to the seventh floor. The clanky car climbed the levels, making me twitch with each crank of the old-fashioned elevator. Eventually, the doors creaked open, and I continued through to my apartment's smashed-in door.

Inside, I heard Patrick Swayze shouting at Jennifer Grey to hold the position. Just as she screamed and fell into the water with a splash, I held my breath and stepped inside, hoping that Macavity hadn't awoken and overpowered Valentine.

The sofa bed lay unfolded with Valentine sitting on the end engrossed in Dirty Dancing. Next to him sat a gigantic but conscious leopard with his spotted tail curled like a question mark.

They looked more like old friends than a pair of supernatural monsters who'd just engaged in a bitter fight.

My mouth dropped open. "What's going on?"

Macavity turned around and shot me the same narrow-eyed glower he used whenever I interrupted his fun. I reared back, trying to process the scene unfolding on my sofa bed.

Valentine twisted around, holding what was left of my chicken. "Did you see the dead assassin?"

"What do you mean—" A memory tumbled into the front of my mind. That strange man I'd bumped into earlier this morning appearing on the fourth-floor landing. Macavity dashing to the door, looking suspicious.

What if Macavity hadn't been trying to scam me out of extra salmon but had sensed an intruder? What if the reason he'd eaten so much was to power his transformation?

I glanced from the vampire to the giant cat. "What's happening?"

Valentine picked up a broken collar. "Macavity needs to borrow a slimline belt."

A hysterical laugh bubbled from my throat. "My cat's just turned into a monstrous leopard, and you're worried about the state of his accessories?"

Macavity hissed, but the sound just sent shards of

irritation across my skin. The cat just killed a man and wanted me to stop spoiling his enjoyment of the movie?

Valentine rose from the bed and walked across the room, fixing me with eyes that were now a deep violet. Heat bloomed across my skin. He used to gaze at me like that before we kissed, before he would spiral me into a whirlwind of desire with lips that never failed to deliver pleasure.

The pulse between my ears thudded hard enough to drown out the movie. This wasn't happening. I wouldn't melt at the sight of this wretched vampire, wouldn't let him charm me into staying quiet.

I didn't spend the past three years working hard to overcome a crushing heartbreak just to let myself get hurt. I stepped back, hitting my shoulder against the doorframe.

"Now do you believe me that your life is in danger?" Valentine's deep voice curled around my senses like hookah smoke. He cupped my cheek, the warmth of his palm adding to the heat of my skin.

My heart lurched into my dry throat, and my eyes longed to flutter shut and savor his touch. I rolled his question around in my mind, savoring the nuances of his words.

"There was a man on the fourth-floor landing earlier," I murmured.

Valentine frowned. "I had people watching the back of the building."

I raised a shoulder. "He stepped out of shadows and grabbed me."

His gaze swept down my baggy t-shirt and bare legs. "Did he hurt you?"

"He didn't get a chance. Macavity's roar distracted him and I ran." At least that was what I remembered. Adrenaline still coursed through my veins, making everything seem fuzzy.

He was probably a shadow mage. I sensed their energy as devoid of heat, bending and stretching and fading the way shadows do in changing light.

"Now do you believe there's an assassin?" Valentine asked, his eyes softening.

Something inside me flipped at the way he looked at me, but I lowered my lashes. Being a shadow mage didn't mean the man had come to kill me. I was a nobody with no power, missed by no one. What if Valentine had hired him to attack me in the hallway?

I shook off those thoughts and focused my gaze on Valentine's beauty mark. The mage was dead. I saw the blood and the disembodied fingers.

"Morata," Valentine drawled.

"Don't call me that," I snapped.

If Valentine hadn't lied about something as huge as his love for me, I wouldn't be standing here in a grubby t-shirt with a patch of blood three floors below me and a gigantic leopard on my bed.

He exhaled a weary breath like I was the one with the problem. "That man you encountered was an assassin sent to kill you. This apartment is no longer safe."

"Why?" I met his gaze.

His brows furrowed. "Did you miss what I said about the assassin?"

I narrowed my eyes. "You know exactly what I'm asking." I flung my arm to the side. "Why did Macavity turn into a leopard? Why is he suddenly tame when he's just killed a man, and why were you lurking outside my building?"

Valentine drew back, letting his gaze skim me once more, starting from my messy hair, down my shapeless t-shirt, bare thighs and to my bare feet, which were now probably encrusted with dirt and dried blood. His gaze swept up on my body, lingering on my erect nipples.

I curled my shoulders, wrapped an arm around my waist and fought back a flush. "You still haven't answered my question."

"Did you not agree to a vampire guard?" He raised a dark brow.

"Yes, but I thought you were talking about one of your security vampires," I said.

The corner of Valentine's mouth lifted into an amused smile.

Alright, maybe I was getting the terminology wrong, and the males were vassals or footmen or some other word to indicate they were working for a king, but that wasn't the bloody point.

"Are you complaining that I came to save you tonight?" he asked.

"No—"

"Then I don't know why you're making a fuss."

"You didn't answer my question." I pointed at the leopard, who now lay on his front, taking up the entire bed. "What about Macavity?"

Valentine's smile faded. "Your aunt thought he should watch over you in case someone hostile came to your apartment."

My eyes widened, and I met Valentine's gaze. When I was growing up, Aunt Arianna never let me have a cat because she was allergic to the creatures. Macavity had been with me since I'd moved into Grosvenor Square.

"She sent him?" I asked.

Valentine's hand on my cheek slid down my neck and onto my shoulder, leaving a trail of delicious warmth. "Pack your things before they send another assassin."

"Who?" I asked. "But I haven't—"

"Mera," he growled. "Get changed or I will transport you as-is to the safe house."

I stared down at my too-short t-shirt, bare legs, and filthy feet. "You wouldn't dare—"

Before I could complete that sentence, I was over his shoulder, traveling at the speed of sound through the hallways, and deposited in the warm leather seat of a limousine. Moments later, the limousine door opened, and Macavity stalked inside.

I ground my teeth. Was Valentine really going to leave me alone with a fully transformed and ravenous werecat?

CHAPTER NINE

Valentine didn't join me in the back of the limo. I thought Macavity would set upon me during the car ride through the London streets, but the leopard stared at me through a green eye and went to sleep. Perhaps he'd been tired out by a night of shifting and murder.

I stared out of the window, trying to work out where we were going. We passed the edge of Grosvenor Square and entered Upper Grosvenor Street, which ran parallel to the crystal shop's stretch of road. At Park Lane, the limo turned right and continued along the east side of Hyde Park.

By now, my heart rate had returned to normal, and I rubbed a patch of cold on my arm where the shadow mage had grabbed me. A line of residual power pulsed around my throat.

Back then, I'd been pumped full of adrenaline and

was too terrified of what Macavity might become to notice what the man was doing. Now that I was calm and no longer in danger, I could focus on the sensation clinging to my skin.

The only way to describe it was the feeling you got when the sun disappeared behind a cloud on an autumn day. In the middle of summer, clouds were a respite from the sun, but autumn had a tendency to make a person miss the warmth. The shadow mage's touch wasn't just an absence of heat. It was an absence of love.

And what was the light that had caused him to release his grip? I glanced down at the firestone tattoos, wondering if they had attacked the man.

I turned my gaze down to the lounging leopard taking up the entire length of the limousine's L-shaped seat. "Macavity?"

The leopard's right ear twitched to say he was listening but not interested enough to raise his head.

"Were you sent to protect me?" I asked in a small voice.

Macavity nodded.

I swallowed hard and stared at his golden fur. I longed to feel if it was as soft and rich and luxurious as it looked. My hand twitched toward his shoulder, but I curled my fingers into fists and forced it back.

This was the same creature who had reduced a man to a puddle of blood. He probably didn't want my grubby hands over his majestic fur.

"Are you a werecat?" I asked.

He shook his head and snarled.

I sucked in a shocked breath through my teeth. "Right. Because a werecat would be human throughout the month and a cat on the full moon."

Macavity let out a soft snort, and his breathing deepened, indicating that he was asleep and not to be disturbed.

I glanced out of the window, watching the north side of Hyde Park race by on the left and Lancaster Gate station on the right.

In the Supernatural World, there were werewolves, humans who transformed only on the full moon, wolf-shifters, who could transform any time they wished, and then variations of beings with similar transformational abilities.

So, that meant were-tigers were only tigers once a month, while tiger-shifters could choose whenever they wanted to revert to their animal forms.

None of this explained Macavity, a cat who transformed into a huge leopard. As far as I knew, there was no such thing as a supernatural animal.

Perhaps Aunt Arianna had granted him a one-time transformation to help me when I was in need. It would explain why the cat seemed to eat more than was appropriate for his size and was always on the prowl for more food.

Hyde Park Place turned into Bayswater Road, and I wondered how far this safe house would take me away from the crystal shop. We passed Queensway Station and reached the end of the park, and continued into Notting Hill.

A breath caught in the back of my throat. Notting Hill was just a bus ride away and was a great place to live and socialize, but I thought the safe house would be outside London. The limousine cruised down a street of restaurants and bars and boutiques, which then turned residential, where we slowed to a stop.

I stared into the open doorway of a detached three-story villa that looked like something Hugh Grant and Julia Roberts would have occupied in the Notting Hill movie.

A short fence of wrought iron spanned its exterior, creating a small paved garden. Two tall windows stood beside the house's portico entrance of slimline pillars holding up an ornate stone plinth. A white balcony spanned the entire floor above, making me wonder what this place would be like during the carnival.

What on earth was I thinking? I shook off thoughts of exterior decor and focused on the leopard twitching himself awake. Macavity raised his head and stared through the villa's open door. This had to be the safe house.

I pressed my thighs together and smoothed down my t-shirt, expecting Valentine to open the door with a smirk, but the leopard raised his head in a let-me-out glower.

"Fine." I opened the door, letting in a gust of cool air.

Macavity stepped out first and stalked down the villa's short path with his head up and his tail curling like a satisfied snake. He paused at the door, pushed it open with his head, and disappeared into the house.

I glanced from side to side down the residential street, checking that nobody was around before dashing down the path and into the warm house.

A bright entrance hall of marble floors and painted walls stretched out the length of the villa. It was large enough to fit my apartment, the crystal shop, and all its treatment rooms.

I followed after Macavity, passing two doors on my left and right that I assumed led to large rooms of some sort, but my gaze was fixed on a wide, circular staircase that curved along the back wall.

The cool stones felt smooth underfoot as I followed Macavity up the stairs. He appeared to know where he was going, and while I didn't trust him around my meat and fish, he seemed to want to keep me safe.

Who knew what the cat did during the day when I was at work. I'd always thought he went back to his owner for cuddles and gourmet treats, but he might have come here.

"Valentine?" My voice echoed across the walls.

Macavity made a high-pitched purr in the back of his throat that almost sounded like pity.

I gulped, wondering if this safe house would be my prison. Someone was definitely out to get me but I didn't know if it was some mystery assassin, Mr. Masood, or Valentine working with my supposed cat.

The staircase took us past a huge drawing room that looked like it spanned the entire house. A fire crackled in a white marble hearth, illuminating a room of ivory sofas, mahogany floorboards, and a sumptuous white rug.

Tall floor lamps shone their dim light over the low tables dotted about the room, also highlighting the floor-to-ceiling windows and balcony that overlooked the street.

Gulping at the splendor, I continued up the winding staircase. This was nothing like Aunt Arianna's little cottage in Logris. That place was small and cozy and felt like home. This house was like a miniature version of Valentine's palace.

At the next floor up, Macavity left the stairs, padded across a marble floor, and pushed open a door with his head. We stepped into a bedroom nearly twice the size of my studio in Grosvenor square, with a king-sized bed covered in a quilt of ivory and white silk.

Another fireplace warmed the room, providing gentle light over silver picture frames of myself, Aunt

Arianna, people around the coven, and my long-dead mother.

Before I could react to seeing items from my old house, a pulse of power caught my attention. My heart skipped several beats, and I rushed to the bedside, where a dagger the size of my palm lay on the dresser. The note attached to it said:

This metal is forged of solid flame and will kill any supernatural being except those who wield fire.

Keep it with you at all times. It may save your life.

Valentine.

I placed a hand over my mouth and gasped. Its handle looked and felt like ivory but its blade was of a metal so fine that it appeared transparent. I held it up to the fireplace, watching the flames drift toward it like sunflowers following the sun.

"Why would any assassin want to target me?" I muttered under my breath.

Macavity padded toward the bed, gently knocking me aside with his warm, furry body.

"Hey," I snapped. "Don't get on that—"

It was too late. The oversized leopard had already taken up the center of the king-sized bed and curled into a ball as though he was still a Bengal cat.

"Aren't you supposed to sleep in the trees?" I muttered.

A knock sounded on the door, and a sensation of smoke curled around my senses. Valentine stepped inside with a mug of something steaming and smelling of chocolate and vanilla.

"I came to tuck you in," he said.

I folded my arms across my chest. "Will you explain what's happening now?"

"Is that the thanks I get for saving your hide?" he asked with a raised brow.

"Macavity saved me from that man," I said. "And you just saved Macavity from getting noticed by everyone on Grosvenor Square."

Valentine set down the mug on the bedside table and walked toward me with the sinuous gait of a predator. When he wanted to, he could move swiftly and silently, pouncing out of nowhere and pinning a girl down for pleasure that could make her heart explode with lust.

His gaze lingered on my lips. "The Inamorata I used to know wasn't so abrasive."

"She learned one of life's greatest lessons and grew up," I said.

"Enlighten me," he drawled.

"Never trust a vampire bearing safe houses."

His face split into a grin that made my pulse quicken. This was just a game to him. An attempt to wear me down until I gave in to his advances and let him break me for a second time.

Aunt Arianna had warned me about getting involved with a vampire, and I hadn't taken her words to heart. Not because I'd been foolish but because Valentine hadn't come at me with a silver tongue and seductive eyes.

When I was sixteen, Valentine's assistant had plucked me out of a classroom of twenty others to become an intern at his property holding company, and Valentine had barely noticed me for the first two years of my employment.

It was only when I attended a few work-related events in the human world that we had even spoken, but I had stuttered so badly I thought he would fire me on the spot. He didn't.

When I turned eighteen, he talked to me a little more, but he'd kept our conversation on neutral subjects like human books and art. Little did I know that those innocent conversations had been part of a long-term strategy of seduction.

I tore my gaze away from his twinkling violet eyes and away from those full lips. Lips that had kissed me everywhere and had me begging for more. Lips that had featured in my most erotic dreams.

Turning away from the man in my bedroom, I picked up the mug of hot chocolate he'd left on the bedside and held it in front of me like a shield.

Valentine was a mystery wrapped up in a dark and sexy and enigmatic package. I never understood the point of his pursuit of me.

All that effort for one afternoon of sex with a virgin and a few mouthfuls of my blood? What was the point when there were so many willing blood cows?

Some Neutrals survived by selling their blood for a living. Most bottled their blood and delivered it to their vampire patrons and others preferred to sell through a broker for maximum discretion.

The most dangerous way to supply a vampire was letting them feed from the vein because their saliva contained thrall, which heightened arousal, but it was even worse to let them bite.

A vampire's bite created the most intense high and left a part of the vampire within their victim. The more bites the victim experienced, the deeper the bond they'd create with the vampire.

There were people so addicted to the bite of a vampire that they spent their lives chasing that high until the vampires bored of their company. Then they'd turn to the black-market faeries who could synthesize thrall in exchange for six months of a person's youth. Prematurely aged and shunned, those people would live on the fringes of society as outcasts.

I took a step back, trying to slow my breaths. "What do you want from me?"

"To keep you safe." He loomed over me, filling my nostrils with his smoky, masculine scent.

My pulse fluttered in my throat like a trapped bird. "You still haven't explained why."

Valentine took my right hand and skimmed his

fingers over the firestone tattoo, sending a line of sensation across my flesh. "A clever young woman should have worked it out by now."

"Apparently, I have a blind spot when it comes to deception."

His soft chuckle caressed my skin. "What makes you think I'm not being honest?"

Nature, or rather supernatural magic, had honed everything about the man for maximum seduction. His scent, his voice, the very way it teased my eardrums set a rush of dopamine to my brain, urging me to demand more and more until I was willing to offer him anything in exchange for a few more caresses, a few more moments in his presence.

I squeezed my eyes shut and focused. Focused on the hurt and heartbreak and humiliation of opening my heart and body to him, of being rejected in front of his vampires. The first time had been devastating, but I couldn't blame myself for being an inexperienced girl wanting love.

These three years, I'd come to terms with what he had done and I wasn't about to allow myself to experience the heights and depths of emotion associated with Valentine Sargon.

Valentine made a questioning hum in the back of his throat, indicating that I hadn't elaborated on why I thought he was being deceitful.

Opening my eyes, I focused on the bridge of his perfect nose. "You abducted me into this safe house against my will, and now you've brought all my favorite things as a distraction."

His grin widened. "I only brought you a cup of hot chocolate… And myself."

My cheeks burned with mortification. Valentine was my least favorite thing, ranking somewhere below those disembodied fingers floating in a pool of blood.

"I was referring to Macavity."

The cat in question raised his head and made a curious sound. Perhaps I hadn't been so charitable toward him before his transformation, but now that I knew he'd protected me from that shadow mage, I loved him more than ever.

"Morata," Valentine drawled.

"Please don't call me that."

"It's what you are to me."

A lump formed in the back of my throat, but it wasn't out of nostalgia or a rush of positive sentiment. This feeling reminded me of my younger days at the academy, when I hadn't developed enough magic to qualify for Logris University. Each time someone made a barbed comment that I wouldn't amount to anything, my throat would thicken with a lump of sorrow.

"My darling, precious inamorata," he said.

He probably wanted me to melt at the words, the way I usually did when he used to say them, but they hit with a sting hard enough to make me flinch. I didn't want him to know how much his taunting had affected me, but my indifferent act only encouraged him to push and flirt and mock.

"How dare you," I snarled from between clenched teeth.

"Mera?" he said, the skin between his brows creasing with a frown.

My gaze slid to the beauty mark on his cheekbone. "How could you call me that word after how you left things?"

Valentine drew back and peered into my eyes as though trying to delve into my sould. "Are you alright?"

Flinching, I stepped back and folded my arms across my chest. "I will be after you tell me if anyone's really trying to kill me."

"But the assassin—"

"There were three fingers and a pool of blood," I snapped.

He cupped my cheeks with both hands, a look of urgency crossing his features. "Please, tell me what you're talking about."

My brows drew together. "Did I dream that you cast me out at our engagement ball in front of the cream of vampire society?"

He said. "No, but—"

"Even if I feel nothing for you, the humiliation you put me through still burns."

Valentine flinched. "But you said—"

"Enough. I'm tired of dealing with you." I walked around the bed, looking for a patch that Macavity hadn't taken up with his selfish sleeping position. "Tomorrow morning, I'm finding myself somewhere else to stay. After that, you're going to leave me the hell alone, and I'll tell my aunt to stop bothering you."

The air shifted, and Valentine appeared in front of me. "Will you tell me what's changed between us?"

"Me," I snapped. "Now get out of my way before I stick you with my new dagger."

His lips pressed into a tight line, and he stepped back. "We will speak tomorrow."

Every muscle in my body trembled and my lungs spasmed, holding in a gust of air. Valentine seemed so convinced that he'd done nothing wrong, even after admitting that he really did dump me in public. This had to be an advanced form of gaslighting because he was making me doubt if my perception of what he had said had been wrong.

He walked around me and moved across the room at a pace even a human would find slow. I didn't bother to watch him leave, but when the door clicked shut, I exhaled a long breath.

Maybe there had been a huge miscommunication at the ball and a supernatural trickster had made me imagine Valentine's words as harsher than they'd been that night.

That couldn't be right. If Valentine hadn't ended

our relationship, he would never have waited three years before coming after me.

Someone was definitely meddling with my life, and if it wasn't Valentine, I wanted to know who.

~

Sleeping with a big cat wasn't the ordeal I had imagined. Macavity moved to his side of the bed and curled around me like I was his kitten. With his protective presence, I drifted off to an uninterrupted sleep and awoke curled around a purring Bengal cat.

A change of clothes lay on the dresser—new jeans, a tank top, a sweater of the softest burgundy cashmere, and a lambskin jacket in my size, along with a change of underwear. My eyes widened at the designer labels, and a breath caught in the back of my throat. These were the kinds of brands Beatrice could only afford in the sales.

Biting down on my bottom lip, I glanced over my shoulder. It was just like Valentine to buy me luxuries. But what did he want from me in return?

After showering and dressing, I walked downstairs, following the scent of freshly-brewed coffee.

The kitchen was through one of the doors I had passed on my way to the stairs and was a long space that spanned the house's entire length. White, lacquer units ran along its right side, with a middle island containing a double-sink unit. I groaned at all the dishes I could cook from scratch in a kitchen as large as this.

Morning light streamed in from an entire wall of windows at the back of the room. Steam billowed from a coffeepot on a table overlooking a paved garden, and I hurried past the unit to get a taste.

Enough food for four lay at one end of a mahogany table large enough for eight, including a large serving bowl of fruit salad, a plate of Danish pastries, and serving bowls of granola with a cold jug of milk. Bowls of blueberry and raspberry jam sat among half-slices of grapefruit and an entire baguette.

I picked up the silver coffeepot and poured myself a cup, wondering if whoever had set the table had meant for Valentine to be eating with me.

Next to my place setting was a china bowl filled with the juiciest-looking sashimi and another bowl containing water. Macavity jumped on the table and pawed at his water before tucking into his fish.

I stroked his soft fur with one hand and nibbled at a cinnamon whirl with the other. The poor cat had gone through a painful transformation the night before. He deserved the best.

After eating, I patted Macavity on the head. "Thanks for taking care of me last night."

He met my gaze with a solemn nod.

"Could you transform again?"

Macavity tilted his head to the side, and I swore the cat frowned.

"Not right away," I blurted. "If there's danger another time, would you change to protect me?"

He nodded and continued with his breakfast.

"See you later, then?" I said, not quite knowing where I would end up tonight.

I stared at the cat alternating between his water and sashimi. Valentine's behavior had been puzzling. Admitting to dumping me but expecting me to be fine about it. There was something missing in this scenario.

Even if he was right about the assassin being real, I was certain he was hiding something extremely important. And I was sure it was related to the firestone and the flash of light that had made the shadow mage flinch.

I walked through the marble hallway with a newfound determination. If I couldn't work it out myself, perhaps I could enlist the help of Istabelle.

CHAPTER TEN

The crystal shop was only a short bus ride away. I walked down to the end of the road, hopped onto the number twenty-three bus, which took me past Paddington Station, and got off at Marble Arch. After that, it was a seven minute walk down Park Lane to Upper Brook Street.

It was my first real commute. Staying over at Beatrice's place didn't count as I only did that on the weekends. When I first arrived in London, I stayed in Istabelle's spare room until I got the studio apartment in Grosvenor Square.

I arrived at the shop, feeling refreshed and finding no peculiar men in black, curling shadows or any other sign of supernatural beings. If someone had followed me, they were either wearing Cleopatra stone or had used another method to cloak their magic.

I peered through the window display of rose-quartz necklaces arranged around studded earrings. Once again, Istabelle was already standing behind the counter when I arrived. She'd even opened the shop.

Today, she wore a pink suit that looked like she'd bought it in the late sixties or early seventies. It consisted of a round-neck tunic that fell mid-thigh and wide-legged pants with a light flare. A cerise-and-white neckerchief in a flamboyant pucci design finished off the entire ensemble.

Today, she wore a silver headband at her hairline, pulling back her white puff of dandelion fuzz. For a century-old woman, she was in better shape than human women half her age.

I pushed the door open, walked around the pamphlet display and stood at the other side of the counter. "Are you alright?"

She offered me a weak smile. "I had trouble sleeping last night. Did you notice peculiar flares of power around ten?"

"Oh."

Istabelle raised a painted eyebrow. "I take it that you did notice something?"

I told her everything from Macavity transforming to the shadow mage I'd encountered on my escape down the stairs, ending with bumping into Valentine and being abducted into a safe house.

Istabelle placed her hand on her chest and listened

to my account of last night's events with parted lips. When I finished, she shook her head, walked around the counter, and turned the shop sign to CLOSED.

I stared after her, wondering what she was about to say that was more important than keeping the shop open for business.

"You must come with me at once." Istabelle grabbed my hand and strode around the counter.

I thought she would take me to the basement library, but instead, we went into treatment room one. It was a rectangular room of white walls and white linoleum floors, containing a full-sized hydraulic massage table with enough space to move around its perimeter to perform healing.

Two framed posters hung on the wall. A Traditional Chinese Medicine diagram that depicted the body's meridians and acupuncture points and a Vedic diagram that depicted the chakras.

Spanning the entire back wall was a counter where we kept flower remedies, boxes of crystals, and sound bowls. It curved around to the wall on the right-hand side, where there was a sink for cleansing hands and crystals along with a huge roll of paper for the table.

Daylight streamed in from two skylights, providing scant illumination. This was fine in the winter when creating a relaxing atmosphere, but in summer, we needed blinds.

"What's going on?" I leaned against the wall and folded my arms.

Istabelle pulled out a long strip of paper and laid it flat on the bed. "Lie down."

"Are you going to check me for magic?" I asked.

She nodded. "Intrinsic magic, curses, psychic attacks, and energetic attachments."

A breath whistled through my teeth. While deliberate psychic attacks were rare, energetic attachments were often executed on purpose. Disembodied spirits could latch onto people, using the life force of their victim to cling onto the mortal plane.

Most people didn't notice the attachment at first, but over time, it caused a drain that suppressed the immune system, blocked the dopamine receptors, and resulted in a spiral of bad luck, poor health, and depression.

"Do you think something's clinging to my aura?" I asked, trying to keep the tremble out of my voice.

"That's what I want to find out," Istabelle replied. "Get on the table."

My throat dried, and I sucked in shallow breaths. Some species of fae and demon also attached to people out of a need to feed.

I wouldn't call it consensual because they never explained outright what they did to their victims. Instead, the victim would think they were getting one thing, such as a relationship with someone richer and far better looking than they'd expect, only to end up being fed upon over months or years before finally being discarded.

"Alright," I said, my feet dragging as I walked to the treatment table. "You'll tell me if you find something, right?"

She inclined her puffy head. "Of course."

Sometimes, knowing too much was bad for the brain. Take the situation with Valentine and me. He was a bloody king, ridiculously handsome, powerful, and rich.

I wasn't plain, and with a bit of makeup and the right styling, I could look great. Some nights, I lay in bed, wondering if Valentine had fed on me in the same way.

After climbing on the table's cushioned surface, I lay on my back, and closed my eyes. We had done this over a hundred times before, both as part of my vampire detoxification program and part of my training to become a new age healer.

Istabelle always said that the only way to learn how to heal others was to get treated myself.

"Sound bath first?" I asked.

"I'm going to sense your aura and see if I can find something—foreign or new—that might cause concern."

Gulping, I let my eyes flutter shut. "Alright."

Istabelle placed a warm palm on the space between my brows, right above the third-eye chakra.

The other, she placed on my solar plexus chakra below my breastbone.

She sucked in a huge breath, her way of connecting with her own third eye. Like me, Istabelle couldn't see or wield energy, but her ability to feel it was far more developed than mine.

Istabelle described it as being able to read braille, but instead of feeling raised dots under her fingertips, her entire energy body was a conduit for reading magic.

When she exhaled, she moved the hand on my third eye down to my throat and placed her fingers on the medallion of black tourmaline I always wore to ward off negative energy.

"That's the first piece of foreign magic," she muttered. "This crystal is almost full, so you should cleanse it immediately."

"Right," I croaked. "Thanks."

The fingers on my solar plexus moved to my right hand and skimmed the tattoo over my wrist.

"There's a tiny hum of residual power on your skin here, but nothing significant enough to warrant any attention."

"Do I have any magic whatsoever?" I asked.

Istabelle stepped back and sighed. "You're exactly the same as you were when you arrived. Unable to store and wield magic. Unless…"

I cracked open an eye. "You've thought of something."

She shook her head and turned to the sink, where she washed her hands. "It was a ridiculous suggestion and virtually impossible."

"What?" My other eye opened.

"I don't want to get you alarmed."

The lining of my stomach fluttered with trepidation. "I still don't know if Valentine was lying about the shadow mage coming to assassinate me, but the cat I've lived with for the past three years transformed into an oversized leopard before my eyes."

Istabelle rubbed her chin and stared at me through narrowed eyes, as though she was assessing whether I'd freak out over whatever she wanted to say.

I sat up and met her gaze. "Something terrible is about to happen, but I don't know what. If there's anything you can tell me—"

"It's just a theory," she said.

"I'd love to hear it."

Istabelle exhaled a long sigh. "When you do, don't run off and lose yourself to despair."

My breath caught. She was about to tell me I'd been cursed, wasn't she? Or something a hundred times worse. I bit down on my lip, trying to act casual. If I acted scared, she'd withhold that information, and I'd never discover what was on her mind.

"I promise not to overreact," I said. "What is it?"

Her gaze wandered to my wrist, making me wrap

a protective hand over the tattoo. "You said the shadow mage attacked you with his magic?"

"I'm sure he did."

She raised her brows. "But a flash of light made him back away?"

My pulse quickened. "Right."

"What if someone gave you the firestone to absorb fire magic?"

I shook my head. "But I've never been to a volcano—"

"You could be a fire mage."

I slid off the table, pulled off the paper sheet, and placed it in the wastepaper basket. Istabelle was right. Her theory wasn't just impossible, it was outlandish and could get a person killed. The penalty for wielding magic was death. No trials, no mercy, just a swift execution.

"Fire mages are extinct," I parroted from a history lesson. "The last fire mage burned out his magical core—"

"While trying to take over the world," she said. "Yes, I also got that lesson. I've also been in the human world long enough to learn about genetics."

My teeth worried at my bottom lip.

Istabelle folded her arms across her chest. "Magical ability is a dominant gene, which is why supernaturals can mate with humans and produce magical children."

I pinched the bridge of my nose. "But I come from a long line of witches, not mages."

"You come from a long line of witches and humans who might have had mage ancestors," she said. "Some magical traits are recessive."

I ran a hand through my hair and blew a breath through the side of my mouth. The Supernatural Council was mostly tolerant about the needs and bloodthirsty peculiarities of its citizens as long as they didn't raise the dead or expose the world of magic to humans. The one thing they couldn't abide was a supernatural who wielded fire.

It didn't matter what kind—hellfire, actual flames or illusionary fire. Even witches, who could create the chemical reactions to produce fire, refrained from performing fire-based spells for fear of inciting the council's wrath.

The last fire mage was a man called Kresnik, who burned himself out half a millennium ago. After that, all supernaturals who even had a hint of fire magic were destroyed at birth. It meant that there were no dragon shifters, fire mages, salamanders or ifrits. According to my history teacher, they now all dwelled in hell.

"Can we not talk about this?" I said. "Anyone under suspicion of harboring that sort of thing gets disappeared."

Istabelle inclined her head and walked toward the door. "It's just a thought."

"Let's keep it that way, please." I followed after her.

She opened the door, and bumped into a tall young man with honey-blond hair swept off his face, sharp-as-dagger cheekbones, and the most startling aquamarine eyes.

"What are you doing here?" she said.

The boy's gaze wandered over Istabelle's shoulder, landing on me. "Watching out for Miss Griffin."

I stepped back, examining his symmetrical features. Even though I couldn't feel an ounce of magic on him, everything about his appearance was perfect from his flawless alabaster skin to his full lips, and his square chin.

He was beautiful but without the dazzling sparkle of faeries or the smoldering heat of a demon. The boy had to be a baby vampire—one whose fangs hadn't yet descended.

Istabelle dropped into a curtsey, holding the door for balance. "It is an honor to meet you, young man. May I have your name?"

Pink spots appeared on his cheeks. "Kain Shepherd, and there's no need to curtsey. I'm no one."

My eyes narrowed. Was he a royal nephew or something? Istabelle could recognize people's exact species, but she had never told me she could differentiate between a regular vampire and one related to Valentine.

Kain stood back, letting us walk around the

corner into the shop. I stared at the peculiar vampire boy, wondering why Valentine had sent someone so young to watch over me.

"Mera, dear." Istabelle pointed at the shop's glass door. "Will you bring in that package and see what's inside?"

A foot-high cardboard box sat in the doorway, presumably dumped there by a delivery driver who didn't want to make a second round. I huffed an exasperated breath at the audacity of the man to dump our stock where anyone could have picked it up. What if it contained something valuable?

Kain strode around the counter and opened the door. "I'll get it."

"No." Istabelle placed a hand on her chest. "My apprentice is more than capable…"

Her voice trailed off because Kain had already reached the door and picked up the box. I glanced at the older woman, wondering what she saw in the boy that I couldn't. His magic was so weak it barely registered through the power of the crystals. Kain was just like any other vampire at the academy.

As he returned to the counter, I shouldered on a white coat, slipped on a pair of protective goggles, snapped on a pair of gloves, and picked up a box cutter. "Let's see what's arrived today."

The door opened, and Jonathan stepped inside, his blond hair blown in all directions by the wind.

His eyes bulged, and his face broke into a smile. "Mera?"

Bile rose to the back of my throat. Only twenty-four hours ago, I told him to leave me alone, and now he was back. "What are you doing—"

"They've cordoned off Grosvenor Square," he blurted. "Someone reported seeing a large cat as they drove past. When you weren't in the shop, I thought the worst."

My lips formed a tight line. "I'm here now."

Jonathan stepped inside, blowing out an exaggerated relieved breath. When I continued glaring at him, pink spots bloomed across his cheeks. "Thank goodness for that," he said, his voice trembling with nerves. "Where were you this morning? I waited outside the cordon—"

"Are you stalking Miss Griffin?" Kain growled.

Jonathan's mouth fell open. "Stalk—" He turned to me with shocked eyes. "Mera, is that what you're saying to people about me?"

I rolled my eyes. Who had time to dwell on a nuisance like Jonathan in the light of shadow mage assassins, Bengal cats that transformed into monstrous leopards, and annoying vampires whose intentions may or may not be nefarious?

"Anyone listening to you can work that out from what you're saying," I snapped. "Now, for the third time, will you please leave and never return?"

Jonathan sniffed. "Actually, I'm here to buy some rose quartz."

Kain placed a hand on Jonathan's shoulder. The young man was about five-ten, looked sixteen or seventeen, and probably hadn't finished growing. "Try eBay." He marched Jonathan toward the exit and opened the door, letting in a gust of cold wind and busy traffic. "This place doesn't serve stalkers."

Jonathan gaped at me over his shoulder. "Another man, Mera? How old is this one?"

I bit back the urge to tell him it was none of his business, but doing so would only give him some sort of validation.

I had no idea what was wrong with Jonathan. He was persistent beyond reason. While most men gave up after two or three attempts, he kept going and going. Someone needed to teach him a bit of self-restraint.

After giving Jonathan a hard shove, making him stumble onto the sidewalk, Kane waited at the door with his arms crossed.

Jonathan stood on the other side of the display with his mouth flapping open and closed, looking like an abandoned bear. He stuffed his hands into his pockets and trudged in the direction of Starbucks.

Kain turned back to where I stood behind the counter. "Are you alright?"

Nodding, I picked up a box cutter. "Thanks for getting rid of him."

"What was that guy's name? I need to report all unsavory characters who come after you to Valentine."

"You can tell Valentine that who I associate with is none of his business," I snapped, immediately feeling guilty for being rude.

Kain raised his shoulders and walked around the store, picking up stones and rolling them around in his hands.

I glanced at Istabelle, wondering what she thought of this newcomer, but she gazed at him with the same soft-eyed admiration she used to look at Valentine. I pursed my lips and tore open the box with the cutter. Kain had better not be Valentine's secret son.

Inside the box were angel figurines made of opalite. It was a man-made substance created to mimic opal with an iridescent sheen that also mimicked moonstone. They held no magic—not even a trace of the bright light associated with the power of angels. I dusted them off and placed them on the shelves.

Istabelle remained in the shop for the rest of the morning, trying to engage Kain in conversation. The young vampire remained polite, giving her one-word answers.

As I tidied and rearranged the shelves, I discovered that he'd grown up in Glastonbury, was new to

Logris, and hadn't yet enrolled in the academy. A secret lovechild?

I only listened with half an ear because Istabelle's words kept swirling through my mind. There was no way I could be a fire mage. Someone would have noticed sparks flying from my fingers by now. Besides, even the latest of developers came into their power by the age of twenty-one. I was three years overdue.

Excusing myself, I walked around the counter, through the door that led to the library, and down its wooden steps.

The floor-to-ceiling mahogany shelves beckoned, and the cleansing scent of the crystals that maintained the books filled my nostrils. A layer of stress I hadn't felt before melted away, loosening the tension around my chest and shoulders.

Exhaling my relief to finally be alone, I walked alongside the collection of books, looking for anything I could find on fire users.

Istabelle kept a few history books among her tomes on magic and healing, but usually sold anything of particular interest on Supernet, our equivalent of the World Wide Web.

History wasn't my favorite subject. It was mostly tales of politics and battles and plots to drag the earth into hell.

With every species having their own ruler and each

ruler having an equal amount of power within the Supernatural Council, Logris enjoyed five hundred years of relative peace. Some of the Council members were older than humanity, with some of the younger members ruling in proxy for ancestors in other planes.

Next to a leather-bound tome called *Laws and Treaties for Supernatural Separation* was another called *Dragon-Kind*. I skipped over it as the last dragon had died three thousand years ago, and I wanted something from around the time of Kresnik. My gaze landed on *The Witchcraft Act of King Henry VIII*.

I pulled out the book and flipped through the heavy parchment. Henry VIII was the ruler of England in the sixteenth century, who introduced the witch trials that drove both mages and witches underground. I placed the tome on the table for later, continuing my search.

Twenty minutes later, I found another book called *Fire Suppression Through the Ages*, and returned to the table.

As I flipped through the first few pages of the fire suppression book, footsteps creaked from above. I glanced up to find Kain descending the stairs.

My brows pulled together in a frown. "The basement is perfectly secure. I'll be safe down here."

"I brought us some hot chocolate from Paul Young's," he said.

Saliva flooded my mouth. The hot chocolate from that bakery was one of the best in London.

Unlike the overly sweet, milky concoction available from places like Starbucks and Pret a Manger, Paul's hot chocolate was deeply delicious and darkly decadent.

My gaze darted up the stairs. "Istabelle doesn't let me have food or drink down here."

"She said it was okay." Kain offered me a shy smile.

I moved the leather tomes to the far end of the table, away from the armchairs. "Thanks." My gaze lingered on the paper bag in his hand. "That was really thoughtful."

Kain raised a shoulder. "Valentine said it was your favorite."

"How do you two know each other?" I licked my lips, wiping my palms on my white coat. "You told Istabelle that you didn't grow up in Logris."

"He tracked me down to a foster home, saying he was a distant cousin." Kain pulled out two insulated cardboard cups, letting out warm gusts of cacao that made my stomach gurgle.

I was only vaguely aware of foster homes from what I picked up watching television. Most people in Logris belonged to covens, clans, houses, packs, legions, or choirs.

Supernatural children were precious and it was rare for one to grow up outside some kind of family unit. In the Natural World, orphaned children were handed over to strangers paid to provide care.

"What was it like, growing up on the outside?" I asked.

"What was it like to grow up in Logris?" he asked with a smile.

I smiled back, realizing my question had been dumb. Neither of us had any comparisons since we'd both experienced a single world as children.

"May I ask you a question?" he asked.

"What?"

"Why do you work in a place like this when you have Valentine?"

All my good humor drained to the soles of my shoes, and I set down my cup. "What's he said about me?"

"Not much," Kain said, his tone defensive. "Only to watch out for you here and at your house while he was away."

"Where's he gone?" I asked.

"The Supernatural Council called him in for an urgent meeting," he said with a shrug. "He left a group of guards watching the shop from across the road and around the back."

"Why?" I asked.

He flinched. "I wouldn't presume to question Valentine."

I leaned forward. "Why did he send a young vampire?"

Kain glanced away, his lips forming a tight line. "He trusts me."

My eyes narrowed, and I remembered something Valentine's servants had told me on the steps of the palace. "Are you his heir?"

Kain arched his brow. "You mean the Dick Grayson to his Bruce Wayne?"

I tilted my head to the side and frowned. "Who?"

He huffed a laugh. "Never mind."

Brushing that aside, I took a sip of the hot chocolate, enjoying how its bitter flavors mingled with the sweet creaminess to create the perfect mouthful.

Something was different about Kain. I'd grown up with young vampires and they didn't come into their power until their fangs had descended.

Earlier, his power had seemed weak but up close, it varied from barely registering to as strong as Valentine. I narrowed my eyes, wondering what was so special about this boy to have been taken in by the King of the Vampires.

As if inspiration had struck, the words tumbled from my lips. "You're a pure-blood."

Kain's lips tightened. "If you mean that my parents were both vampires, they were."

My brows rose. "Does that mean you'll become the next king?"

"Hopefully not for a few centuries," he muttered under his breath.

We fell silent for several moments, and I wondered if Valentine wanted to retire from ruling the vampires at some point in the future.

Kain cleared his throat, making me meet his sapphire eyes. "I don't know what happened between you and Valentine, but he wouldn't put all this effort into you if he didn't think you were special. Give him a break, alright?"

CHAPTER ELEVEN

Kain's words stuck with me the entire day. As Grosvenor Square was still cordoned off due to the sightings of a large cat, Kain and I took the bus back to the villa in Notting Hill, where he gave me an official tour of the safe house.

Afterward, we shared a meal of gourmet burgers, while Macavity joined us for a bowl of chopped tuna.

I expected Valentine to have made an appearance by now, but he was probably giving me space. It had been clever of him to introduce me to someone who'd grown up in the human world and hadn't been in Logris at the time of my humiliation.

Kain might be a pure-blood vampire, but everything else about him seemed mostly human… at least it would be until he came of age.

Valentine was probably grooming him for rulership, as pure-bloods automatically gained the status of king, no matter the circumstances of their birth.

At the end of the evening, another vampiric presence drifted into my awareness. It wasn't as powerful as Valentine's, and I guessed he was still busy with the Supernatural Council.

Kain rose from the sofa. "Good night."

"Where are you staying?" he asked.

"With a group of others in the villa across the road," Kain murmured.

I bit down on my lip. Normally, I would have sensed those vampires if they were so close. Perhaps they were wearing Cleopatra stone.

After Kain left, I went upstairs with Macavity on my heels and stepped into my room.

The cat bounded across the wooden floor and leaped on the bed. He circled the middle, kneaded the quilt with his paws, and settled into a little ball of leopard skin fur.

I stood at the doorway and smirked. It didn't matter where he lay. When he was in his Bengal form, I was the giant who could push him around. "Sleep anywhere you like."

The bedroom's square windows overlooked the villa's garden, a paved space of white slabs, raised flower beds, and potted trees. In between them and opposite the bed stood a dresser with an ornate mirror etched in gold. I opened a drawer, hoping that someone had transferred my night clothes from home, but found it filled with brand new clothes.

I pulled out a silver nightgown of washed silk and read the label. "La Perla?"

This was Beatrice's favorite brand. In the drawer above were lots of bra and knickers sets. The one that caught my eye was a rich green that contrasted with the red of my hair. With an excited giggle, I laid it on the white quilt, took a photo, and I sent it to my friend via text.

Her reply was immediate. *Where did you get that?*

I texted back. *My temporary pad in Notting Hill.*

What happened to the old one? she replied.

I stared at the screen, wondering how I could explain things to a girl forbidden to know anything about the Supernatural World. *Pest control issues. There's a pool and sauna downstairs. Want to come around and play?*

You had me at pool. What's the address?

I sent her the location via google maps. *See you in the morning?*

Guess who's back on the app, prowling for new conquests? His headline says he's looking for a special relationship!

What's wrong with these men? I shook my head. One of these days, he would mess with the wrong woman, and she would teach him not to fake a long-term interest when all he wanted was a fling.

She messaged back. *I know. See you tomorrow.*

On the right side of the room was the door that led to the bathroom, but I hadn't yet explored the door on the far left on the same wall as the head of the four-poster.

I walked around the king-sized bed, keeping my gaze on Macavity, whose ribs rose and fell with deep breaths. Cats were so lucky with their ability to take long naps. He probably tired himself out with last night's transformation.

The door led to a walk-in wardrobe with its own window, a dressing table and open closets running along three of the walls. Some of the closet contained garment rails long enough to house full-length dresses and coats, some were shorter and held shirts, jackets, and bottoms.

Among the rails were racks for shoes, shelves for accessories, drawers, and spaces up high for luggage. I turned in a circle, looking for clues as to Valentine's true intentions.

The closets were half-full of clothing in my size and the style I used to wear when we were dating. It was as though this was my starter wardrobe and he would permit me to buy additional items.

My throat thickened, and I gulped several times in quick succession. I didn't know if I should be troubled or touched. The portraits from my cottage, the brand new clothes, the sexy lingerie. This wasn't a temporary safe house.

It looked like Valentine intended for me to stay here... either until the crisis was over or until he tired of keeping me.

The old me would have been thrilled at these wonderful gifts but the new me needed answers. Answers about what happened that night, answers about the threat hanging over my head, and answers about his intentions.

In the restaurant, he spoke as though Aunt Arianna had begged him for help, but this was going beyond a favor for an old flame.

~

I thought through my situation for hours that night, shifting position until Macavity got sick of my restlessness and slept on the windowsill. No amount of coaxing could get him to return, and I ended up lying on my back, staring at the ceiling until my eyes became too heavy and dry to stay open.

What seemed like moments later, sunlight streaming in through the blinds woke me the next morning.

Since I couldn't get back to sleep, I stepped into the ensuite, a gray-marbled space twice the size of the walk-in wardrobe that boasted a clawfoot tub, two sinks and a walk-in shower the same length and width as the bathroom in my studio.

I stood beneath the hot spray, letting the water

pressure pummel my skin. No matter how much I thought about it, I couldn't work out what Valentine wanted from me. If he ever showed his face again, I would ask him if he suspected me of being a wielder of fire. Then, I'd examine him for microexpressions to work out the truth.

Afterward, I changed into a bright-blue bikini and examined myself in the mirror. The warm shower brought out some color to my skin, removing some of the paleness that dulled my complexion during the winter.

I'd lost a little weight since the last time we had travelled to Madeira in Valentine's yacht, but I still managed to retain enough curves to fit the bikini.

The doorbell rang. I slipped on some sandals, shouldered on a dressing gown, and nearly tripped over an outraged Macavity as I dashed through the hallway and ran downstairs.

A faint presence lurked close to the house. Since it had the smoky texture of a vampire and not a shadow mage's absence of heat or a shifter's jagged edges, I continued across the downstairs hallway to find Beatrice at the doorstep.

She wore her hair in a high bun with wavy tendrils framing her heart-shaped face. Her calf-length navy peacoat was buttoned up to the neck, and her long boots didn't betray a glimpse of what she wore underneath. The morning traffic whizzed past, busy even for a Sunday.

Beatrice spread her arms out and grinned. "You invited me over for a day of unbridled luxury?"

I pulled her inside. "It's nice to be able to treat you for once."

Beatrice stepped over the threshold, her eyes wide and her mouth falling open as she took in the high ceilings, marble floors, gilded portraits. "Do you know how much a place like this costs?"

"A million or two?" I said with a shrug. "Three?"

She looped her arm through mine. "More like fifteen! I'll bet this place costs tens of thousands in monthly rent."

"Wow."

Not all supernaturals were rich, but some of the older families had owned land in the Natural World for centuries and had amassed a tremendous amount of wealth. Most witches were more concerned about power as they could gather anything they needed through magic and nature.

I led Beatrice into the kitchen and opened a built-in refrigerator crammed with groceries. Whoever had prepared breakfast the day before had supplied us with Marks and Spencer finger food—perfect for eating by the pool. My face split into a grin. This was just like Beauty and the Beast, but without the surly monster growling over Belle's shoulder. I much preferred my real-life version of the movie.

"Ooh, cheese and onion." Beatrice pulled out a

tray of miniature quiche slices. "Did you say there was a pool?"

"Actually…" I shook my head and pulled her toward the stairs. "Pool is an understatement."

We reached the basement, and Beatrice clutched at the handrail with a gasp. Last night, when Kain had shown me what was in the lower level, I'd been tired and hungry and a little overwhelmed. I'd seen the pool illuminated by spotlights in both the water and the ceiling, but the space looked larger and more spectacular this morning. It spanned the property's entire footprint, stretching beneath its back garden to accommodate a thirty-foot pool.

The color scheme consisted of pale neutrals, from the off-white walls to the gray stone floors that contained enough texture and grit to prevent slipping. On its right side was a decked area housing a small sauna, a round sunken jacuzzi, and a glass steam room.

Beatrice clasped her hands and squealed. "Did you faint when you first saw this place?"

"Not quite," I said with a chuckle. While this villa was luxurious, Valentine's palace boasted at least a hundred times the size and splendor.

I exhaled a sigh. Valentine's palace was a fairytale. The sort of place a girl would move into, even if its owner was a frog or a slathering beast. But all the wealth paled in comparison to how Valentine had made me feel.

He'd looked beyond the Neutral no-hoper, and over our three-year courtship, helped me blossom into a confident young woman... What a shame that destroying that had taken a mere three minutes.

Beatrice rifled through her bag. "Alright, then. Where do we get changed?"

"Don't you want some brunch and a glass of buck's fizz?" I asked.

She gestured at a refrigerator recessed into the wall. "I'm happy with water. Right now, I'm dying for a swim, a sauna, and a soak!"

The pool turned out to have a current that worked against the body, so the swimmer always stayed in the same position. Beatrice said it was an exercise pool that people with smaller houses used so they could have a continuous swim without needing to constantly stop and turn around. I'd thought it was magic, but if she knew about it, it had to be human technology.

After the swim, we climbed out of the pool and brought our water bottles to the steam room, a square space with a U-shaped bench. The air was thick, and condensation soaked the walls. Trying to breathe in all that steam wasn't as relaxing as we'd imagined, so we headed for the sauna, a gorgeous wooden enclosure heated with burning coals.

The sauna was arranged in an L-shape, with two tiers of benches for us to lie or sit. I stretched out a fluffy towel on the top row and lay on my back. Beatrice sat resting her back on the wall with her legs stretched out at the bottom.

"We had saunas every day in Finland." She picked up a ladle of eucalyptus-scented water and poured it on the coals, filling the tiny room with a flare of menthol and heat.

I raised my head. "You didn't tell me you worked there."

She smoothed her wet hair off her face and hummed. "It was a short project I did a few weeks before meeting you, but more importantly, whose house is this? Does it belong to your ex?"

"Yes," I said, keeping my features neutral.

Beatrice twisted around, her eyes wide. "You moved in with him?"

"He doesn't live here. At least I'm sure he doesn't." This was his house, and he could install himself here at any time.

Concern creased the corners of her eyes. I couldn't blame her. To anyone on the outside, it looked like I'd spent three years pining for a mystery guy, only to uproot myself the moment he and his limo swept back into my life. By anyone's standards, changing one's lifestyle at a man's whim was perilous.

"It's not what you think," I said.

"When will you return home?" she asked.

"As soon as we've dealt with the pests," I muttered.

She paused for several heartbeats before saying, "Don't be like me—"

"No, it's not like that." I rose off my seat and placed my hand on her damp shoulder. "Valentine and I aren't dating. We're not even friends."

She raised a brow, the corners of her mouth lifting into a smirk. "Valentine? Are you sure that's not a pseudonym?"

His full name was Valentinus Sargon de Akkad, but telling her that would lead to more questions I wasn't permitted by the Supernatural Council to answer.

Dry heat swirled around my head, so I lowered myself onto the bench, scrambling for a way to explain. I'd had the entire night to think up an excuse for being here as Beatrice was bound to ask.

Only a watered-down version of the truth would work because Beatrice knew me well enough to tell if I was lying.

"Do you remember that morning you called me?" I didn't want to ruin things by mentioning Christian by name and I hoped she would know which day I was talking about.

"Yes, which is why I thought you'd have learned from my disastrous experience and thought twice before giving a guy exactly what he wants."

"But I'm not." I twisted onto my side and met her dark eyes. "One of the things I most admired about you was how you can bounce back from anything."

She wrinkled her nose. "Really?"

"Compared to me, yes." I nodded for emphasis.

"It's what makes you so courageous. You don't overthink decisions. You jump in knowing that you're capable of taking care of yourself and dealing with any consequences."

Beatrice huffed a laugh. "I've got to have some spontaneity somewhere."

I snickered. It was strange that such an exciting woman would have such a boring sounding job. Maybe tax was the dynamic part of accountancy and her work-life was more like Wolf of Wall Street.

"Anyway," I said. "Speaking to you that morning made me decide to move on."

"By moving in?" she whispered.

By the time I stuttered out an explanation, Beatrice was totally unconvinced that I was no longer in love with Valentine. She also pictured him as a domineering old guy with ogreish tendencies toward women. The worst part was that everything she thought about him was true. Valentine's attitudes were old world, even though he tried to keep up with modern times.

"Why couldn't you stay with Mrs. Bonham-Sackville while they're fumigating your studio?"

"She's an old lady," I blurted. "What if she got affected?"

Beatrice pinched the bridge of her nose, seeming like she thought I was lying to myself. "Why don't we get a drink and talk about it later?"

My heart plummeted, and I felt all Beatrice's notions of me being a paragon of strength and willpower float into the ether. That was the downside of keeping secrets. Not even a half-truth could sound convincing.

We stepped out of the sauna to find a wooden table on its side, laden with a platter of finger food, two glasses of buck's fizz, and bottled water within a bucket of ice.

"Does he have servants?" she asked.

"Yes, but I didn't see anyone this morning," I replied with a frown.

Beatrice and I moved the tray of food close to the hot tub, and we climbed inside the warm bubbly water with our cocktails. I took a sip of my drink, letting the sweet liquid slide down my tongue. This was actually a mimosa, which was made with one-part orange juice and another part champagne. Buck's fizz contained two-thirds of the alcoholic beverage.

"How have you been?" I asked.

"Oscillating between anguish and anger." She took a sip and exhaled a satisfied breath. "Alcohol helps."

"So do naughty nibbles in the jacuzzi." I picked up a canapé topped with cream cheese and gestured at the tray for her to get something to eat. "Have you been tempted to call him?"

"Every time I felt like firing off a furious text, I

asked myself what you would—" Beatrice's mouth dropped open, and she drifted forward, nearly spilling her mimosa into the warm water. "Bloody hell."

"What's wrong?" I turned around, catching more than a glimpse of Valentine striding toward us, his perfect bronze body glistening with water.

Clenching my teeth, I snatched my gaze away, but afterimages of that glorious body still branded themselves into my mind's eye. Broad, muscular shoulders, bulging pectoral muscles, a sculpted six-pack abdomen, and defined thighs.

Beatrice's face darkened with a deep flush that spread down to her cleavage. She panted through parted lips, "Who is that?"

"Valentine Sargon." He reached out a large hand. "You must be Beatrice. I'm delighted to make your acquaintance."

A rush of shock hit me in the gut, and I spun around to meet his smiling eyes. In the basement's artificial light, they appeared more indigo than violet.

Valentine brought Beatrice's trembling hand to his lips, all the time gazing at me with the tiniest of smiles. I pressed my lips into a tight line and breathed hard to expel the heat rushing between my legs.

This reaction didn't mean a thing. Vampires were built to attract victims, and everything about them was seductive. I was only flesh and blood. One could get excited about the male form and not like or trust its owner.

"I thought you had business somewhere far away?" I said.

"Surely you don't expect me to work on a Sunday," he drawled.

"But we don't want to keep you from important business," I said with a little more bite in my voice.

Beatrice batted at me in a silent plea to stop trying to chase Valentine away.

My eyes narrowed. If the vampire wanted to stick around and make a nuisance of himself, nothing I could do or say would stop him. He had that in common with Macavity.

I turned my head, which only made him grin wider in the periphery of my vision.

"Ladies, I will take my leave," he said. "When you've finished exercising, I would be delighted to take you both out for a late lunch."

"We're not hungry," I snapped.

Valentine chuckled and strolled away. I glowered at the rippling muscles of his broad back, and at the trunks clinging to his ass. The laugh he made seemed to say the lady doth protest too much. He opened the door, making the muscles of his shoulders bunch in a way that caused a tiny groan to reverberate in the back of my throat, and disappeared into the stairwell.

I brought my mimosa glass to my lips and took a

long drag of champagne-infused orange juice to moisten my dry throat.

Beatrice leaned into me and whistled. "Forget everything I said earlier. With a body and a face like that, I'd jump on that dick, ride it to the sunset, and damn the consequences."

I spat out a fountain of mimosa but half of it went down my throat. "It's not like—"

Beatrice gave me several hearty claps on the back, trying to dislodge errant drops of orange juice and champagne. "There's no need to explain yourself. Just breathe."

The more I protested, the more the mimosa travelled down my throat. The bubbles raged as I leaned forward, gasping and coughing and spluttering for air. Damn that vampire for flaunting himself. What did he bloody want?

"Seriously, you're going to have to give me some tips," she drawled. "I wouldn't want any of the London riffraff after drinking from the font of Valentine."

"Beatrice," I hissed.

She turned to me and smirked. "Give us a few juicy deets."

I rubbed at my temples. "Men like Valentine know they're gorgeous and sought after. To them, women are wholly and utterly disposable."

Beatrice blew out a long breath and downed the rest of her drink. "I should know."

"Sorry." I turned to my friend and frowned. "I didn't mean to remind you—"

She raised a hand. "I was being insensitive. It's obvious that you're still hurting. He must have really gotten under your skin."

"And into my heart and soul." I finished my mimosa, now wishing it was a buck's fizz, or better still, straight alcohol.

Beatrice set down her glass and wrapped her arms around my neck. "Forgive me?"

I hugged back, letting the heat from the jacuzzi engulf our bodies. "That's the thing about true friendship. There's nothing to forgive."

Beatrice's hand fell away, and she drew back, trying to scramble out of the water. I raised my head to see what had upset her but couldn't see her through the thick clouds of steam.

Steam?

The jacuzzi was supposed to be warm, not hot.

"Mera," Beatrice croaked.

My heart leapfrogged into my throat, and I rose to my feet, waving my arms about.

"What's happening?" I followed her toward the steps, where the steam was less intense.

Beatrice's skin glowed a deep shade of red, making my breath catch. It looked like she was having an allergic reaction to something. Her limbs trembled as she stumbled up the steps, breathing hard and fast.

Once she was out of the water, she straightened, seeming a little calmer. I exhaled a relieved breath and climbed out after her.

"Are you alright?" I placed a hand on her back.

Her eyes rolled to the back of her head. "I'm—"

Beatrice fell face-first in the roiling water with a hard splash.

CHAPTER TWELVE

A scream tore from my lips, and everything happened in a blur. I jumped into the water, and tried hooking my arms beneath Beatrice's to pull her to the edge of the hot tub, but Valentine appeared and rushed her into the pool. With his other hand, he was already on the phone to emergency services.

Two suited vampires rushed to the poolside, and Valentine barked such rapid instructions at them that it was impossible to tell if he was speaking French, Italian, or Arabic. I could barely see anything through the clouds of steam billowing around the jacuzzi.

What the hell was happening? The water wasn't even that warm.

Clutching the edges of the tub, I climbed out, my limbs trembling in sync with the pulse booming between my ears. As I rose, someone placed a dressing gown over my shoulders and pressed a freezing bottle of water into my hands.

"Drink, Miss Griffin," said a female voice. "And please come with me to get changed."

I couldn't go anywhere. Not with Valentine standing in the pool, holding Beatrice in the water. Her unmoving body floated to the surface, her usually tan skin now even redder.

"Is she—" The words caught in the back of my throat.

Valentine turned around with grave eyes. "She's still breathing. The paramedics are on their way."

"Please tell me what's wrong," I said.

"Come away, Miss Griffin." The vampire female wrapped an arm around my shoulder, trying to guide me toward the changing room, but I shrugged her off and rushed to the side of the pool.

I fell to my knees, not trusting myself in the water when every muscle in my body quivered. Steam still billowed from the jacuzzi but it was less dense, proving that something about me had caused the water to boil.

"Valentine," I said.

He raised a palm, still balancing a prone Beatrice on the water. "Don't come in."

My throat thickened. Even Valentine knew it was my fault.

The door flew open, and a pair of paramedics stepped inside, a tall Black woman with cornrows and a gray-haired man with a short beard. Both wore uniforms of bottle-green fleece jackets with matching shirts and pants, and each carried down bulky medical backpacks and a pair of cases.

For a heartbeat, they both gaped at the basement before rushing to the poolside.

"Sir?" The woman's case landed on the stone tiles with a thud. "Please move her slowly to the edge of the pool. Has she had fluids?"

"She's still unconscious," Valentine replied.

The male paramedic knelt beside me, and I backed away from the pool. As soon as Valentine brought her up to the ledge, the paramedics raised her feet onto a block, attached a blood pressure monitor to her arm, and stuck a thermometer in her ear. By now, the color of her skin had bloomed to a livid red.

Numb shock spread through my body. If I knew how to take it back, I would. What if I'd just damaged my best friend's internal organs?

A moment later, Valentine maneuvered my arms into the dressing gown and guided me away from the paramedics. As we stepped onto the sandstone floors and muted brown walls of the basement's dressing room, I realized he was trying to protect me from watching Beatrice die.

"I have to be with her," I croaked.

Valentine guided me to a wooden bench and knelt at my feet, holding a pair of white panties. That's when I glanced down and found he'd already taken off my bikini.

He wrapped his fingers around my ankles and threaded my feet through its openings. "Get dressed, so you can accompany her to the hospital."

Hope filled my chest, and I inhaled a breath deep enough to pull back my shoulders and expand my chest. "She'll survive?"

"The ambulance people are doing what they can for your friend." He turned to a wall of mirrors to fetch something from the pile of clothes left on the counter.

I eased the underwear over my hips. "What happened?"

Valentine handed me a pair of loose, black leggings and a tank top. "It looks like Beatrice overheated—"

"No." I pushed myself off the bench and stumbled toward him.

He caught me in his strong arms and guided me back to the bench. "Careful."

"Don't lie to me," I said with a sob. "Something terrible just happened to Beatrice, and I'm sure it's something I did."

Every muscle in his body stilled, and he stared down at me through thick black lashes. "Have you done this before?"

"Made someone unconscious by sharing a hot tub?" I shook out the leggings, but my fingers trembled so much that the garment slipped to the floor.

Two people getting boiled in a jacuzzi was a freak occurrence, but one burning up while the other felt nothing was signs of a supernatural who had lost control of their magic.

Valentine didn't answer, instead helping me with my leggings, a bra top, and a thick sweater that he assured me I would need for the cold weather. I tried to leave the room, but he held me in place and dried my hair with a towel.

We emerged from the changing room just as the paramedics had wrapped Beatrice with metallic cooling sheets and loaded her onto a stretcher.

At the top of the stairs, four of Valentine's employees stood against the hallway leading to the open door. Kain was one of them and gave me a slight nod as we passed. I still couldn't believe someone so young and vibrant could go from normal to unconscious within mere seconds.

"Stay at Beatrice's side," he murmured into my ear. "My people are already at the hospital checking for signs of enforcers."

"Will you please tell me what's happening?" I whispered.

"Not here."

We followed the paramedics wheeling Beatrice out of the house and onto the sidewalk, where a small crowd of onlookers had already gathered.

Dense, noisy traffic curled around a fluorescent-yellow ambulance parked directly outside the villa.

The female paramedic slid open the back door, revealing the ambulance's crowded interior, and her male colleague wheeled Beatrice into the back.

It was larger than I'd imagined but small enough to induce a bout of claustrophobia. Supplies and devices covered every scrap of wall with rows upon rows of cupboards that stretched to the ceiling. They parked her bed on the right side of the ambulance and pulled on some kind of brake, and while the woman sat on a green leatherette seat behind Beatrice's bed, the man strapped her in.

I hopped aboard the ambulance and took one of two spare seats on the left, hoping they wouldn't kick me out and tell me to catch a cab to the hospital.

The ambulance doors slammed shut, encasing us in what felt like a cluttered tomb, and something beeped. I glanced around to find a monitor flashing with her vital signs. Her blood pressure was 150/186 compared to a normal of 120/80 and her body temperature 41.50°C compared to a normal of 37°C.

When the paramedic fastened her seatbelt, I did the same, and the vehicle pulled out, sounding surprisingly silent for an ambulance.

"Could you answer a few inquiries about Beatrice?" asked the paramedic.

"I'll try," I replied.

She asked a bunch of questions for which I

couldn't give definite answers. For example, if there was a chance Beatrice could be pregnant. I had to say yes, in case Christian had slipped up during those intense few days.

While I answered the other questions as best as I could, my gaze fixed on Beatrice lying within those metallic sheets, looking like a roasted bird. My chest ached, and I gripped the handrail, trying not to throw up. The paramedic explained that they often got cases like this in the height of summer, but never in autumn and never from anyone in their twenties unless they'd taken recreational drugs.

Poor Beatrice didn't even look like she was breathing. Only the numbers on the monitor above her head indicated that she was still clinging to life.

After what felt like an eternity, the ambulance stopped, and its doors opened, letting in a gust of cold air and drizzle. Silently thanking Valentine for helping me get dressed, I stepped out into an outdoors parking bay within the tall buildings that made up the hospital and waited for the paramedics to lower Beatrice's stretcher to the ground.

I pulled up my collar and hugged my arms, watching the dozen or so ambulances parked around us. Two of them contained patients, others contained paramedics wearing masks and white gloves, who cleaned their vehicles' interior. After what felt like an eternity, the woman brought a metallic, yellow ramp, and pushed Beatrice out.

Hoisting Beatrice's bag over my shoulder, I walked alongside the paramedics as they pushed her toward St Mary's Hospital Accident and Emergency, and through an entrance of two sets of automatic doors separated by a twenty-foot-long foyer. I clutched Beatrice's coat to my chest, my heart fluttering with panic. What the hell had this done to her insides?

We hurried through an oatmeal-colored hallway surrounded by wooden double doors. In the three years I'd been living in the Natural World, I hadn't needed to visit a doctor, let alone go to a hospital. It looked just like it did on television, only a hundred times worse.

This was no stranger being wheeled for a dramatic scene of medical magic featuring dreamy doctors and their steamier colleagues, this was Beatrice.

As we stopped at the Accident and Emergency's busy reception area, the smoky energy signature of a vampire curled around my senses. I glanced around the vast space, surrounded by transparent one-bed booths, but found nobody who looked supernatural. It was probably one of Valentine's people.

The paramedics left and handed me over to an Indian nurse, who wheeled Beatrice into a corner booth. Pale sunlight shone through its narrow window, illuminating an entire wall of monitoring equipment.

After drawing the curtains around the bed, the nurse pressed electrodes on various pulse points over her body and covered her with a fresh cooling sheet. Moments later, another came in with a saline drip and attached it to a cannula on her hand.

"Beatrice?" I sat at her bedside on a moulded plastic chair.

She didn't even twitch.

Clicking footsteps sounded from behind, and a middle-aged blonde doctor strolled in, clad in a white shirt and pencil skirt. Flanking her were three male junior doctors a few years older than me, each wearing stethoscopes around their necks and white coats. One of them pushed in a laptop on a trolley the height of a standing desk.

"Good afternoon, my name is Dr. Louise Bigger." She walked around the back of the trolley and glanced at the laptop's screen. "The patient is Beatrice Pala, aged twenty-five, in general good health. After spending the morning in a spa, drinking champagne cocktails, she overheated and collapsed with heatstroke, and is now exhibiting signs of hyperthermia and first-degree burns."

She turned to the most handsome of the trio, a dark-haired young man with a soul patch. "Doctor Tyler?"

He straightened. "Most likely brought on by dehydration and the overuse of sunbeds."

I bit down on my lip, desperate to tell them all

what had really happened. She wasn't drunk and wasn't sitting under a source of direct heat. One minute, Beatrice was helping me dislodge mimosa from my windpipe, and the next, she'd collapsed in the water from having gotten boiled.

A statement like that would lead to too many questions, the exposure of the Supernatural World, and possibly the arrival of enforcers to remove chunks of memory from every natural—including Beatrice.

Valentine had warned me to go along with whatever the doctors diagnosed before disappearing when the ambulance arrived, saying he would fix things.

The senior doctor turned her attention to me. "We're going to admit Ms. Pala for overnight observation."

"Will she be alright?" I asked.

"With a little more cooling and saline, she should awaken and make a full recovery." Dr. Bigger cast Beatrice a pitying look. "When Miss Pala awakens, I hope she better understands the perils of seeking an all-year tan."

"Beatrice isn't vain enough to sit under sunbeds," I snapped. "She's brown because her father's Indian."

The doctors offered me tight smiles and swept out of the little room. Perhaps they were used to patients and their families saying anything to present a better version of themselves. I lowered myself to the seat and reached for Beatrice's hand. The skin was so raw, I didn't dare to touch it.

"Can you hear me?" I murmured. "You're going to recover from this."

Two sets of supernatural energy approached from a distance. A vampire and a powerful witch, whose magic blazed with a clean, slicing energy that almost felt angelic.

"Here's Miss Pala," Valentine said from the doorway.

He stepped inside with a woman with red hair a few shades lighter than mine, veering toward a strawberry blonde. She was about five-eight—three inches taller than me—with turquoise eyes that looked like they would glow the moment she activated her magic. No lines marred her face, not even the fine lines people got when they smiled. It was hard to tell if she was fifty or five hundred.

My gaze dropped down to the diamond-shaped crystal she wore around her neck, the source of the blazing power. A breath caught in the back of my throat. Valentine had brought a high-level witch who could wield the healing magic of an angel.

Her eyes fell onto me. "And this girl?"

"One of us," said Valentine.

The healer nodded. "May we have some privacy?"

I rose off the seat and turned toward the door.

"Not you." The healer flicked her head over her

shoulder, indicating that everyone walking past had a view through the clear windows of Beatrice's booth.

"Oh," I glanced around the room for ideas, my gaze landing on the blinds. "We could obscure the window—"

"Do it," she said.

Valentine walked to the door and twisted a lever that lowered the blind and sealed its slats, while I did the same on the right side of the exit. After shutting the door, the healer raised her hand, creating what felt like a crackling seal around its frame.

"Let's have a look at this patient." The healer lifted the metallic blanket from Beatrice's legs, placed her hands on the soles of her feet, and flinched. "What is the meaning of this?"

"Pardon?" Valentine said, his face devoid of emotion.

The woman stepped back, her face pale. She turned to Valentine. "This human carries residual magical fire in her veins. Do you know what could happen to her if she dies?"

I clapped a hand over my mouth. "But the doctor said she'd be alright."

"Not the point!" The healer whirled on Valentine. "Your Majesty, how is such a thing possible?"

"Can you heal this human or not?" Valentine growled, making the healer flinch.

Wrapping my arms around my middle, I edged toward the wall, letting the healer's words percolate in my brain. Magical fire somehow burned Beatrice from the inside out, and now she might die. A sob caught in the back of my throat.

Valentine appeared at my side. "Nobody's going to die." He turned to the woman and said in a harsher voice, "Healer Dianne was speaking hypothetically."

She inclined her head. "I can heal this young woman, but I will need to report my findings to the Council."

Valentine bared his teeth and snarled, "I am the Council."

The healer stiffened as though suddenly remembering that Valentine was one of the seven monarchs who governed Logris.

My insides quivered. Whatever she had discovered in Beatrice's body had to be serious if she had forgotten her place. I stepped in front of Valentine, pulling the woman's attention back to me. "Will anyone damage Beatrice's mind?"

Healer Dianne's eyes softened. "His Majesty tells me that neither of you saw the creature that attacked from behind. It's fortunate for us that it decided to strike in private instead of at that bar."

I glanced at Valentine, who made a subtle nod for me to go along with that story. Valentine was trying to pin what happened to Beatrice on Mr. Masood, the shifter who sent us the champagne with the enchanted glasses. I nodded back, still not knowing what on earth was really happening.

"Let's get started, then." The healer placed her palms on Beatrice's feet and inhaled a deep breath.

As she exhaled, magic curled around the room, feeling like being licked by invisible flames. My gaze caught the healer's crystal, which glowed like the sun hitting a prism. It illuminated the woman's arms, hands, and Beatrice's feet an incandescent white.

Tiny pulses of power travelled up Beatrice's legs in the same pattern as the energy pathways depicted in the healing room of the crystal shop. They zigged and zagged up her belly, down her arms, and ended over her face in a network of crossing lines.

I gulped. It was one thing to believe in the meridians of Traditional Chinese Medicine—it was like believing in diagrams of the blood vessels without dissecting a cadaver to see for yourself. Witnessing the meridians glowing like this just made them so real.

Valentine gazed down at Beatrice with a furrowed brow. I couldn't tell if he was concerned about the woman's ability to heal her wounds or what had caused her to collapse and emerge from the water covered with red burns.

Somebody knocked on the door, making me flinch.

"Hello?" asked a gruff voice. "Porter."

I turned to the healer, who continued pouring energy into my friend. Valentine crossed the room and stood in front of the door with his arms folded and furrowed his brow into an even deeper frown.

"The doctor just admitted Beatrice for an overnight stay," I said.

"When I've finished with this patient, she won't need any further medical attention." The healer's crystal pendant rose off her chest as it brightened. "However, I'll leave some superficial redness to make the humans think their medicine has worked."

All the tension left my neck and shoulders in a relieved breath. I pressed the heel of my hand into my aching chest. Even though Beatrice would make a full recovery, I still put her through a terrible ordeal. If Valentine hadn't been there—

I cut off that thought. Beatrice and I had been friends for years and I'd lost count of the number of times we'd shared a bed. Nothing had happened to her then, so something else must be happening. This time, when I confronted Valentine I would do whatever was necessary to get those answers.

Moments later, Dianne released my friend's feet and sagged. "I've healed the damage and obscured the last few hours in the human's mind. She'll think she fainted from exhaustion."

"Thank you," Valentine and I said at the same time.

The woman straightened, smoothing down her camel-colored coat. "This incident will need to be reported."

"Of course," Valentine said in a voice as slippery as massage oil.

The healer walked to the wash station in the corner of the room and turned on the taps. Instead of shoving her hands under the running water, she ran her palms up and down its flow as though cleansing the energy around her extremities.

"And she'll spend the next few years monitored by enforcers," she added.

My mouth dropped open. "Why?"

After turning off the tap, the healer turned to me and frowned. "I only performed the triage necessary to get Miss Pala up and running. Removing the fire in her veins will require an extensive transfusion."

I glanced at Valentine, who stood as still as death, his face an unreadable mask. Since this expression and body language wasn't telling me anything apart from a need to exercise caution, I turned back to the healer, who tilted her head to the side with a soft crack.

"Why do the enforcers need to know about Beatrice if her memory is fuzzy?" I asked.

She paused to stare at me as though I'd asked her to explain something obvious. "Any being who dies with fire in their veins rises as the undead."

The words hit me like a kick to the gut. "What?"

Healer Dianne tutted. "Don't they teach you children anything in that academy? The male you encountered a few days ago is obviously a very powerful and unscrupulous wielder of fire. It's just like the days of Kresnik. That man loved to raise the dead to fight his battles."

I shook my head from side to side. There was that name again. "What about when she dies of old age? She can't turn into a zombie!"

"The fire will eventually die out if not stoked," the healer replied.

My lips parted to ask what that meant, but Valentine stepped forward. "Thank you for coming at such short notice," he said in that slippery voice. "May I see you to your car?"

Pink boomed across Healer Dianne's cheeks. She tilted her head to the side and offered him a coquettish smile. "It was an honor to be of assistance, Your Majesty. Will you settle now or shall I invoice your private secretary?"

"My driver will settle in whichever currency you desire." He swept his arm toward the door. "If you would release the enchantment securing the room, perhaps the porter can take Miss Pala upstairs to recover?"

"Of course." Healer Dianne raised a hand, and the magic over the door released in a rain of invisible sparks that crackled against my skin.

Valentine rushed behind the woman, spun her around, and locked eyes. "Beatrice Pala encountered a magic crystal that backfired."

I sucked in a breath through my teeth. He was mesmerizing a powerful healer.

Dianne's eyes glazed. "I've told these enforcers to gather up all these dangerous crystals but they have no jurisdiction over stones that naturally absorb power."

He gave her an approving nod and placed his hand on the small of her back.

"Valentine?" I whispered.

His eyes softened, and the tender look he gave me made my heart melt. It spoke of love and sympathy and yearning, but beneath the expression was a touch of fear.

My heart ached, and I longed to ask Valentine what was happening, but the words died in my throat.

"Do you trust me?" He cupped my face with his large hands, filling my chest with a giddy warmth.

"No," I whispered.

The corners of his lips curved into a sad smile. "I will explain everything when I return." He stepped back, leaving me yearning for his touch. "But know this, Inamorata. I will protect you until the end of my days."

Valentine swept his arm out for Healer Dianne and walked her out of the room.

I stood at the door, staring after the pair as they strolled through the long passageway of the Accident and Emergency Department. The part of me that still clung to past hurts urged me to run after Valentine and demand answers right now, but I'd already pieced together most of the story.

It was me who had attacked Beatrice, and something within me that would turn her into a zombie if she died while that fire magic still coursed through her veins.

A shudder ran down my spine. Valentine just mesmerized a healer to protect me, to cover up what I did, and to make sure the enforcers left Beatrice alone. Chasing after them now would undo his efforts and alert Healer Dianne that something was off.

I shook my head and stepped back into the room. Maybe it was time to start trusting Valentine. Regardless of what happened between us three years ago, everything about him suggested he had my best interests at heart. Besides, some things were worth more than getting immediate answers. One of them was keeping the Supernatural Council's enforcers off all of our backs.

CHAPTER THIRTEEN

After checking on Beatrice and finding her breathing with ease, I paced up and down the hospital room, clenching and unclenching my fists. Valentine would probably use the excuse of getting rid of the healer as a means to escape without giving me answers.

How dare he swoop back into my life and withhold the truth?

I raised my wrist, glowering at the source of all my problems. The tattoo seemed to have faded into a bright orange instead of its usual brown, but still looked stark against my pale skin. Each facet of the crystal hearts etched its own pattern, looking like a diagram of the crystals that had encased my wrist.

That bloody bracelet had probably been infused with a curse. Istabelle said it was firestone but what if it also contained something neither of us could detect? Crystals didn't just melt into a person's flesh and stain their skin.

I clenched my teeth. Why had I let him walk out of the hospital room without giving me an explanation? Because he was an old-as-sin vampire, and a magicless twenty-four-year-old couldn't make Valentine Sargon do a damn thing. I could bark and yap at him however much I wished, only for him to smirk at me like I was his evening's entertainment.

All the bluster and anger escaped my lungs in an outward breath, replaced with a wave of helplessness. I walked to Beatrice's bedside and lowered myself into the plastic seat. My relationship with Valentine had never been one of equals, no matter how well he had treated me. I'd always been subject to his whims.

Even though the redness of her skin was an enchantment and Healer Dianne had restored her to health, seeing her so helpless made my throat thicken.

I did this. I did this to an innocent human who had been nothing but kind and sweet and generous. Beatrice hadn't deserved an ounce of what had happened to her but because she got involved with a supernatural, she was now lying in a hospital bed.

Worse, if she died between now and the time my magic wore out, she would rise from the dead.

A sob caught in the back of my throat, and my eyes blurred with tears. What would happen to her soul? My breath came in shallow pants. I would have to work out a way to protect her.

"Beatrice, I'm so sorry." I slid my hand beneath the metallic blanket and wrapped my fingers around hers. "If I'd have known I'd become a danger to you, I would have kept my distance."

Guilt clutched at my chest with its sharp talons. The one time I'd allowed myself to get close to a human had resulted in something catastrophic.

Back in the academy, our teachers had told us about human-supernatural relations and the importance of keeping our world secret. While many supernaturals needed humans to reproduce, they had to choose their partners carefully. No casual encounters, no confidences, and certainly no platonic friendships. I'd left Logris to do the complete opposite.

A magicless supernatural like me had no need to leave our world when I'd be compatible with all the other species. We were supposed to be prime breeding partners—vessels of inert magic to be harnessed into producing powerful offspring.

The only reason they hadn't dragged me back was because I was formally apprenticed to Istabelle—a registered Master of Crystal Magic. And what did I do the moment I settled into the Natural World? Befriend a human woman and nearly get her killed.

I blinked, and two fat tears rolled down my cheeks. What would I do about Beatrice? If I couldn't remove this accursed bracelet, I might hurt her again and again, until one day, I ended her life.

My thoughts drifted to my last conversation with Istabelle, who had examined my energy body, identified the black tourmaline crystal that needed cleansing, but hadn't picked up any sign of the firestone bracelet lurking under my skin. What would she see if I stood in front of her now?

More tears rolled down my cheeks, and I choked back a sob. How on earth would I explain this to Beatrice when she woke up?

The door creaked open, and Valentine stepped inside, his features grave.

I bolted off the seat and rushed toward him with my hands curled into fists. "Will you please tell me what the hell is happening?"

Drawing his brows together, he placed a large warm hand on my cheek. "How much do you remember of your last week in Logris?"

"Don't change the subject," I snapped. "If I'm some sort of killer, I need to get as far away from people as possible."

His thumb brushed over my cheekbone. A gesture like that would normally have made my heart flutter, but even my body was in agreement that there was no time for romance after having nearly boiled an innocent girl to death.

"Please answer my question," he said. "It will help me answer yours."

"Everything," I said from between clenched teeth.

"Then why do you act like you've changed your mind?"

My stomach dropped. "What are you talking about?"

"We all agreed that you would spend time in the human world until—"

"Wait." I stepped out of his embrace. "Aunt Arianna and I decided I should leave Logris after you humiliated me in front of every high-society vampire, including your brothers."

Valentine's frown deepened, and he shook his head as though I'd somehow misinterpreted the cruel words that had tormented me for years. My insides roiled with fury. I knew when I was being gaslighted, and no amount of confused or concerned stares would make me doubt what had happened on that terrible evening.

"May I see your memories?" he asked.

"Why?" I stepped back and raised my palms. "You want me to relive those horrible words? Once was enough for a lifetime."

"Mera," he said with a sigh.

Angry heat rose to the surface of my skin. "Stop changing the subject and tell me what's going on. My life was going great until you sent me a bracelet and you haunted me like a ghost of Exes Past."

His lips thinned, and red striations flared across

his irises, making them appear crimson. "Will you behave yourself?"

The condescension in his tone made me flinch. I stepped back, my features twisting into a scowl. How dare he suggest I was some kind of unruly child having a tantrum?

Inhaling deep breaths, I tried to slow my frantic heart and get myself to calm. Valentine wouldn't avoid giving me answers by reducing me to a defensive screaming and crying mess. I wouldn't allow it.

I turned my gaze to the room's white wall, trying to clear my mind of Valentine's presence and its resulting resentment. If he wanted a civil conversation, I would give it to him, but that didn't mean agreeing to his every demand. "I don't consent to you rummaging through my mind."

"Alright," he murmured.

"Now, if you'd like to tell me what you know about the firestone bracelet and what happened to Beatrice, it would help me tremendously in not becoming a murderer," I said from between clenched teeth.

A muscle in his jaw flexed, and the nostrils of his perfect nose flared. He was trying to suppress his frustration. Was it because I hadn't escalated my tantrum or because I was back to demanding answers? Perhaps if he could answer a direct question, he wouldn't need to feel so exasperated.

I folded my arms across my chest and turned to look him full in the face. "Please."

Valentine's violet eyes roved my features as though trying to solve a puzzle. "This is what we agreed on," he said in a slow, even tone people used for explaining complicated concepts. "How could you forget?"

I shook my head from side to side, partially out of denial and partially to dislodge the surge of disbelief. "No sane person would willingly play the fool to such a large audience."

Even saying the words made my insides roil with a mix of hurt and fury. All my life, I'd been the subject of barbs from supernaturals my age who would inherit wealth, status, and become productive members of our society.

Aunt Arianna tried to tell me that the role I would play was just as important as theirs, but it was hard to accept that all I could ever amount to was a blood cow or a breeder. Even harder to have others judge me based on my plain human looks.

Beauty was important in Logris but secondary to magical and political power. An ugly-as-sin demon could stand proud beside the most beautiful of angels and fae if they possessed a unique gift that could impress others with its utility or its horror. Someone born and bred in the gutter could rise to the highest echelons if they worked hard and honed their innate talents. But not people like me.

It's hard to explain how it is for those without magic without using words like 'breeding stock' or conjuring images of farmers inspecting the teeth of a horse. Powerless supernaturals were considered little more than humans. A person's parentage didn't matter. Without magic, they could only survive on the charity of their families or the generosity of a wealthy benefactor.

When others taunted me at the academy, Aunt Arianna told me never to let them see me hurt because my pain would be their entertainment. I had been strong and rolled my hurt and anger into a ball to maintain a facade of serenity, which bored even the most persistent of bullies, but standing here alone with Valentine made something inside me crumble.

I'd worked through the pain with Istabelle as she had told me that I'd be incapable of healing others without healing myself. What I couldn't release, I kept in a kernel deep within my heart. Now, everything I had suppressed threatened to erupt, all because of the way Valentine stood before me and gazed into my soul.

After what felt like forever, Valentine finally spoke. "I think someone has tampered with your mind."

"Why?" I whispered.

"You know how difficult it is for your kind to leave Logris?" he asked.

I nodded. Aunt Arianna had appealed to the

Witch Queen on my behalf, explaining what had happened. The queen had only signed off on my permit to enter the human world because I would be under the formal guidance of an accredited master like Istabelle Bonham-Sackville.

Valentine stepped toward me, filling my nostrils with his masculine scent. My pulse quickened, and I took another step back, not wanting the distraction.

"Why do you think I agreed to being dumped in public?" I asked.

He walked over to Beatrice and placed a hand on her head. Vampires had the power to put people to sleep with a single touch.

After checking over my friend, he walked back to me and asked, "Did you know fire users develop their powers well before the age of twenty-one?"

A tight fist of panic squeezed my heart. He was about to say what I didn't want to hear from Istabelle —that I'd become some fire-wielder who would be hunted to death. I clamped my lips shut and shook my head, this time forcing myself to listen.

His features hardened with determination. "Each Neutral is assigned an enforcer at birth to monitor their progress until they come of age. At various stages in your life, they will have assessed you for signs of developing fire magic."

My throat dried. I couldn't be a fire mage. Up until today, I hadn't so much as overheated. A little voice in the back of my mind reminded me of the assassin who had seized me with his shadow. It was me who drove him back, not Macavity, who was still thrashing behind my closed door.

I met his somber eyes. "Valentine—"

He placed his fingers on my lips. "Let me finish."

I nodded.

Valentine launched into a story that spanned back beyond the cradle of civilization. Humans had their origin stories such as the Big Bang, and God saying 'let there be light,' but supernaturals had the Cosmic Clash, when the three Noble elements—air, fire, and water—collided to create the earth.

Over time, the elements combined, so that earth plus water made wood, earth plus fire made metal, and air plus fire made ether—an early form of magic. Any Magical Sciences teacher at the academy could demonstrate this in a magical laboratory. I guess this was the equivalent of humans' scientific theory of elements versus compounds.

The elements formed sentient beings, who roamed the earth in their purest forms, such as phoenixes and ifrits, beings purely composed of fire. They mated among themselves and produced offspring that combined all the elements, and then those beings mated.

Over thousands of generations, they created humans, animals, and supernaturals. Supernaturals were the beings who contained high levels of the element ether.

Nowadays, the closest thing we have to the original supernaturals are the elemental mages, beings who wield a single element, such as water or shadows.

"Are you following me?" Valentine asked.

I nodded. What he explained pretty much covered what I had learned in the academy, but his deep, hypnotic voice made the origin story vivid and less like a myth.

"The most powerful element of all to wield is fire," he said.

"Why, when it's just as old as air and water?" I asked.

He shook his head. "Fire is so much more than just an element."

"I still don't understand why the Supernatural Council fears it," I murmured. "They told us about Kresnik at the academy, but lots of supernaturals turn into tyrants. That doesn't mean people who share his category of magic should be hunted."

A bitter taste rose to the back of my throat. I was such a hypocrite. While growing up, I'd swallowed those lessons, also believing that fire wielders were a danger to our society. It was only now that I suspected I was such a supernatural that I bothered to question the humanity of not allowing them to live.

"Fire is the only element that sparks life," Valentine said. "Kresnik didn't just fight with his own power. Every person he killed with his magic rose from the dead and wielded their innate power against his enemies."

I placed a hand over my mouth.

Valentine nodded, as though approving that I was taking this seriously. "At first, it was easy to identify his puppets, but Kresnik honed his gift to a level of sophistication that made it impossible to know who he had animated until it was too late."

I gulped. "Necromancy?"

Valentine shook his head. "A necromancer animates a corpse. Kresnik's fire could breathe life into the dead, making them indistinguishable from the living."

"That's why the Supernatural Council hates fire users?"

"He was just the most recent tyrant in a long line of Light Lords, Lords of Fire, Ladies of Flame. Even though dark lords have risen, none have used their power to infiltrate Logris at such high levels."

Every ounce of moisture left my throat. These fire wielders seemed to have the power over life and death. "Why do you think I might be one of them?"

"I noticed how your temperature would rise when we were intimate." His hand cupped my cheek.

My eyes widened. "Did I hurt you?"

He shook his head. "It just rose a little above the level of a shifter or a demon."

I swallowed back a question about how he'd

grown familiar with the base temperatures of other beings. It wasn't like I was jealous or anything. Valentine had lived centuries and had a life before meeting me.

My tongue darted out to lick my dry lips. "That still doesn't explain—"

"The scene outside my palace?" he asked.

I nodded.

Pain creased the corners of Valentine's eyes, and he cupped my cheeks with both hands. "The last thing I would ever do is hurt the purest, most precious being in my life."

An ache formed in my heart, and I lowered my lashes, unable to withstand the love infused in his words. Even if he hadn't intended the words he uttered on the palace steps to wound, the rejection had cut deeper than any knife.

"I still don't understand," I whispered.

"We planned this." His voice strained with a plea for me to understand. "You, me, and your aunt."

I shook my head. "When I returned to Aunt Arianna in tears, she would have reminded me that we'd been acting. She was as upset as me."

"Did you tell her what I'd said?" he asked.

"No," I whispered. "Somehow she already knew."

A flash of realization flickered across his eyes. My nostrils flared, and every muscle in my body stiffened, ready for a fight. If Valentine so much as suggested that the woman who raised me had engineered a situation that would leave me in so much pain, I would walk out right now.

He paused for several heartbeats, his eyes roving my face. Perhaps he was thinking of a more delicate way to tell me that Aunt Arianna had tampered with my memory.

"Are you sure she didn't mistake your distress for sadness at having to leave Logris?" he asked.

Relief whooshed out of my lungs, and all the tightness loosened from my chest. This time, when I met his gaze, it was to see the beauty in his dark eyes and not the accusation.

Right now, they were an indigo so deep it was hard to differentiate the shades of red and blue. White flecks filled the irises, both reflecting the sunlight streaming through the hospital room's window and shining with the light of the truth.

My throat thickened. Part of me wanted to cling to the notion that he had courted me under false pretenses for years until he'd taken my virginity, made love to me, and then cast me aside once he'd gotten what he wanted. Part of me wanted to believe that I'd been duped.

Holding on to those beliefs was what kept me safe, stuck in a continuous cycle of suppressing my pain. They were what stopped me from getting hurt.

Somewhere deep in my heart, I shed the last vestiges of numbness, and a question spilled from my lips. "How do I know this isn't some elaborate plan to see how far you can dupe a stupid Neutral?"

Valentine's brows furrowed. "In all the time we've been together, have I ever reveled in tormenting someone whose position in our society was weaker?"

"Is that how you see me?" I asked, my voice brittle.

"Focus, Mera." The hands around my face clutched me tighter. "Our circumstances of birth are different, making me wield more supernatural power than most vampires. I'm wealthy, immortal, and was born into the Royal House of Sargon, but even that pales next to the beauty and strength of your soul."

On the inside, my heart dissolved into molten metal, but I tightened my features into a scowl. "How do you expect me to believe that I would agree to such public humiliation?"

"It had to be terrible enough to convince the Council and its enforcers that you weren't escaping Logris to hide your burgeoning fire," he said.

A breath caught in the back of my throat. My humiliating rejection had been the reason why the Witch Queen hadn't called me in for an interrogation when I'd applied to leave Logris. But only one thing plagued my mind.

"Why don't I remember this?" I asked.

Valentine's eyes softened, and the pad of his thumb caressed my cheekbone, sending a ripple of pleasure down my spine. "Please, will you let me look into your mind?"

My heart pounded so hard that I felt its reverberations in my toes, the tips of my fingers, and even against the outer layer of my skin. "I won't let you have free rein—"

"Someone must have gotten to you before you reached the palace," he said. "I want to search your memory for anything that might have happened between after we made love and then."

I squeezed my eyes shut. Maybe he was right and someone erased that plan from my mind, letting me walk into a public rejection. But why?

"Alright," I whispered.

"Thank you." Valentine's hands rose to my skull. "Open your eyes. I swear I won't venture further than the time I specified."

I met his gaze, making sure to focus on his expanding pupils. The ring of violet darkened and shrank until all that was left were deep pools of black. This was the power of a vampire. They combined smoke and ether to curl around the senses and beguile the soul. Creatures of seduction who could delve into a person's inner recesses and emerge as exactly what they desired.

As promised, Valentine brought up an image of us walking hand-in-hand through the marble-and-gold hallways of his palace. It was three years ago, and the person I was back then felt a hundred times lighter than the person I had become. I recognized this scene because I wore a white sundress with a red sash that I now clutched between my fingers.

Valentine and I had just made love for the first time, and it had been bittersweet. The most pleasurable experience in my life, but also a goodbye. I wouldn't see Valentine again until he and Aunt Arianna had found a way to control this terrible power that might one day get me executed.

He walked me down the palace's external steps, and outside into the sunny courtyard, where a black car awaited to take me back to the cottage I shared with Aunt Arianna. There was a ballgown for me at home, and in a few hours, I would return to the palace to enact a performance to save my life.

The driver walked around the door and bowed, but my chest ached so much that I couldn't keep my eyes from Valentine's face. This was going to be the last time he looked at me with any semblance of love —at least until we had managed to find a way to suppress my power.

Valentine cupped my cheeks, not giving the driver any hint of our plan. His sad violet eyes implored me to go.

A lump formed in the back of my throat, and I swallowed several times to fight back a sob. Lowering my gaze, I turned to the car and let the driver open the door. As soon as I scooted inside and let the driver shut me in, I stared out at Valentine standing at the bottom of the palace steps, his eyes reflecting the pain in my heart.

As the car sped through the courtyard and down the long drive out of Valentine's estate, a chill snaked around my neck, and a shadow crept into the edges of my vision until everything turned gray.

Flinching, I snapped out of Valentine's gaze, nearly falling onto the floor of Beatrice's hospital room. "What on earth was that?"

He cupped the back of my head, his eyes turning red. "It's as I thought. Someone has tampered with your memory."

CHAPTER FOURTEEN

Blood roared through my veins, and the pulse in my throat thrashed a furious beat. I stared into Valentine's eyes.

The dark ring around his irises blackened and the white flecks flashed like lightning across the spectrum of violet. His eye color only changed so drastically under intense emotional strain, and he was probably thinking the same thing as me. Who could have tampered with my mind, and why?

Silence stretched out between us, broken only by the beeping of Beatrice's monitors. She slumbered at the edge of my vision, still in a Valentine-induced sleep.

He smoothed a lock of hair off my face and tucked it behind my ear. "It's no wonder you were so hostile when I visited you in the shop. Those words I said to you…" He winced. "They weren't real."

I nodded, my ears still filled with the sound of rushing blood. "Do you recognize the driver?"

Valentine nodded. "He has worked for our family since before I was born, but I will have his mind examined."

My gaze dropped to the gray linoleum floor, and I swallowed over and over as though trying to digest the truth. Someone had violated my mind and condemned me to three years of heartbreak… Why?

I ran a trembling hand through my hair and blew out a long breath. This was unreal. I was a nobody. A nobody destined to marry the King of the Vampires. Was that why they'd attacked my mind or was it related to the fire magic?

Some of the pressure that had made a permanent fixture around my chest loosened. Knowing what had really happened felt like being reborn. Threads of self-doubt and recrimination that would weave through my mind in moments of silence turned to ashes in the fire of truth. I hadn't been stupid and naive and hadn't allowed anyone to dupe me over a period of years into falling in love, I hadn't been the sport of a cruel vampire king.

Outside, the trundling of a passing trolley snapped me back to the present. Now that I'd eased the pain of the past, I still had to face the perils of the present.

Valentine placed a soft kiss on my forehead. "For everything you've suffered, I am truly sorry. The time we spent apart was going to be hard, but if I'd known you were suffering—"

"Stop." I placed a hand over his chest, marveling at the way his heart reverberated against my palm. "It's just a relief to finally have answers." I still didn't know who had tampered with my mind or why, but at least I could let go of all that hatred.

It had festered in my heart, caused me to hate myself for dreaming about Valentine, thinking about Valentine, doing anything but suppressing the memory of Valentine.

At least now, I could finally accept that he genuinely worried about my problematic magic. Now, I could stop resisting his attempts to help.

His violet eyes shimmered with hope. "Now that we know the truth, perhaps you will allow me to court you again?"

A rush of emotion made my chest swell. Of all the things I expected him to say, I hadn't imagined him asking for a second chance. Could things work between us? My gaze dropped to his full lips, and a memory of how they had felt against mine drifted to the forefront of my mind.

I shook off that thought. Everything was happening too quickly. "We've got to find out who did this—"

"They will die for hurting you," he said, his voice full of steel. "Regardless of everything that's transpired between us, you are still the fiancée of a king."

His words curled around my heart, seeming to repair some of the damage it had suffered since the night of the ball. Whoever had done this must have known we would carry out a pretend break-up but wanted me to believe it was real. I asked myself for what felt like the tenth time: Why?

I thought back to all the girls in my academy who had disparaged me for having no magic. Some of them had been vampires. Were they upset to see that their king had chosen me for courtship and not them? No one had made a comment, but then, they probably wouldn't if they were planning on sabotaging our relationship.

Aunt Arianna had tried to warn me—I shook off those thoughts. She wouldn't go so far to stop me from marrying a man I loved.

We stood at the foot of Beatrice's bed, staring into each other's eyes and drinking each other in. What manner of mind manipulation could have made me believe Valentine capable of such cruelty?

His magic lingered in my mind like tiny wisps of smoke, still making connections, still healing, still uncovering the truth. It would take time to undo the spell woven into my unconsciousness, but I had faith in Valentine's power.

A knock sounded on the door, and Valentine stepped back to answer it.

"Porter," said the same voice from before. "I've got instructions to send this patient to an upstairs ward."

I turned to the monitors and checked her vital signs. Blood pressure 118/79 and temperature 36.4° C. Normal, if a little low from the cooling blankets. Healer Dianne's enchantment had made her retain the coloring so the doctors wouldn't be suspicious of her quick recovery.

We followed the porter through the hospital's winding back-corridors, into a metallic elevator large enough to fit two beds, and through the double doors of the Emergency Medical Unit, where the porter handed the nurse at the reception desk some papers.

The nurse turned her gaze to us. "We can't let you in just yet. Visiting hours start at five."

"Then I will say goodbye." Valentine placed his hand on Beatrice's temple and removed the sleeping enchantment.

I placed a kiss on my best friend's cheek. "Hang on, Bea. I'll be back with snacks and hot chocolate."

St. Mary's Hospital was a half-hour walk from the villa, and Valentine waved away the offer of a car from a black-suited vampire employee who had been tracking our movements throughout the day.

We walked out into Praed Street and continued down the road toward Paddington Station. Black cabs and double-decker busses rumbled past, but warm sunlight filtered down through the gaps in the crowds, making it feel like September rather than the first days of November.

A smoky presence moved several paces behind us,

and another across the road. His vampire guards. I edged toward Valentine, secure that I'd be safe from potential shadow assassins.

"How many of your people are out here?" I asked.

"Dozens." He wrapped an arm around my back and tucked me under his arm the way he used to while we were courting. "Someone will watch the healer to make sure she behaves, another group is still in the hospital, and there are six walking the streets."

Warmth filled my chest, making my heart swell. This was strange yet so familiar, dangerous yet safe. "I can't believe how one memory can unravel three years of confusion."

A growl reverberated in the back of his throat. "We will get to the bottom of this. When this is over, I will present to you the culprit's heart."

"Right," I murmured.

More concerning was the illegal magic festering beneath my veins. Everything Istabelle had said about firestone suddenly made sense. If supernatural nations used it to store firepower for weapons, I supposed that Valentine and Aunt Arianna had intended the bracelet to lock away any magical flares in case I had an outbreak in front of whoever had been watching me.

As we passed under the burgundy awning of a Costa Coffee, I stared up into his chiseled features and asked, "What are we going to do now? I guess the firestone bracelet was supposed to contain my magic. It didn't work."

Valentine hummed his agreement. "Arianna assured me that it would have been enough to keep you hidden, but perhaps she underestimated the extent of your power."

The clouds thickened, taking away the warmth of the sun. My feet ground to a halt. "Is Kresnik my father?"

He paused and stared at me with wide eyes. "Why would you ask such a question?"

"It took you ages to tell me what was happening, and if I'm more powerful than you both thought—"

"No." He placed both hands on my shoulders. "That man died five centuries ago. There is no possible way he could have risen from the dead to father you."

"What if he didn't die?" I gulped. "Aunt Arianna said she didn't know my father, and my mother didn't have any relationships in Logris…"

Valentine shook his head. "When Kresnik killed my father, my brothers banded together to release him from his slavery."

My mind flitted to the four vampire princes I'd met during my relationship with Valentine. Ferdinand, Sylvester, Constantine, and Lazarus seemed more interested in pleasure than in war. "Those four went into battle?"

"Not them," Valentine said with a chuckle. "I had two older brothers."

"What happened?" I frowned. He'd never mentioned them before.

Valentine inhaled a deep breath. "By the time Kresnik had killed my father and taken control of his corpse, he'd already entered the Supernatural Council and slaughtered the Wizard King, Mage Queen, and Shifter King. My brothers and two uncles tracked him across the country to destroy his body and put his soul to rest, but they lost their lives freeing my father from Kresnik's magic."

I squeezed Valentine's hand. "They didn't tell us that at school. I'm so sorry."

"Nobody in the Council is proud of how Kresnik took control of over half their number," he murmured. "Least of all me."

A wave of lightheadedness swept over my body, making me cling to Valentine to stay upright. The healer had described my power in similar terms.

It was no wonder the Supernatural Council wanted to destroy fire wielders before they came into their power. That didn't mean I agreed with them. Killing hundreds of innocent people in case they turned out like Kresnik was still barbaric.

Valentine's features seemed to sag with remembered grief, but warm gratitude filled my chest. Despite losing over five family members to the Light

Lord, he still wanted to protect me from the Supernatural Council's wrath.

I resisted the urge to lean my head against his shoulder, wrap both arms around his waist, and melt into his hard body. There was still so much to puzzle out, and I still needed to work through my feelings.

"It must have been a terrible time," I murmured. "Was that when you became the King of the Vampires?"

Valentine shook his head. "My uncle Draconius stepped in as the regent until I reached my sixth century."

His uncle lived in New Mesopotamia, a small kingdom between the rivers Tigris and Euphrates in what is now Turkey, Iraq, and Syria. Unlike Logris, New Mesopotamia had been ruled by the Sargon Dynasty of vampires that dated back over five thousand years.

I had only met Prince Draconius a few times, and one of those times had been outside that terrible ball. The man was always polite enough, but the seriously old vampires had an uncanniness about them that could make the flesh crawl. It was something in the way they stared at a person for minutes without blinking, making one feel like prey.

My phone buzzed.

"Answer it." Valentine paused at the junction of Praed Street and Eastbourne Terrace to let a black cab trundle past.

I pulled it out of my pocket and examined its screen. The number came from the crystal shop. "Hello?"

"Mera?" The sharpness in Istabelle's voice made me startle. "Where are you?"

"Walking the streets of London," I said, trying not to sound wary. "Why?"

"A group of people in black knocked on the door, asking for your whereabouts."

A boulder of dread dropped into my stomach, and I clutched at Valentine's arm. "What did you tell them?"

"The truth," she replied. "I've never kept track of my apprentices after work hours and I don't intend to start on their account."

"Did they give their names or say where they were from?"

Her snort filled the speaker. "No, but I know the look of an enforcer. Even if they pretend to be delivering a gift from His Majesty."

I glanced at Valentine, meeting his worried violet eyes. With his vampire hearing, he would have heard Istabelle's every word.

"They're heading toward the apartment," she said. "I can't promise they'll not be there when you return from your walk."

"Thank you," I murmured.

Istabelle hung up, and I stared at the phone.

Valentine slung an arm around my shoulder. "Let's get you to the safe house."

Gulping, I glanced from left to right. "You don't think they've tracked me down, do you?"

"Anything is possible," he muttered. "There are enough tech-wizards and witches working for the Council to track a person through their phone."

Valentine raised a hand at an approaching taxi, only for it to continue past and turn right into Paddington Station.

"Damn it," he hissed.

"I think there's a rule that says they can't pick people up from within a few feet of a taxi rank," I said. "We're going to have to go into Paddington Station."

"Come on." The arm around my shoulder lowered to my waist. Instead of rushing back through Praed Street, he continued down the road, glaring intently into the traffic.

"What are you doing?" I stared into his determined features.

"Catching us a cab," he said in a voice of steel. "We can hardly run back to the villa."

I gulped. Hadn't he heard what I just said?

The entire journey back to Notting Hill would have taken minutes using his vampire speed, but even members of the Supernatural Council were forbidden to exercise their power in view of humans and, more importantly, in view of all the surveillance cameras they installed through the streets.

Up ahead and across the road, a black cab approached with its orange light glowing. Valentine stopped walking to raise his hand, this time staring directly into the cab. The vehicle made a U-turn and stopped in the bus lane.

I gulped, shuddering at some of the penalties the Supernatural Council dished out to those who threatened the secrecy of Logris. A pair of vampires at the academy went out on a school trip to the Jurassic Coast and decided to stay the night and pick up human girls.

After using their fledgling powers on a pair of veterinary students to bite their necks, the Council decided to remove their fangs. It had happened two years before I'd met Valentine. As their king, that punishment would have been his decision.

Valentine opened the door and gestured for me to get inside. I lowered myself into the black cab's back seat and waited for him to sit next to me.

When the cab pulled out of the bus lane, I leaned into him and whispered, "What did you do?"

"Just a little charm and persuasion." He wrapped an arm around my shoulders and pulled me into his side.

My entire body melted. It had been years since Valentine—or any man—had held me like I was precious.

"Pembridge Villas, Notting Hill," Valentine said to the driver.

Anyone watching his actions on close-circuit television would just see an extremely handsome man hailing a cab. He hadn't done anything to flout the laws of the Supernatural Council. Besides, it probably wouldn't matter. Valentine was their vampire representative.

The taxi turned down Westbourne Terrace, a leafy, four-lane road bordered by tall, Georgian townhouses rendered in white stucco. This part of the road would have made for a beautiful, romantic walk with the sunlight filtering through the trees.

I shook off those thoughts and focused on the people in black who had tracked me down to the crystal shop. Anyone with access to my records would have known I was apprenticing under Istabelle, but why so many and why did they pretend they were working for Valentine?

My throat dried. I would bet my entire collection of black tourmaline that they were colleagues of the shadow mage who had met his end at the teeth of Macavity.

At the end of Westbourne Terrace, the taxi took a right and drove down Bayswater Road, which ran along Hyde Park.

I placed a hand on Valentine's muscular thigh. "Are you sure the villa is safe?"

"The houses in that development have been in my

possession since they were built in the eighteen-hundreds," he murmured back. "During their construction, some witches in my employment tied the wards to my life force. Whenever I want, I can lock every living being out."

"Of all the houses?" I pictured all the people unfortunate enough to have purchased a house on that road being kicked out of their own home.

"I can select which house I want to secure," he said with a confident smile.

"What about magical objects?"

He raised a brow. "Like fire and shadows?"

I nodded.

"The house will eject anything attached to the magic of anyone other than myself and my nominated guests. You will be completely safe while you bring forth your power."

"And if I accidentally set it on fire or make something else overheat?"

Valentine chuckled. "Everything is fireproof." He pressed a kiss on my forehead. "Your aunt even stopped by the villa after you left Logris to place your hair into ward stones she buried deep within the earth. Nothing you can do to the house would damage it. Trust me. I've thought of everything."

I wasn't quite sure about that and a few questions lingered in my mind. If nobody could stop me from developing into a fire mage or some other kind of wielder of fire, who would stop me from going mad with power?

My eyes fluttered shut as the taxi drove us through the streets of London. Maybe I was thinking about this the wrong way. Magic was just a tool that was neither good nor bad. Everything depended on the intentions of its user. If a maniac gained the power to wield flames, they would use it just as Kresnik had.

All my life, I'd just wanted to be the same as everyone else—magical, and not someone anyone could consider a broodmare. But the price for such illegal magic was too harsh. I couldn't spend my entire life being chased by the Supernatural Council's enforcers.

"What happens if the precautions you took don't work, and I turn into something terrible?" I asked.

Valentine flashed me a grin. "If you make it through the transformation without getting yourself caught or killed by the enforcers, you will no longer need my protection."

CHAPTER FIFTEEN

What did he just say? I twisted around in the taxi's leather seat and stared at Valentine's perfect profile of high cheekbones, a beautifully straight nose and parted lips. One of his violet eyes rotated to meet my gaze, and he raised his brows in question.

"What's that supposed to mean?" I asked.

He turned his head and frowned. "Mera?"

"You're going to let me transform into a…" I raced through my mind for the correct words.

Kresnik sounded like a monster, an anomaly, a supernatural freak. There was no way I would become any of those, even if I ended up developing the same power as the man who had taken control of Valentine's father.

"So, I'm going to turn into a fire mage and there's nothing anyone can do to stop it?" I asked.

Valentine exhaled a sigh and took my hand. "Your aunt has spent the past three years thinking of ways to reverse your development and halt it altogether. Did you ever eat her special homemade chocolates?"

"Of course." I frowned. "Did she put something in them?"

"Nullweed mostly, to suppress your magical development. It's a common practice among parents wanting to delay their children's development for betrothals or political alliances."

I stared out of the taxi's window, watching the traffic whizz by Hyde Park. There were fewer red double-deckers on the road, and more regular cars traveled among the black cabs and open-top hop-on-hop-off tourist busses. By now, the sun had disappeared behind white fluffy clouds, casting Bayswater Road in a November gloom.

We'd learned about nullweed in the academy, and some of my classmates had been taking it from birth because an important person they'd been betrothed to was either a decade younger or hadn't yet been born.

Back in my younger years in Logris, such practices were commonplace, and it was only when I'd come to live in the human world that I realized that suppressing children's development was barbaric. People weren't bonsai trees that needed pruning.

The thought that Aunt Arianna doctored her weekly box of chocolates with such a substance made my heart sink. It was no wonder she told me not to share it with anyone else.

"Mera?" Valentine squeezed my hand.

"I'm fine," I replied with a sigh. "She just wanted to protect me. I get it."

"Then why the frown?"

"She should have told—" I stopped myself before I could finish that sentence. "She probably did and I lost that knowledge in the mind control."

Valentine nodded. "Whoever tampered with your memory also didn't want you to know about your power."

"I thought it was strange that I didn't get any chocolates this month," I muttered. "Do you think it was that shadow assassin?"

"It's possible," Valentine replied. "If they discovered what your aunt put in the chocolates, withholding them for a few weeks would remove the nullweed suppressing your magic. It would also trigger your development."

I nodded. There was no point in raging at anyone. Except for whoever was working behind the scenes to sabotage Valentine's and Aunt Arianna's efforts to hide my power from the Supernatural Council.

The knowledge that Macavity had killed the assassin was no longer a comfort because a bunch of enforcers had tracked me down to the crystal shop. What if they found traces of the dead man?

The taxi turned right at Notting Hill Gate Station,

which at this time of the afternoon was crowded with people moving to and from Portobello Market. As we passed a bakery with glossy pastries in its display, my stomach rumbled. We hadn't eaten since the hot tub.

"You can't go to work tomorrow," Valentine said, his voice grave.

My gaze dropped to my lap. He was right. The flare of power that had heated the water and boiled Beatrice was probably the first of many. Maybe the next time, I would erupt in flames and hurt a human.

For everyone's safety, I needed to stay hidden. "I know."

Something he said earlier plagued my mind. "What did you mean when you said I wouldn't need any protection?"

Valentine's eyes glimmered. I would have thought the expression was admiration, but after hearing about what Kresnik had done to his family, he might have been looking at me with apprehension.

"Fire wielders are the most powerful of all supernaturals," he replied. "Kresnik's power was unusual and immense. Nobody in written history has animated the dead with such lifelike precision, but supernatural flames can burn through magic and have a destructive power that rivals volcanic explosions."

"Walking nuclear bombs?" I muttered.

"Once you've reached maturity, it will take a small

army to kill you," he murmured. "The Council will then convene to decide if attacking a peaceful fire wielder is worth the potential casualties, and I will vote against going to war."

I stared at his profile, my chest filling with awe. "Sometimes it's hard to remember that you're part of that group of elders."

Valentine chuckled, the sound tickling my ears.

The driver pulled in outside the white villa, and Valentine pulled out a credit card and held its chip to the passenger section's card reader. After tapping the display to add a tip, he thanked the driver for a pleasant ride.

The taxi's interior dropped a few degrees in temperature, and I turned my gaze back to the window. Outside, the clouds darkened, looking like it might rain. Goose pimples prickled across my skin, even with the tracksuit top and woolen coat.

Maybe it was a deep supernatural dread seizing my body or a reluctance to embark on this next stage of my life. Maybe something terrible was waiting for us at our destination.

As Valentine reached for the door, I grabbed his arm. "Wait."

He glanced at me over his shoulder. "Is anything wrong?"

"All the heat has been sucked out of the cab."

Valentine frowned. "You sense something?"

I nodded, not needing to explain. In the three

years we'd been together, we'd spoken at length about my ability to sense magic. Valentine found it fascinating and would often take me to far-flung places around the Supernatural World just so I could describe how a person felt.

He'd said it was like looking at the world through a different pair of eyes. I might lose that insight once I came into my power.

"Let me go out first, alright?" he said.

"Alright," I whispered.

Valentine opened the door and stepped out into the street. He turned back to me with a gentle smile. "Are you ready?"

My throat dried. I gulped over and over, staring at the villa looming ten feet behind him. It was only a few steps away, but those short iron gates now looked like the walls to a prison. With one thought, Valentine could lock everyone out. I knew how wards worked. With that same thought, he could also lock me in and keep me there until he decided to release me or he lost his life.

Right now, I felt like the ugly duckling about to transform into a raptor. Once I stepped through those doors, I'd probably endure days or weeks or months of pain and emerge the kind of creature everyone would hate and fear.

It wasn't like I had much of a choice. This development was going to happen whether I wanted it to or not.

"Let's go inside," I said, my voice already weary.

He offered me his hand and helped me out into the street.

As I stepped onto the curb, something cold snaked around my ankle, leaching the warmth from my foot. My heart jumped into the back of my throat. It tugged, making me stumble forward.

"Valentine," I said with a gasp.

In the blink of an eye, he scooped me into his arms and ran through the gap in the villa's metal fence. It hadn't quite been vampire speed, but fast enough to outrun a gold-medal sprinter.

"You're safe within the villa's wards." He paused at the doorstep. "What happened?"

"It felt like a shadow," I said.

Valentine spun around, and we both glanced down the street. Humans dressed for autumn walked past on their way to the stops and bars of Notting Hill, paying us no attention. Traffic wound around our black cab, which still remained parked outside the villa. We had left the door open, and the driver walked around to close it.

My gaze dropped to the curb. A thick, tentacle-like shadow stretched from beneath the taxi to the villa's threshold, forming the shape of a T alongside the metal railings separating us from the street.

"Look at the ground," I whispered.

Valentine snarled through his teeth. "Don't worry. Whatever that is, it can't pass the wards."

Turning us around, he pushed open the front door and carried me over the threshold of the villa. Warm air engulfed my body, melting away a layer of tension. I rested my head against his broad chest and sighed.

The old Mera from three years ago might have fluttered at the symbolism of Valentine's gesture, but that girl had never been hunted by an assassin or wanted by enforcers of the Supernatural Council.

A quick glance through the gap in the open door told me that the shadow was still trying to find its way inside. It lengthened, thickened, and rose off the ground the way Macavity did when begging for treats.

I could still feel the absence of heat from where that shadow grabbed my ankle. The wretched thing reminded me of a two-dimensional slug, leaving a trail of slime along my flesh.

Valentine kicked the door closed and carried me across the hallway and up the curving staircase. "Are you alright?"

"Thanks," I murmured. "That thing must have followed us from the hospital."

"They must have been monitoring you for longer than I thought," Valentine muttered under his breath. "Either that or someone working in the hospital contacted the enforcers about a suspected supernatural injury."

"That happens?" I asked.

Valentine stepped into the living room and approached the crackling fire. "Low-level enforcers work in human law enforcement and the health service. They're our most effective way to catch supernaturals who come to the human world to cause harm."

The heat of my heavy garments, the warm villa, the open fire, and Valentine's body made my skin itch, and sweat gathered on my brow. He still clutched me to his chest as though I was something precious, and the tip of his nose ran down my neck. A deep hum reverberated in Valentine's chest, making him feel like a cat who had caught its prey.

I cleared my throat. "Thanks for carrying me through the wards. You can put me down now."

Valentine's lips grazed my neck, sending tingles racing across my skin. "Have I told you recently how wonderful you smell?"

"Ummm." My pulse quickened, my nipples tightened, and I squirmed on his lap. "Valentine?"

"Inamorata."

His deep voice resonated through my body and settled at the most sensitive spot between my legs. What on earth was he doing? We had a shadow assassin, shadow curse, or whatever that thing was, lurking outside the house. We needed to call someone to get rid of it, not hole up in the villa sniffing each other's necks.

I placed a hand on his hard chest to give him a

shove, and his rapid heartbeat thudded against my palm. My mouth dropped open, and my gaze met his smoldering violet eyes, which radiated an intense and naked hunger. All the moisture left my throat. Did I really have such an effect on him?

"Valentine," I tried to keep the tremble out of my voice. "We should be fighting what's out there—"

"My wards are old and absolute," he said in a deep, melodic voice that curled around my senses like a cat. "No one will enter."

"Alright." My tongue darted out to lick my dry lips, and his eyes tracked the movement.

I gulped. The Valentine who had courted me had always shown restraint and had never been so openly passionate. Maybe it was because of our three years of absence. Maybe I would have felt the same intensity of desire if that shadow thing hadn't wrapped around my ankle and tried to drag me under the taxi.

"Could you put me down, please?" I murmured. "I need to sit away from the fire."

Still cradling me to his chest, Valentine backed us toward an armchair and lowered himself into the seat. He raised the arm around my back, and threaded his fingers through my hair, cupping the back of my head.

"Is that better?" he asked.

My heart pounded so loudly that his voice distorted through my ears. "A little," I replied, "but I really wanted to sit on the sofa."

He grinned, staring at me through sparkling eyes. "You're already sitting on me."

"Yes, but—"

His lips descended on mine in a soft kiss that sent a jolt of electricity through my insides.

"Oh," I said with a moan.

Before I could repeat my request for him to let go, he kissed me again, this time parting my lips with his. Valentine shifted beneath me, and his hardness pressed into my ass. My lips parted with a gasp, and he slipped his tongue into my mouth.

Valentine's lips were both soft and firm, coaxing and demanding, his tongue caressing mine in a series of languid strokes that sent spirals of pleasure racing through all my most sensitive spots. The rapid pulse of my desire boomed through my skull, its echoes drowning out a tiny voice that whispered at me to slow down and focus on the assassin outside the door.

Vampire saliva contained enough thrall to subdue even the strongest of supernaturals, and with each kiss, each curl of his tongue, I melted further in his arms and surrendered to desire.

Warmth gathered between my legs, bringing with it a surge of moisture that dampened my folds. Right now, my entire world coalesced into the strong arms securing me to the broad hard body, and the waves of pleasure Valentine incited with his lips and teeth and tongue.

My heart pounded. My blood roared. I wanted more. Needed it.

With a desperate moan into the kiss, I ran my palms over the contour of his hard pecs, over his broad shoulders, and around his thick neck. Valentine groaned in response, deepening the kiss. He devoured me, consumed me, subdued me, and muffled my cries with more of those toe-curling kisses.

"You are most intoxicating," he drawled.

My only response was a muffled groan as I clung onto his neck.

With one hand, he unbuttoned my coat, and with the other, he held me in place, his kisses now traveling along my jawline and down to my neck.

The pulse between my legs quickened. Would he bite me? Would he let me taste his blood? Excitement rippled through my insides, and with it, a bout of terror. Exchanging saliva with a vampire was dangerous enough, but blood…

"Valentine," I murmured.

"Shhh," he whispered, his kisses traveling down to my collarbone. "I know exactly what you need."

Relief loosened my muscles, and I released the arm around his neck, but Valentine lowered me onto the floor and sat me on the rug.

"Do you know how much I have yearned for you, Inamorata?" he growled.

"No," I whispered.

All those years, I imagined Valentine had moved on to another girl, another challenge, another bit of sport. It had never occurred to me that he would even cast me a second thought except to perhaps laugh at the stricken expression I made on his palace steps. Now that I knew we had an enemy who had sabotaged our relationship, it had erased half the pain I had endured.

Valentine pulled back my coat and slipped his hands beneath the fabric of my sweater. His fingertips blazed a trail of pleasure over my belly and ribs, and my nipples tightened, eager for his touch, but he pulled the garment off my body and tossed it to the side.

Warm air swirled around my naked top half, and I pulled my arms over my B-cup breasts. Maybe if I was a cup size larger or as curvaceous as Beatrice, I'd flaunt myself, but with months of absence from the sun, I was blue veins and milky white skin.

"Don't hide yourself from me." His gaze roved my form. "Even after committing your body to memory, I still couldn't capture the extent of your beauty."

Heat rose to my cheeks, and I lowered my arms.

Valentine's eyes lingered over my body as though he was caressing me with his entire gaze. Licking his lips, he laid me flat on the soft, silk rug. "You are, without doubt, absolutely exquisite."

As his fingers slid down the sensitive skin on my breasts, I arched my back, aching for more.

His eyes glazed, and he hooked his fingers beneath both my leggings and knickers before pulling them down my thighs. When his gaze fixed on the red curls between my legs, he parted his lips and moaned, "Let me taste you."

A whimper reverberated in the back of my throat as he divested me of my shoes and tossed my clothes across the living room.

The thud of them landing snapped a part of my mind out of my daze, and I stared up into Valentine's lust-filled eyes. Eyes that were now a deep crimson with no hint of the indigo I'd seen in them before.

All the moisture left my throat and coalesced between my folds. My heart made rapid palpitations as his lips parted and his hands slid over my knees.

Valentine parted my legs, and I sucked in a shuddering breath. He was going to see how wet he'd made me—the full extent of my arousal.

His eyes dropped to my sex, and his fingers made a slow, torturous descent down my inner thigh. My core twitched and spasmed with need, and that tiny voice in the back of my head told me we were moving too fast. Valentine's fingers brushed my outer lips, and a breath caught in the back of my throat.

His satisfied rumble sounded almost like a purr. "You are so deliciously wet for me."

I squeezed my eyes shut, my cheeks heating with a mix of discomfort and desire. This was one time I couldn't hide my feelings from Valentine.

"Look at me." His deep voice resonated through my insides.

One of my eyes peeped open.

Valentine raised his brows, looking every inch the commanding vampire king. "I want to see every moment of your pleasure."

"Really?" I murmured.

"I want to see the ecstasy in your eyes when I do something like this." His fingers brushed over my outer lips.

Pleasure spread across my sex and pooled low in my belly, arousing the fire that had been threatening to ignite. My back arched, and I bit down on my bottom lip to stifle a moan.

"Inamorata." His tone was chiding. "I want to hear your moans."

A nervous giggle burst from my throat. "You don't ask for much."

Valentine's face broke out into a broad grin. "When it comes to you, I want it all."

His fingers glided through my folds, circling my entrance before traveling up to my clit. My breath came in shallow pants. I'd touched myself a thousand times since we'd been apart, always thinking about a faceless stranger, who certainly wasn't a vampire. But no self-pleasure could even match the effect his fingers had on me.

As he reached the base of my clit, a whimper reverberated in the back of my throat. Round and round his finger went, with a punishing slowness, barely skimming my sensitive bundle of nerves. I panted through my parted lips, trying to catch my breath. Pleasure swirled through my insides at his touch, but it wasn't enough.

"I need…" My tongue darted out to lick my dry lips.

"Tell me," he growled.

A pleasant shudder skittered down my back, settling where I needed him most.

"Touch me," I whispered.

"Where?" His fingers made a wider circle, giving me the barest hint of the promised pleasure.

I clenched my teeth. Bloody hell… I was three years out of practice with all the dirty talk. "My clit," I said in a much stronger voice. "I want you to touch me there."

Valentine's gaze dropped to my sex. "As you wish, Inamorata." He lowered himself on top of me, positioning his broad body between my legs. Before I could utter a word to ask what he was doing, he said, "But first, a kiss."

"I can do that."

He swooped down and captured my mouth in a kiss that was harder, deeper, infinitely more demanding than the ones we had shared earlier. Valentine devoured me with his tongue, lavishing my mouth with wicked, long strokes that made me moan.

The fingers circling my clit now glided over it, each revolution building me to new heights of sensation. As I lost myself to the kiss, my core spasmed and clamped as though crying out to be filled. Valentine had just awoken something in me, and it was ravenous.

My head spun with a combination of his saliva and the fingers teasing me to distraction. I clung onto his broad shoulders as though they were the only things keeping my consciousness from spiraling out of control. Pleasure wound tight, like the dial of a clock, and just when I thought something would snap, he removed his hand and drew back.

"What's wrong?" I said, my voice trembling through rapid breaths.

He slid down my body, kissing one nipple then another, until he reached my belly button. "I want to hear you moan."

"It's hard to make noises with your tongue down my throat—"

Valentine's tongue swiped down the length of my sopping slit, and a shockwave of pleasure lanced through my insides.

"Oh." My eyes bulged first then darted from side to side. I'd forgotten how good this could be.

The tip of his tongue grazed the top of my clit, and a bolt of sensation shot to my core. With a noisy gasp, I threaded my hands into his hair.

"That's it." His breath fanned over my folds as he

placed his palms on my inner thighs, laying me completely bare. "Sing for me."

There wasn't even time to feel embarrassed because Valentine's tongue flicked up and down my clit, sending sparks of pleasure deep into my core and down my inner thighs. My lips parted, letting out a long moan.

Valentine quickened his pace, tormenting me with the most delectable strokes of that silver tongue. My thighs trembled, my core pulsed, igniting a wildfire in me that spread across my every nerve ending. My eyes rolled to the back of my head and I moved my hips against his relentless tongue.

Every few moments, it would slide down to my opening, lapping up my arousal as though he found it more precious than blood. The thrall in his saliva coursed through my veins, driving me to heights I hadn't experienced in years.

I lost track of time, lost track of history, and lost track of the events of the day. Right now, it was just Valentine and me and his clever tongue.

"Exquisite," he growled, his warm breath fanning over my folds. "I could do this forever."

"Mmmm!" Apparently, I'd also lost track of the ability to speak.

Valentine laid the flat of his tongue against my clit. This time, the pleasure became even more intense.

Every red blood cell racing through my veins felt like it was on fire. My hips ground against his tongue, chasing the sensations. Valentine's fingers dug into my thighs, holding me in place as the pressure inside me mounted. I was so close. Close to releasing the pent-up frustration from all those years we spent apart.

Valentine's appreciative growls reverberated across my sex, adding to the mounting heat. "Come for me."

My gaze dropped down to the head between my legs, and Valentine's crimson eyes met mine in a look that said he wanted to consume every morsel of me until there was nothing left. Something within me snapped, and I lost myself in an explosion of ecstasy that shattered my soul.

A cry tore from my throat, ringing through my ears in staccato bursts as Valentine kept licking, lathing, lashing at my clit. My core muscles spasmed, and molten pleasure burned through my body, setting everything alight.

"Valentine," I managed to say through gasping breaths. Whatever I was going to utter next lost itself as my body convulsed with a second climax.

This one was mercifully shorter than the second, but just as powerful. After it quickened through my body, I melted into the rug. Spent.

It took several moments for my breathing to return to normal, and for the ripples of my core muscles to calm. That had been one of the most intense experiences of my life.

"You were delicious. Delectable, an absolute delight." He licked his lips. "But I want more."

I stared up at him through a haze of euphoria, wondering if we were going to have sex.

Then his fangs descended.

CHAPTER SIXTEEN

I was a relative stranger to post-coital bliss, but we were becoming acquaintances pretty fast. My mind was far too relaxed to worry about a pair of fangs. Especially when they were attached to someone as ravishing as Valentine.

He knelt between my legs, his large hands sliding down my thighs. The sensitive nub between my folds pulsed once more, and I held my breath, waiting for his next move.

Valentine lowered his head to my neck and pressed several kisses along the sensitive flesh. His tongue slid up and down my vein as though he could taste the blood coursing beneath my skin.

"Now, I want to feel the force of your climax around me," he drawled.

My lips parted with a moan. It had been three years. Three long years since I'd felt the touch of a man, the weight of his body against mine. I hungered for Valentine as much as he hungered for me. My current state of euphoria and the vampire saliva soaking into my skin was just making matters more desperate.

Whatever resistance I might have clung to now drifted into the ether, and I fumbled with the buttons of his silk shirt. "Take it off."

In the blink of an eye, Valentine was shirtless and pinning me to the rug. As he continued laving my neck with open-mouthed kisses, he caressed my breast, rolling my nipple between his thick fingers. Sparks of pleasure flew across my skin, settling into the nub aching between my legs.

I ran my hands down the smooth skin of his broad shoulders, over the muscles rippling on his back, enjoying the way he moaned at the taste of my skin. My fingers trailed down his spine, and by the time they reached the curve of his ass, he'd already removed his pants and boxers, leaving me squeezing his firm glutes.

Valentine's hardness pressed against my belly, the trail of dampness seeping into my skin, making my folds flood with moisture. With one shift of his hips, the tip of his length brushed against my slick folds.

I parted my legs, my breath coming in shallow pants. "You said something about wanting more?"

His deep chuckle resounded through my body, making my hungry core muscles ripple. Still nipping and sucking at my neck, the hand caressing my breast slid beneath my shoulders, holding me in place.

With his other hand, he lined himself against my opening, and my hungry core clenched with need. "You want this, Inamorata?"

"Yes," I whispered in his ear.

"As you wish." He pressed into me.

The intensity of the stretch was incredible and made my breath catch in the back of my throat. I'd forgotten how long he'd spent preparing me with his fingers that first time. The most intense pleasure made my insides quiver with need. I was no longer that frightened virgin. I was too blissed out from his kisses and from that climax to interpret these sensations as anything but ecstasy.

"More," I whispered.

Valentine's satisfied purr reverberated across the entire length of my body, making my nipples tighten. He pushed in a little further, intensifying the stretch. Just as my muscles trembled around his girth, he pulled out.

I wrapped my arms around his neck and clutched at his silken hair as he moved back and forth, taking me inch by excruciating inch. Rocking against him to deepen the penetration, I reveled in the sensations. This was proving to be even more wonderful than the cunnilingus.

The next thing I knew, his sharp fangs pierced my skin.

Molten ecstasy exploded through my insides, triggering wave after wave of pleasure rippling through my core. Adrenaline flooded my system, making my heart clench.

Valentine moaned, his hips moving back and forth and his thick, pulsing length sliding in and out of me, driving me to another climax. A second burst of sensation tore through my insides, even stronger than the first. My muscles seized, and fire raced down my every nerve ending, making them hum. I struggled to catch my breath, riding out pleasure and waiting for his fangs to slide out of my veins. Valentine was still hard, and thrusting into my core, pushing me to a third orgasm.

My mind spun out of control. My blood roared, and the frantic beat of my heart kicked up several notches. Valentine's lips remained clamped to my neck.

"Valentine?" I slid my palms over his biceps and dug my nails into the tense muscles.

"Hmmmm." He continued moving his hips back and forth, still pushing me toward yet another climax, and cradling me to his body the way a cat might grasp a delicious fish trying to escape.

My eyes snapped open. Something was off. Vampires only needed the barest amounts of blood to survive and got most of their nutrition from food.

The Valentine I knew wouldn't take more than a mouthful, yet my ears filled with the sound of his continuous gulping.

Realization hit me like a hailstorm. Valentine wasn't just tasting me—he was feeding.

I clutched at his broad shoulders. "What are you doing?"

Valentine's hips quickened, his strokes becoming deeper, harder, more frenzied.

Panic lanced through my chest, or maybe it was pleasure. The signals firing through my brain were frazzled. As I opened my mouth to yell, that third orgasm tore through me like a firestorm.

"Valentine!" My eyes rolled to the back of my head, and every muscle convulsed with an unending pleasure that kept going, even as I slapped at his arms, even as I screamed.

He roared into my neck, shuddering through his mouthful, while still drinking my blood.

As that climax freed me from its grip, my mind returned to normal, and I exhaled several ragged breaths.

"Enough," I croaked. "You're going to kill me."

Valentine hummed as though he hadn't heard a word of what I'd just said. Cold sweat broke out across my skin. I'd been a fool and I was going to die. What if everything—from the person following me that morning through Grosvenor Square to the shadow assassin, to Beatrice boiling in my supposed magic—what if all of that had been a charade to make me enter a warded house of my own accord so he could drink from me without consequences?

Even the people in black who visited the crystal shop made sense now. When I eventually went missing, Istabelle would assume that enforcers dragged me back to Logris for a swift execution or that I had died resisting arrest.

I slapped at his arms, tried to push him off but he was too big, too heavy, too determined to drain me of my blood.

A sob caught in the back of my throat. I'd been a bloody fool.

Valentine sucked harder at my neck and groaned. Tears stung the back of my eyes. Maybe draining the lifeblood of a Neutral was a secret vampire rite of passage they didn't teach us in the academy. What if he'd needed me all along to boost his own power?

The little voice in the back of my head screamed at me not to give in to speculations or despair. Even if everything Valentine told me about developing firepower might have been a ploy to take my blood, I couldn't just lie on the rug and become a vampire's meal.

"Valentine?" I said, this time trying to keep my voice clear of rising panic.

"Hmmm?" He held me tighter.

I clenched my teeth. Charming him wouldn't work.

Words wouldn't distract the ultimate apex predator from his prey. Bitterness coated the back of my tongue. That's all I was to him. Prey. Prey to stalk, prey to trick, prey to beguile. Prey to humiliate in front of a crowd of other predators and win back, only to take me to the edge of ecstasy before draining my blood.

Every ounce of my fear transmuted to a fury that burned hotter than molten lead. It swirled through my chest, burned through my veins, and surged along the edges of my taut nerves. Sparks as long as my fingers flew from my hands, filling my nostrils with the scent of burned flesh.

Valentine stiffened, and with a startled gasp, his fangs withdrew from my neck. "Mera." He pulled back, his crimson eyes wide. "What just happened?"

"You tell me." I held out a sparking hand, pointing my fingers out like daggers, and scrambled to my feet.

Valentine remained sitting on the rug, staring at me with confused eyes and parted bloodstained lips. "I didn't mean to bite you."

"Liar." A foot-long flame flared from my fingernails.

He flinched. "Morata, please—"

"Call me by that nickname once more, and I'll burn off your lying tongue."

His chest rose and fell with rapid breaths. I stepped back, heading out toward the hallway with my arm outstretched as though it was the only thing keeping him from pouncing.

"You're changing," he said from his seated position on the rug.

"What?" I snapped.

"You're expressing your magic."

The moment I stared down at my hand, the flames vanished. My stomach plummeted to the wooden floor.

"I'm so sorry," he said.

A heartbeat later, Valentine stood in front of me with his hand around my wrist.

Fresh panic pierced my chest, and I yanked my arm out of his grip. "Don't touch me."

He jumped back several feet, the rapid movement making me flinch. "I don't know what happened. One minute, all I wanted to do was kiss you and the next…"

Every instinct called at me to cover up, but I didn't dare scramble about for my clothes in case Valentine decided he wanted more blood. "Have you drained a girl before?" I asked. "Is this a vampire thing you guys keep a secret?"

He shook his head. "Something seized control—"

"What?" I stepped back.

Valentine pointed at my leg. "You have a cursed mark."

Baring my teeth, I held out my palm. "If this is a ploy to make me—"

"Mera, please."

There was absolutely no way I would break eye contact with Valentine. This was just like a game Macavity and I always played. I'd lie low and hide around a corner, poking my head out, trying to catch his eye from across the room. When I disappeared, he would take a few steps and then freeze the moment I emerged to make eye contact. Each time I hid, he would take more steps toward me until we were nose to nose.

Closing my eyes also made Macavity come closer. It was a fun enough game with a house cat. But with a vampire who had just consumed mouthfuls of my blood and only stopped after getting burned, it was downright dangerous.

"Just tell me what you see," I said through clenched teeth.

"A black band around your ankle." His voice strained with desperation. Desperation to do what, I didn't want to know. "Your blood is irresistible and it tastes incredible."

"You want more, don't you?" I asked, my voice flat.

"It must be the cursed mark," he replied.

His lack of response to my question was answer enough. If I didn't get away from this vampire, I might never leave this house except as an exsanguinated corpse.

"Put your clothes on," I said in a tone I might use to calm down a feral beast. "Slowly."

As he backed away, I forced my gaze to remain on his eyes and not on the taut muscles that rippled as he moved, and not on the way the sun streamed through the window, warming his bronzed skin.

Everything about a vampire was a lure to distract, seduce, beguile, including the long, thick erection I could see on the edge of my vision, protruding from a thatch of black hair.

Valentine edged around the sofa and bent behind the broad piece of furniture. Flinching, I readied myself for a covert attack but he emerged holding a pair of black boxer briefs.

"I have to call back Healer Dianne," he said as he slipped them on. "She'll remove the curse—"

"Just get dressed and get out," I snapped.

Nodding, he placed his legs into a pair of dark pants and pulled them over his hips. "If you hadn't triggered your magic when you did…"

"You would have drained me dry." My chest tightened as I said the words, as I realized that I'd come so close to death.

Valentine closed his eyes, his nostrils flaring. "Mera, I am capable of many things, but hurting you is not one of them." A muscle in his jaw flexed as though making that declaration was at odds with what he wanted to do to my neck. "Please stay in the house while I go out and fetch help. And trust no one."

My lips pressed into a firm line. The trusting no one part would be easy. While I could feel cold, foreign magic writhing around my ankle, I still wasn't sure about Valentine's motives.

Maybe shadow mages really were hunting me and this wasn't part of an elaborate plan to trap me here as some kind of blood slave. But I couldn't trust him not to reattack, knowing he would never have stopped consuming my blood without the threat of being burned by my flames.

Flames. My throat spasmed. I was a fire mage or something worse. Right now, I couldn't complain. That power was the only thing keeping me alive.

Valentine shouldered on his black shirt, slipped on his shoes, and walked around the perimeter of the room toward the door. I stepped several paces to the side, nearly tripping over my coat as I put as much distance as possible between us.

As he passed, his eyes bored into mine, and their pupils were dilated, surrounded by a tiny ring of crimson. Valentine's steps faltered for a beat, making my outstretched fingers spasm, but he passed into the hallway and continued down the stairs.

I crept after him to make sure he didn't double back and stood at the top of the stairs.

Halfway down, he paused again, making my heart clench. "I placed the solid flame dagger in the pocket of your coat. Use it to protect yourself, even from me."

I nodded.

He raised his head, meeting my gaze with eyes that still glowed the color of blood. Something in the way he breathed and in the white knuckles of his fists clenching around the handrail told me that it was taking Valentine every ounce of willpower not to rush at me again with his fangs.

"Go to your room, lock the door, and stay there until Healer Dianne or another female healer knocks."

"Alright," I croaked.

Valentine continued down the curling staircase until he disappeared from sight. His footsteps were deliberately loud as though trying to communicate that he really was leaving. I knelt toward the coat at my feet and slipped my fingers into the pocket. He was telling the truth about the dagger.

As soon as the downstairs door closed, I clutched the coat, dashed across the marble hallway, and bounded up the next flight of stairs. I opened the door, looking for signs of a Bengal cat, but Macavity was either downstairs or must have gone out for the day.

I shut the door and turned the lock, even though metal and wood meant nothing against the might of a vampire. After throwing the coat on the bed, I pulled open the drawers, and slipped on a pair of panties, jeans, a tank top, and a pair of sneakers.

"Oh, shit," I whispered to myself. "Bloody, bloody shit!"

This had to be one of the most perilous situations in my life. It was even worse than the time Macavity turned into a giant leopard. What if Valentine decided he didn't like the smell of fresh air and wanted to finish the job he'd started? What if he wasn't even outside but was standing right on the other side of that door, debating whether to break into the room and take what was his?

I fumbled through the coat's pocket and pulled out my smartphone. The only person who would tell me what was happening was Aunt Arianna. I tapped her icon and pressed the phone to my ear, waiting for her to answer.

Three rings later, a voice said, "Mera?"

"What's happening with Valentine?" I blurted.

"Did he find you?" she asked.

The entire story spilled from my lips, starting with the bizarre encounter with the unseen vampire and ending with nearly being drunk. When I finished, Aunt Arianna went silent.

"Are you still there?" I asked.

"Yes."

"Well? How much of what he said is actually true?"

Aunt Arianna's sigh fanned across the smartphone's speaker. "We did discuss a plausible way to get you out of Logris without arousing the suspicions of the council, and I did put nullweed in your chocolates. I thought you already knew all this."

"Do you know who might have tampered with my memories?"

She paused for several moments. "Another vampire?"

I rubbed at my temples. A vampire might have overheard what Valentine and I were planning. So far, all indications pointed toward the man who had driven me home from the palace. But that solution seemed too simple, especially considering the driver was still working for Valentine while most would have disappeared, fearing they would be caught and punished.

"You said there's shadow magic around your ankle?" Aunt Arianna asked. "Why didn't the wards catch it?"

"The shadow stayed behind on the street, but it still managed to curse me for the second or so it took hold of my leg," I replied.

My aunt fell silent for several moments before saying, "I'm so sorry."

"What for?"

"We thought the firestone would contain your magic. Those beads were supposed to hold the power of four mages."

Cold spread through my insides. "I'm powerful?"

"It would appear so." Her voice broke. "No matter what King Valentine says, the Supernatural Council will never stop hunting one with so much magic."

"Because of Kresnik?" I asked.

"For such a diverse group of people, they can be horrifically narrow minded when it comes to a minority with a specific power."

My heart sank, and I lowered myself into the ivory armchair by the window. The way Valentine talked about things, he thought the Supernatural Council might leave me alone if I proved to be peaceful. It sounded like Aunt Arianna thought they wouldn't stop until I was dead.

"Is there anything I can do to protect myself?" I whispered.

"Perhaps," she replied with another sigh. "It's risky, but then so would be leaving the wards of the safe house."

"And staying within them when there's a hungry vampire on the prowl," I muttered.

"Give me a few days," she said. "I've been experimenting with a new way to absorb your magic. If I can tweak things, it might even absorb your curse."

"What will you do?" I asked.

Aunt Arianna paused the way she did when trying to describe something she thought I might find unpleasant. She'd also acted this way years ago when trying to warn me away from Valentine, saying that vampire males couldn't be trusted, and that associating with a king would bring an unwanted spotlight. I guess she was right about the spotlight part, but I still hadn't fully decided about Valentine.

"It's best that you don't ask," she said. "If I can make it work, you'll be completely rid of that power and nobody will ever need to investigate you again."

Before I could press for details, the line went dead. My fingers fumbled for her shortcut, but I couldn't get through.

I slipped the palm-sized dagger into the back pocket of my jeans, strode into the bathroom, and turned on the cold water. The liquid streamed out of the tap, and I splashed handfuls over my face, trying to cool the hot red blotches.

What a day. After seeing those flames erupt from my hand and smelling how I had burned Valentine's skin, there was no doubt that I had been responsible for boiling Beatrice this morning.

My gaze darted to the bathroom's white ceiling, and I looked for signs of a clock. The hospital's visiting hours would start soon, but I couldn't leave the house in this state. Even if Valentine was right and the Supernatural Council wouldn't kill me for wielding fire, they might execute me for being spotted around the human world throwing accidental fireballs.

I raised my right leg to the edge of the clawfoot tub and pulled up the leg of my jeans. A black mark snaked around my ankle in a curved line that pointed up toward my knee. While the skin around it felt warm, my cursed flesh was devoid of heat—just like the magic of a shadow mage.

My chin dropped to my chest, and a sigh heaved from my lungs. Valentine was probably right about me being cursed. It was the only way to explain why he both pounced on me to drink my blood and why he became so apologetic afterward and left for a healer.

What I didn't understand was why a shadow mage would go so far as to curse me with delicious blood? Was it an underhanded way of making Valentine my executioner?

I folded down the jeans leg and lowered my foot to the ground. There were some things about the Supernatural World I would probably never understand, and one of them was the politics.

After turning off the cold water, I headed into the bedroom, only to find Valentine standing in the open doorway.

My heart somersaulted into my throat. What the hell was he doing back so soon?

"Mera." His brow furrowed into a deep frown. "I've walked around the house, tried all the exits, and cannot leave. You and I are trapped."

CHAPTER SEVENTEEN

I reared back, hitting my shoulder against the doorway and forgetting all thoughts of how Valentine managed to slip into my room after I'd locked the door. Being in close proximity to a vampire who craved my blood was bad enough, but what on earth was this new development?

He stood a few steps into the room, an imposing figure in black. With his eyes still burning with crimson fire, and his muscular chest rising and falling with deep breaths, he was more dangerous than ever. Right now, there was little difference between Valentine and the mythical kind of vampire humans depicted in horror movies.

The pulse in my throat fluttered, and my chest tightened to the size of two clenched fists. My head spun, but I clung onto the door frame. This was not the time to feel dizzy or unsettled. One moment of churned with trepidation. Was this stage two of the curse? A mindless, slathering beast?

"Can you leave through the front door?" I tried to keep the tremble out of my voice. The last thing I needed was to be nervous and incite his predator instinct.

"Getting into the garden and the front steps is easy enough," he replied. "Getting out is the problem."

A relieved breath escaped my lungs. Maybe he wasn't as far gone as I had thought. "Have you tried turning them off?"

"But that would expose you to—"

"Please, try it." Right now, shadow mage assassins or enforcers from the Supernatural Council didn't sound so terrible.

"Alright." Valentine fell silent for several moments before letting out a frustrated growl. There was no need to ask if it had worked or not.

My mind whirred, trying to puzzle this out. A single shadow mage couldn't lock down an entire building, overriding wards that had been in existence for hundreds of years.

"Hey," I said.

"Hmmm?" he replied.

"You said Aunt Arianna visited the house with locks of my hair." When Valentine didn't reply, I continued anyway. "What if these latest adjustments she made to prepare the villa got something scrambled?"

He made a noncommittal grunt.

I bit down on my lip. Was he even listening? "Or whatever that mage did to me could have triggered the wards to trap us inside."

Valentine made another low hum that could have been him pondering my words or the appreciative sound people made when about to eat a delicious-smelling meal.

"Valentine?" I hissed.

"I'm thinking about it," he replied. "I also tried your phone. It doesn't work."

Despair washed through my veins like acid. I hadn't just imagined that conversation with Aunt Arianna. Either Valentine was lying about the wards or whoever trapped us in this house had allowed me a single phone call before blocking off all mobile signals. I pressed the heel of my hand into my aching chest. Every instinct told me not to trust Valentine.

"Alright," I said, more to myself than anyone else.

The only way I would survive the next few hours in this villa was by developing my fire magic. From everything I'd learned, the fire produced by supernaturals had just as much destructive power as the element they stored within firestone and employed as weapons.

I inhaled a deep breath, focussing on the feel of his fangs sliding through my veins. When that did nothing, I brought back the spike of panic that had lanced my heart when I realized that he was gulping down my blood and wouldn't stop.

Flames erupted from my fingertips. They were no larger than those that flickered out of lit candles and glowed a deep crimson color that matched Valentine's eyes.

I clenched my teeth. The paler the flame, the hotter the fire. Red meant cool but white…

Pouring all my frustration into my fingers, I told them to burn longer, harder, hotter. Someone out there wanted me dead and they were prepared to tamper with Valentine's mind to make him my executioner. The frustration surging through my veins heated to anger and then to incandescent rage.

This was the most disgusting, cowardly way to get rid of a person the authorities failed to kill at birth. Because that's what I was—the wielder of a dangerous power that made me the enemy of every member of the Supernatural Council. Right now, I didn't even know if that list of enemies included Valentine.

The flames expanded, engulfing my entire hand to the wrist and paling to an orange-yellow. The firestone tattoo around my wrist glowed white.

Pride flared through my chest, surged through my veins, and erupted from my lungs in a laugh. So much for being a Neutral. So much for being breeding stock only good for bearing strong supernatural babies. I was a bloody fire mage.

As the flames continued to grow, black smoke spread across the bathroom door and up to the ceiling. The scent of burning wood filled my nostrils. Even if fire and heat didn't affect me, I wasn't about to test my new powers against smoke inhalation.

"Mera?" Valentine's voice echoed from the other side of the door.

"Stand back," I said. "I'm coming out and don't want you to get burned."

Valentine paused. "What are you doing in there?"

I slid back the lock with my non-burning hand and flung open the door to find Valentine on the other side.

The yellow of my flames warmed the red undertones in his bronze skin, reminding me of how sunlight bounced off copper spires. Orange light reflected on the ends of his glossy black hair, making him look like he'd been specially lit for a photoshoot.

He stared at the flames dancing off my fingers and spreading toward the ceiling with his full lips parted, looking as mesmerized as a cat. The red in his irises receded, bringing forth dark blue.

I gulped, never having seen Valentine look as beautiful as when he was basking in the light of my power.

"You did it," he said, his voice breathy with awe.

"How do you like the smell of my blood now?" I asked.

Valentine's features softened. "You've always smelled intoxicating, but at least your fire has taken the edge off my desire."

"Good."

He licked his lips. "But we're still trapped."

"I have a theory." I walked toward him, reveling in the way he stepped back as though I was powerful, dangerous, someone to be respected rather than ravished.

"What if the curse was also designed to tamper with your ability to control the magic protecting the villa?" I asked.

"That is a possibility." Valentine's gaze remained fixed on the flames, and he continued edging backward until he stepped out into the hallway. "What do you want to do?"

I curled my fingers, marveling at how his eyes moved to follow the patterns I made with the fire. "What happens if you pull down the wards?"

His gaze darted toward mine. "If enforcers are outside, I might stop them from arresting you, but they will report the sighting of a fire wielder to the Council."

"Do they have the authority to enter your property?"

"If they suspect I'm in danger of being assassinated, then yes," he replied.

I bit down on my lip. "Alright then. Try stepping outside."

Valentine disappeared in a crack of sound. Two seconds later, he returned with a frown. "Still trapped."

"Right," I said with a groan. "Pass me my phone?"

His gaze flicked to my flaming hand with an expression that asked why I wasn't releasing the fire to get it myself. I raised my brows. If I extinguished those flames, the curse would spring forward and he'd be fangs-deep inside me in a second. No, thank you.

Valentine walked to the bed and picked up the phone, holding it screen-outward. "No signal."

I released a frustrated breath. "Right. Then I have a second theory."

He frowned. "What?"

"Could you show me where Aunt Arianna buried her ward stones?"

"You think those are what's keeping us trapped?" he asked.

"Mages don't have the type of magic that affects wards." I released the flames on one hand, slipped the phone in my back pocket, and walked around the four-poster bed, passing Valentine. "Wards are the work of witches, and they take hours to construct."

"I see where you're going with this." He followed me into the marble hallway. "You think your aunt made a mistake?"

"Or a miscalculation." I descended the curved staircase, passing the living room and trying not to shudder at what Valentine had done to me within its pristine white interior. "You admitted that the firestone bracelet was supposed to contain my magic but I overpowered it this morning and boiled the jacuzzi."

"True."

"This new power is throwing everything off," I muttered. "We need to unearth her wards, so they're not tampering with the original magic your people installed when the villas were built."

Valentine placed a hand on my shoulder. "Do you think you can reach the stones?"

I paused on the stairs and met his gaze. Every single trace of red had vanished from his irises, leaving a dark ring of indigo and a deep turquoise I'd never noticed until now.

Was this his natural eye color when there was nothing around to incite his hunger for blood? "Aunt Arianna tied the wards to my hair, right?"

He nodded.

"That means I can touch them."

He stared down at me with something new in his eyes. They were glossy and bright and full of admiration. While we were courting, he'd always treated me as someone to protect, even from his own desires. Now, I felt like Valentine saw me as any other capable supernatural with their own powers.

Something in my chest lightened. I might have been in the biggest danger of my life, but this newfound power had awoken a confidence and pride I needed to nurture. I reached the ground floor and walked across the marble hallway with my steps light.

Valentine placed a hand on my shoulder, making me stiffen. "You can't leave the building with your hands on fire. Nor can you allow yourself to be seen through the windows."

"Of course." I turned to him and smiled. "If I extinguish my flames, and my blood starts to smell—"

"I'll go into the attic and open a window." He disappeared with a crack of sound.

"Thanks," I whispered into the hallway's empty space.

Taking a deep breath, I pulled back my magic and headed toward the kitchen. Magical control was one of the fundamental classes at our academy, where the instructor would make the younger children imagine a pulse of energy flowing from the heart into their fingertips.

There was a toy called a grover that anyone could manipulate with their mind to form shapes. It felt like putty, but if you held it in your hand and concentrated, it would create streams of lights according to your wishes. It was the only way our teachers would know we were following their instructions and how I learned to channel magic I would never develop... until now.

The sun was about to set, and warm light flooded the kitchen's marbled-tiled space, coloring its white units and stainless-steel worktops a deep orange. Ignoring my rumbling stomach, I continued past the island unit and into the dining area where I had breakfasted with Kain.

At the very end of the downstairs space, behind the wall of windows, the patio outside shone a deep orange with shadows that stretched across its paving stones.

A shudder ran down my back at the prospect of those shadows being alive, but I forced myself to remember the property's powerful wards. The sunlight would fade in less than half an hour, and I needed to get started. Even if unearthing Aunt Arianna's wards took all night, I still had my phone's flashlight to illuminate my work.

I stared at the glass wall, trying to work out which windowpane was the door. Frustration welled through my insides, and I pressed my hands on the glass, expecting it to remain unmoving, but it slid to the right, letting out a swirl of cold air.

My tongue darted out to lick my lips, and I stepped out, looking from left to right for creeping shadows cast by raised beds and potted trees dotted about the yard. They all remained still, save for a line of black along the rim of the villa's white boundary wall that rose a foot into the air. My nostrils flared. It was probably the thing that infected me with that curse. Ignoring it, I continued through the patio.

The only supernaturals capable of constructing wards were angels and demons and witches, but only witches made themselves available for hire to other supernaturals. From what I understood from our coven, witches buried ward stones in cardinal points. In the cases of smaller enclosures such as a villa with a limited footprint, they simply used the corners of their boundary.

Paving stones covered the entire space, meaning that Aunt Arianna would have buried the ward beneath one of them. I walked to the far-left corner of the walled garden, and crouched at the square slab. Between the stone and the boundary wall stretched a four-inch gap filled with gravel.

"Meow?" said a familiar voice.

My head snapped up, and I stared into Macavity's green eyes. A breath caught in the back of my throat. "Can you come in?"

He shook his head.

I rose to my feet and stretched out my arms. "Try."

The cat's pupils dilated. He flattened his ears and hissed.

"Calm down." I raised my palms. "It's not like I'm calling you a liar. Could you just try, please?"

Macavity raised himself on his hind legs and pressed against an invisible barrier.

My posture sagged. He'd been right all along, which was a huge pity. Right now, I could use the backup of an oversized leopard. I murmured, "Sorry."

Without a goodbye meow, Macavity jumped down onto his front paws and disappeared from the fence. I shook my head. Whoever had tampered with these wards really wanted me dead.

Returning to the ground, I hooked my fingers beneath the slab, feeling a flare of familiar magic. Triumph filled my chest. I still had some sensitivity to other people's powers, even though I was no longer a Neutral.

The stone remained in place, but I continued pulling until a flare of power engulfed my body and twisted around my heart. It was probably the ward's security magic, but since Aunt Arianna had incorporated my hair into her enchantment, it passed through me as harmlessly as my own flames.

Finally, the stone yielded, allowing me to upturn it and lean it against the boundary wall. Beneath it was what appeared to be solid cement, but I stuck my fingers into it anyway.

This villa was supposed to be a temporary location in case all efforts to contain my magic failed and I had to go into hiding to metamorphosize into... a fire mage, I hoped. There was no such thing as a fire witch because witches practised magic and mages focused on only one element. I certainly didn't want to become a shifter or a demon.

My fingers sank into a cool, grainy gloop. I pushed down, leaning forward until I was elbows-deep in the wet cement and felt around for a stone.

Nothing.

"Deeper, then," I snarled, plunging myself further into the cold substance.

The gloop sucked in my entire arm up to my shoulder, and I still couldn't find any stone. I went in further until my entire left side lay pressed against the ground. Finally, I brushed a stone the size of my fist. I wrapped my fingers around it and pulled it out of the magical cement.

It was exactly as I'd imagined—a gray stone covered in long red strands tied into intricate knots. I put it on the side and replaced the paving stone. With one of Aunt Arianna's wards missing, her entire enchantment would collapse. Now I needed to step outside and see if it was her additional protection or something else keeping me trapped.

I hurried through the warm house, flung open the front door, and stepped out into the villa's tiny front garden. Dozens of people wearing black suits crowded around the metal fence, including Kain.

Slow traffic trundled past, as did passersby on their way to the bars and restaurants of Notting Hill. A black cab stood parked outside with its lights off and no sign of the driver. Since these vehicles all looked the same, I couldn't tell if it was the same vehicle Valentine had caught at Paddington.

Kain rushed forward, his eyes wide. "What's happening?"

"We're both trapped within the wards," I muttered.

Kain glanced at a blue-haired woman within the crowd, who stepped forward.

"Miss Griffin?" She sounded like the one who had placed a dressing gown on my shoulders. "Where's His Majesty?"

"In the attic." When the woman's brows rose, I bit my lip. That came out more sinister than I'd intended. "Is there any way to break through the wards? We're having a few problems."

Her brows drew together. "May I speak with His Majesty?"

I glanced over my shoulder. Calling Valentine while we were out in the open would be detrimental for protecting the Supernatural World. "We really need help with these wards."

The taxi's door opened, and a shadow poured out of the seat. Panic slammed into my chest and a shocked breath whistled through my teeth. I stepped back, hitting my shoulder on the open door. "Look behind you."

Valentine's employees continued staring at me as though I'd eaten their king, and nobody turned around.

Behind them, the shadow morphed into a black-haired woman wearing the black uniform of an enforcer, who stepped out of the cab as though she'd been sitting inside.

"Step aside," she said in a commanding voice.

Finally, Valentine's people turned around, and they made way for the enforcer. I clenched my teeth. Had they called her when they couldn't get through the wards or was she part of the group who had come after me at the crystal shop?

The woman stood about five-ten, with pale skin, a strong brow, and sharp, high cheekbones only made more prominent by the hair slicked back and secured within her protective leather cap.

Her jacket consisted of three magic-proof panels wrapped around her middle, secured by a leather shoulder and collar brace that buckled beneath her arms and stretched halfway up her neck. Even the gauntlets covering her hands were black and stretched up to the straps of her leather brace.

I glanced from side to side at the passing humans, wondering if they were bothered by the crowd or by the same dangerous statuesque woman.

"Hemera Griffin," she drawled in a cold voice. "Mother, Aurora Griffin—missing, presumed dead. Guardian, Arianna Griffin. Granddaughter of the wizard Napoleon Griffin, and a deceased human female."

I bristled, partly because the woman had both accessed and memorized my records, but mostly because she hadn't even bothered to learn Grandma's name. It didn't matter that she had produced two powerful witches, humans were lower than Neutrals and only tolerated as consorts or diversions.

She walked around Kain and stepped up to the low iron fence that made up the property's boundary. "Father, unknown."

I raised my chin, meeting her gunmetal-gray eyes. "Since you know so much about me, why don't you introduce yourself?"

"Captain Zella, shadow mage enforcer of the Supernatural Council." She stiffened, as though the mention of her title was a source of intense pride. "Please step out of the wards and surrender yourself for testing."

My brows drew together. "Why would you be so interested in a Neutral? Since you've already delved into my records, you'll see that I failed every test for magical talent. All I can do is sense power."

The captain's lips thinned. "We need you to come in once more."

"I'm not going back to Logris," I said from between clenched teeth. "Not after…" A rush of pain strangled my words, and I jerked my head to the side. Even though Valentine had uncovered the tampering with my memories, those humiliating words he'd uttered still hurt.

Her gaze wandered to the villa behind me. "Why are you not in your registered domicile?"

Now it was my turn to purse my lips. She had no

right to ask me what I did or who I consorted with. The Witch Queen had given me authorization to leave Logris, apprentice myself to Istabelle, and live in the Natural World. As long as I didn't inform humans that the Supernatural World and all its inhabitants were real, I could do whatever I pleased.

Instead of answering her question, I raised the leg of my jeans, exposing the black mark around my ankle. It had grown an inch thicker and now wound up my leg like a snake.

"Is this your doing?" I asked.

Captain Zella's brows furrowed, and she dropped into a crouch. "This is dark magic."

Valentine's employees gathered around her to take a better look. My cheeks heated. Weren't vampires supposed to have impeccable vision?

"I stepped out of a taxi just like yours," I said, filling my voice with accusation. "And a shadow just like yours wrapped around my ankle."

She tilted her head up, meeting my gaze with wide eyes that telegraphed her surprise. "You encountered another shadow mage?"

"It wasn't you?" I asked.

Captain Zella shook her head. "We're not authorized to curse suspects."

Suspects. The word made the muscles of my stomach tighten. Somehow, they knew I'd come into my powers. It turned out that Valentine's precautions were correct. I really was in trouble, but if the enforcers weren't the ones sneaking around trying to curse me, then who?

My gaze darted across the crowd of vampires. Perhaps they didn't approve of their king consorting with a Neutral? Each of them except Kain would have purchased blood from a being like me at some point.

"Will you step outside so I may take a better look?" Captain Zella asked, sounding perfectly reasonable.

"There's something wrong with the wards," I murmured.

She rose, her gaze darting down to the ground and then up to the villa's roof. "Please try to step out of the wards."

I swallowed back a laugh. Even if Aunt Arianna's magic was what had kept me trapped, there was absolutely no way I would get within ten feet of the enforcer and have her drag me back to the Supernatural Council for testing and a swift execution.

"You still haven't explained why you're here." Her lips parted, presumably to repeat that crap about needing to conduct a few tests, but I spoke first. "The real reason why."

She nodded. "We have reason to believe you're harboring fire magic. Further inquiries indicated that before your mother disappeared, she had been searching for information related to the tyrant named Kresnik."

A bolt of alarm shot through my chest. Behind the enforcer, Valentine's staff exchanged nervous glances. Valentine had told me Kresnik died five hundred years ago. What if he was still alive?

Captain Zella stepped forward, trying to cross the villa's open fence, but she stopped at the invisible ward. "Miss Griffin. Are you resisting my order?"

My survival instincts kicked me in the ass and told me to get the hell out before she really did issue an order for me to disobey. I took another step toward the house. "You can't talk to me like I'm one of your subordinates."

Her gloved hands pressed against the invisible barrier. "Have you experienced sparks, raised temperatures, unexplained bouts of fire? Have you set anything alight?"

Valentine's employees stepped forward, creating a small crowd around the enforcer. Kain stared at me through wide eyes.

"No." I took another step back to the house, crossing its threshold and engulfing myself in its warmth. "And I don't know what you're talking about."

I bumped into a hard body, and Captain Zella dropped to one knee. "Your Majesty."

"Why is an enforcer of the Supernatural Council harassing my guest?" he asked in a voice of steel.

"It was a routine enquiry, sire," she murmured, her voice reverent. "I did not mean any offense."

Valentine placed a hand on my shoulder, offering me a comforting squeeze. He stepped forward, forming a barrier between myself and Captain Zella. "Mera, go upstairs."

I hurried through the hallway, not wanting to wait around to hear the rest of his conversation with the enforcer. The Supernatural Council had already accurately guessed what I was.

My throat spasmed. If I didn't develop my fire magic soon, either Valentine would kill me or Captain Zella would drag me to Logris for an execution.

CHAPTER EIGHTEEN

I was halfway up the stairs when the front door clicked shut, and my heart jumped with a spike of alarm. Focusing on the magic that now swelled in my chest, I pushed it out into my hands, ready to fend off Valentine in case the curse's development caused him to attack.

Nothing happened, not even a spark. Perhaps I wasn't channeling enough emotion.

"Continue to the attic," Valentine said from the doorway. "Your aunt and I have provided you with everything we thought might help you develop your power."

"Alright." I took the stairs two at a time, my heart pumping with a rush of adrenaline from my encounter with Captain Zella.

Valentine was only one member out of a Council of seven. The enforcer would most certainly report what she saw—one of the monarchs consorting with a possible fire wielder—and then what? I quickened my pace, now taking the stairs three at a time.

I passed the living room, passed the level above it with the bedrooms, and reached the top, where a pale wood door stood, secured with glowing light around its seam. Maybe it was a ward or an enchantment to bring out my innate power. All I knew was that if I didn't develop my magic before reinforcements arrived with a team of ward-breakers, I wouldn't leave this house alive.

Worse, Valentine might get hurt trying to defend me or ostracized as a traitor.

With a soft crack of sound, Valentine stood in front of the door. His handsome features were grave, and he stared down at me with violet eyes. I gulped. They were the same shade as usual, which wasn't necessarily a bad thing, but it also wasn't good. Hadn't he just told me that I always smelled nice?

My hand gripped the rail, but I couldn't move. I couldn't speak. I couldn't do anything but stare into the patches of red deepening the blue in his eyes.

Shit. By checking his irises for signs of bloodlust, I'd let the wretched vampire mesmerize me into staying still. That, or the thrall in his saliva was still affecting my judgement. I was sure this inaction was the result of some sort of nefarious vampire power.

Valentine's nostrils flared. "You are so powerful. So beautiful. My perfect mate."

Annoyance flickered through my insides at the implication that we hadn't been completely right for each other when I was just a Neutral.

Shoving that aside, I raised a palm and tried to push my magic into my hand. "Out of my—"

Valentine wrapped his hand around my wrist and pinned me to the door. His muscular body forming an inescapable cage. He stared down at me with glazed eyes, making my nerve endings tingle with terror and anticipation. He leaned down, his hot breaths fanning against the side of my face. His smoky masculine scent filled my nostrils, making my knees buckle.

"Inamorata." His deep voice was a caress that curled beneath my clothes, over my bare skin, and settled between my legs. "Just let me kiss you."

"It's the curse," I said from between clenched teeth. "It's making you crazy."

"I've wanted you for three years, I can wait no longer." He pressed his hardness against my thigh. It was long and thick and pulsing with need.

My core pulsed back, the wretched thing not realizing we were both in mortal peril. "Go downstairs."

"Not until you give me a kiss." His lips ghosted against the shell of my ear.

A wave of desire shuddered through my body, making me clench my thighs together. Valentine always had this effect on me. Seduction was part of a vampire's modus operandi. But while we were courting, he always exercised control, never going further than what he thought was appropriate. Now, with the curse addling his senses, he was willing to take everything, including my blood.

"Let go of me so I can get into the attic." I reached behind me with my free hand, fumbling for a door handle. The wood was grainy and smooth, but with no sign of metal. Focussing my gaze away from his mesmerizing eyes and on the beauty spot on his cheekbone, I added, "Once I've gotten control of my powers, I'll let you kiss me anywhere you want."

His deep chuckle resounded through my chest, making me squirm with arousal. "I do not negotiate."

"Valentine." I clenched my teeth. "If you don't release me right now—"

"You'll what?" he said with a harsh laugh.

A snarl tore from my lips. Damn the shadow mage who cursed my blood. Damn whoever trapped me in this house with a ravenous and horny vampire, and damn the Supernatural Council for posting Captain Zella outside the door so I couldn't even escape.

Valentine's lips grazed my earlobe, sending sparks of excitement down to my nipples.

Damn Valentine for falling prey to the curse and being so seductive.

"Tell me to stop," he murmured.

"Stop," I snarled.

With a chuckle, he sucked my lobe between his

lips, laving it with his tongue. "I can smell your excitement. You don't mean a word you're saying."

"Yes, I bloody do." I stopped fumbling at the door, slipped my free hand into my jeans pocket, and pulled out a pinch of Dharma salt. "This is your last warning."

Valentine pressed a soft kiss on my cheek and chuckled. "Or what, Inamorata?"

I threw the salt into his face.

With a pained roar, Valentine released my wrist and fell to his knees.

My heart jumped. "Are you al—"

"Get into that attic before this salt wears off," he snarled.

I spun around and ran my fingers against the door's glowing seal. Eventually, it clicked open, and I stumbled inside, spun around, and threw my weight against the door, slamming it shut.

The seal flared with bright white light. Right then, I didn't care if it was keeping me trapped inside the attic or keeping Valentine out. At least I had a chance to finish my magical development.

I laid my head against the door, breathing hard. As far as vampire attacks went, that was pretty mild. But I knew three things. One, the curse was worsening by the minute. Two, I would soon run out of salt. Three, this was Valentine's house. A vampire as powerful and as determined as him would find a way through the seal and get at my blood.

"Mera," he said through panting breaths.

"What?" I snapped.

"Thank you."

My heart clenched, and I swallowed hard. If Valentine had engineered any part of this bloodlust, he wouldn't have thanked me for the injury that had caused me to break free. I struggled for words of apology, explanation, gratitude. Without his and Aunt Arianna's intervention, either that shadow assassin would have murdered me in my apartment or Captain Zella would have dragged me to the Supernatural Council.

"I want you to listen carefully," he said. "The more exposure I have to the scent of your blood, the less I can resist feeding from you. This curse has brought forward base instincts I am struggling to control."

I pressed my hand against the wood. "Valentine—"

"Listen to me." His voice was as hard as rock. "A time may come when I break through those wards and take what I want. Do you have the dagger?"

"Yes?" I whispered.

"Use it before it's too late."

"But you'll—."

Valentine's fist reverberated against the door, making me stagger back. "I would rather die a dozen deaths than be responsible for yours."

My throat thickened, and all doubts about Valentine drifted into the ether. He truly cared for me.

This entire house he'd prepared, this beautiful attic, and the fact that he, as a member of the Supernatural Council, was going against the edicts of his fellow monarchs proved the depths of his love.

"Mera," he snapped.

"I'm listening," I replied. "But let's hope it doesn't come to such a desperate situation."

"If you can't get a handle on your magic by then..." Valentine didn't need to complete the sentence. The memory of him pinning me to the living room rug and drinking from my neck had seared itself into my mind.

"Thank you," I whispered.

Valentine didn't speak again, so I turned and took in my surroundings. The attic spanned the entire length and width of the house and was three times as large as the bedroom. A six-foot-high fireplace stood in the middle of the left wall, filled with wood and crackling with orange flames.

I walked across the wooden floorboards, taking in a kitchenette similar to the one in my studio. Its cupboards were fully stocked with canned and dry foods, with both an under-counter refrigerator and a separate freezer filled with the kinds of foods I liked to eat. I swallowed down a lump in my throat, remembering all the conversations I'd had with Aunt Arianna about the wealth of dishes available to regular people in the human world.

On the other side of the fireplace stood three

wide bookshelves containing tomes on every species of supernatural suspected to be capable of wielding fire. Most supernaturals didn't come into their powers until they were in their teens, and their extended families provided spaces where they could undergo their transitions. Sometimes, a supernatural would develop their magic overnight. Other times, it would take a matter of days or weeks or months.

I guess Valentine and Aunt Arianna researched every possible transformation and wanted this place to reflect what other families provided. For my sake, I hoped my maturity came within the next few hours. It was doubtful after three years of consuming null-weed disguised as chocolates.

Pushing those thoughts away, I turned to the leather tomes, finding that some of them were ring-bound folders containing documents. I pulled one out, flipped it open, and frowned at its contents. Someone had printed out all my records—Aunt Arianna's certificate of guardianship, my first magical test, academy reports, my official certificate of classification, and every magical test I'd ever failed. There was also my permit to leave Logris and an official document of apprenticeship signed by Istabelle.

Behind these papers was information on Mom, who according to her magic tests barely had enough power to qualify as a witch. My mouth dropped open. Everyone I grew up around had told me she excelled at light magic. Had they lied to me or had Mom falsified her test results?

I slipped the folder back onto the shelf and took another that contained records of every child executed on suspicion of wielding fire magic. Some had been demons, others mages, a few of them shifters. I worried at my bottom lip with my teeth. How on earth did so many supernatural citizens allow their children to die? It was just so unfair.

The beginnings of a migraine pounded through my head. With a weary sigh, I slipped the folder back onto the bookshelf and continued exploring the attic.

At the end of the space was a raised mattress large enough to accommodate an elephant. Apprehension rippled through my insides. The last thing I wanted to become was a dragon shifter, even though the thought of flying through the skies was awesome.

My gaze wandered to the right side of the room, where five-foot-tall geodes stood among crystals as large as watermelons. Amethyst for emotional balance and spiritual awareness, agate for balance and harmony, and black tourmaline to cleanse my energy and reach my higher consciousness. In the middle of the geodes lay a nest of cushions, beckoning at me to sit. I gazed at the tattoo on my wrist, which no longer glowed, and walked over to the array of crystals.

I lowered myself to the cushions, crossed my legs, and surveyed the smaller stone. Several large pieces of clear quartz sat among the geodes. They were all-purpose crystals that I preferred to use for concentration. Among them was a cannon-ball-sized piece of firestone I suspected the Supernatural Council could use as a bomb.

Each thrummed with power, making me wonder if Aunt Arianna had obtained the crystal from a talented master like Istabelle. Perhaps my boss knew my problem all along and had been trying to help me keep my magic under control. I sat and picked up a foot-long quartz with both hands and concentrated.

Exercises at the academy with grovers were fine in theory. Earlier, when I'd tried to defend myself against Valentine, I hadn't been able to express my fire. I needed to focus on the emotions that got me to reach that power in the first place.

I couldn't remember exactly when I had boiled the jacuzzi but it was probably when Valentine strode toward us wearing a pair of tight-fitting trunks. My eyes fluttered shut, and the image of those rippling bronzed muscles filled my mind. Even though I'd wanted to be immune to his beautiful body, I'd felt an attraction to him that had heated my blood.

It was the same downstairs, when we had been having sex and I'd noticed that he was drinking more than the usual amount of blood. Despite needing him to stop, somewhere deep down, my traitorous body yearned for him to take me. I had wanted more.

My eyes snapped open, and I stared down at the

hands wrapped around the quartz. They remained as pale as ever, without so much as a glow. An annoyed breath heaved from my lungs. Why did I think quartz of all things would bring out my power?

I set down the clear crystal and picked up the massive lump of firestone. While it didn't have the triple-A quality of the bracelet that had melted into my flesh, I doubted that its flaws and lack of clarity would make it less powerful. If this didn't do the job, I didn't know what would.

Closing my eyes, I inhaled a deep breath and pressed the stone into my solar plexus. Whoever had prepared it had polished its surfaces to the smoothness of a crystal ball. I pushed those thoughts aside and focused on my burning attraction for Valentine.

Everything about him was a wonder, from those mesmerizing eyes that ranged from a deep turquoise to a crimson as dark as blood, to those full, sensual lips that lavished me with such pleasure, and his wonderful, strong physique.

He was deadly. Every instinct in my body feared him as a predator, yet my passion for him still smoldered.

When I opened my eyes again, a flame danced within the stone. An annoyed breath huffed from my lungs. I wasn't supposed to transfer my power into the bloody crystal!

"Alright," I muttered to myself. "One more try, and I'll hit the books."

A little voice in the back of my head said that I should have read the books before trying to express my magic, but I'd done it successfully twice before when defending myself against Valentine. Three times, if I counted what had happened this morning. I could be reading all day and not even get close to generating a spark.

Something cold and damp slithered beneath my knee and settled on my inner thigh. I straightened my leg and pulled up my jeans. The cursed mark now snaked all the way around my calf, ending three inches above my knee.

"Shit." I squeezed my eyes shut and focused on my magic.

At the curse's rate of growth, the enforcers at the door would be the least of my worries. What would happen to me if it reached my heart?

Instead of picking up a crystal, I balled my fists and focused on my worst Valentine-related memory. The same car that had taken me from the palace after we had made love drove me back for our engagement ball. Because it was the first time he had decided to marry, Valentine had invited every member of the Supernatural Council, along with several members of vampire nobility.

The car pulled into the palace courtyard, and I smoothed down the voluminous skirt of my gown. Valentine had commissioned the foremost faerie seamstress in Logris to create a dress as green as the forest to contrast with the red of my hair. She had even produced a headdress, which Valentine planned on replacing with an emerald tiara.

My chest swelled with pride, and I sank into the leather seat, unable to contain my happiness. The only thing that would have made this moment perfect was if Aunt Arianna was sitting beside me. I wanted to prove to her that she could trust Valentine, even if she had an innate dislike for vampires.

"Miss Griffin?" said the driver. "Are you ready to step out?"

"One moment," I murmured.

After tonight, I would no longer be an anonymous Neutral. After tonight, everyone in Logris and beyond would know I belonged to Valentinus Sargon de Akkad, Vampire King of Logris. I released a shuddering breath, savoring my last few moments of obscurity.

I turned to the driver, meeting his maroon eyes in the rearview mirror. "Alright."

He opened his door, walked around the car, and held my door open. A red carpet stretched out from where we had parked, up the palace steps, and to the open double doors, where vampire footmen in white livery stood with security wizards, checking their invitations.

"Thank you." I let the driver help me out and made my way on trembling legs over the red carpet.

My heart pounded to the beat of the distant

orchestra, and sweat gathered on my palms. Valentine had taught me to waltz, foxtrot, tango, and a whole host of other dance steps, but what if I messed up in front of Logris high society? I picked up my skirts to navigate the steps, breathing hard from the thrumming of my nerves.

The two footmen at the top of the steps straightened. Each wore long, white tailcoats with silver buttons, silk lapels, and matching pants and waistcoats. The entire outfit was set off with white bowties in shimmering silk.

When I reached the door, the taller of the footmen stepped in my path. "Your invitation, miss?"

I glanced over my shoulder, wondering if someone was standing behind me. Another black vehicle pulled up to the bottom of the stairs, and a tall, blond-haired vampire male stepped out to let out a blue-haired female wearing a gold dress.

"Valentine didn't give me an invitation," I said with a frown. "He's holding the ball in my honor."

The vampire's lips formed a tight line. "Please step aside."

I reared back, my gaze darting from one footman to another. "What?"

"Today's function is a welcome ball to celebrate His Majesty's new heir."

"What are you talking about?" I shook my head. The whole point of getting married was because Valentine wanted to make an heir. With me. "This is my engagement ball. It's been on the calendar for weeks."

Both footmen exchanged annoyed glances. The shorter of the pair turned, looking like he was about to call on the security wizard, a man from another coven I'd seen around witch-related functions.

I didn't give him the chance to have me thrown out. "If you don't believe me, call Valentine."

The taller footman offered me a condescending smile. "I hardly think His Majesty would—"

"Call King Valentine right now." I fumbled through the folds of my voluminous skirt, looking for the pocket. If these people didn't fetch him, I would call him myself.

He exhaled an exasperated breath, making my skin tighten. Didn't he know I was the woman their king had chosen for a wife? In a month, I would be a queen consort.

"I say, what's the hold up?" asked the blond-haired vampire a few steps behind.

"Gate-crasher, my lord," said one of the footmen. "It happens all the time at high-profile events with eligible young men."

Sparks of irritation exploded through my insides. Anyone who genuinely worked for Valentine would have seen me at the palace over the past three years. I'd never seen these two before, but how could they just assume I wasn't telling the truth? My finger brushed the metal of my phone, and I pulled out the handset.

"Never mind," I snapped. "I'll call him myself."

The footman rolled his eyes.

I pressed the home button and searched for the shortcut for Valentine's personal number, but it had disappeared from my phone.

"Have you lost His Majesty's number?" the footman asked, his voice dripping with sarcasm.

"You're making me sound like I'm addicted to vampire bites," I snapped. "Valentine and I are engaged—"

"You?" The blue-haired vampire woman standing behind me placed a gloved hand over her lips. "Why would His Majesty bother himself with a…" Her nose twitched, and laughter exploded from her lips. "My dear girl. You're a Neutral!"

"So what if I am?" I whirled on her, heat exploding across my skin. "In Logris, all races are equal."

"All *supernatural* races," said the blond-haired vampire. "Neutrals are barely a cut above humans."

I turned to the footman, who tilted his head to the side as though telling me it was hard to disagree with the man's words. Disgruntled mutters broke out on the stairs around me, and some of the palace servants stepped out through the doors to see what was happening. Since they were mostly vampires, I guess they could hear my voice.

Among them was Valentine's butler, who had served the royal family for over a thousand years and had always been kind.

"Caiman." I raised a hand.

The butler stiffened. Like most vampires, it was hard to tell his age. Vampires didn't stay the same forever. When born, they grew at the same rate as everyone else until they reached their late teens or early twenties—whatever nature decided was their peak beauty. They'd stay that age for a century before aging about a year for every hundred.

Caiman was starting to get that uncanny look the older vampires got when the experience behind their eyes outmatched their youthful features.

He inclined his head. "Miss Griffin."

Relief escaped my lungs in an outward breath. "Could you please tell them there's been a mistake. Valentine—"

The blast of an explosion knocked me out of my memory with a jolt. Splinters of magic and broken wood hit my skin. My eyes flew open to find the candles flickering. My heart thudded loud enough to fill my ears. What the hell was that?

I turned to the open door, but before I could even register what had happened, a large body pinned me to the cushions and sank his fangs into my neck.

Valentine.

Pleasure flooded my veins, filled my body, and spread across every nerve ending. I let out a low moan as it travelled downward with a rush of sensation and heat.

Valentine moaned, the sound going straight between my legs, which he wedged open with his muscular thigh. As he swallowed mouthful after mouthful of blood, the pressure behind my clit swelled until it was fit to burst.

Somewhere beneath the maelstrom of desire and alarm, I finally understood why some blood cows found feeding vampires from the vein so compelling. Each bite brought a rapture that made me crave him more and more.

My leg curled around his, and without meaning to, I bucked my hips against his leg, riding out the pleasure until it spilled over, and a climax rippled through my core muscles. Waves upon waves of ecstasy crashed against my senses, and I moaned and shuddered beneath the powerful vampire.

A voice in the back of my head screamed at me to break out of Valentine's grip. But my mind spun before I could concentrate on the words, and that part of my consciousness drowned in a whirlpool of lust. I dug my fingernails into his hard flesh, silently begging—yearning for him to take more, to never stop, to keep drinking until he consumed me.

My pulse echoed in my ears, picking up volume with each rapid beat. It was a sign that I'd lost a significant amount of blood—too much. Valentine gulped around his mouthful of neck, humming his desire.

If he continued like this, I would die.

I knew this and I didn't care because Valentine was giving me enough pleasure to last a lifetime.

A whimper reverberated in my throat, and Valentine growled, the sound making the pulse between my legs quicken. Something he'd said earlier surfaced through the vortex of bliss.

Valentine would never be able to live with himself if he killed me. He would fall into misery. I wanted to warn him, but the words caught in the back of my throat.

Then, just as suddenly as he had pounced, Valentine slumped on top of me like a dead weight.

CHAPTER NINETEEN

Valentine's larger body still pinned me to the floor cushions, his heavy weight crushing my ribs. I opened my eyes to find flickers of reflected candlelight dancing across the ceiling. I tried turning my head but the position of his mouth against my neck made movement near impossible.

I couldn't tell if he had fainted, had fallen into a food coma, or if something had gone terribly wrong. Warm blood trickled down my neck, creating an expanding wet patch on the cushions.

It took a few moments to free my hands from beneath his weight, but I placed them on his shoulders and tried shoving him off. The sharp pain of his fangs nicking my neck made me fall back with a wince. Blood trickling down my collar now seemed to pour, and the pounding of my pulse filled my ears like a boombox.

"Valentine?" I slapped his arm. "Get up."

When he didn't so much as twitch, I slapped harder, trying to figure out this peculiar behavior. Had the curse poisoned my blood?

"Valentine," I said, making my voice sharp.

He still didn't move.

Clenching my teeth, I placed my hands back onto his shoulders and pushed all my magic and strength into my arms. Valentine shifted a few inches, but not enough for me to slip out from under his body.

"Wake up," I said. "You're crushing me."

He exhaled a long breath, somehow giving me the momentum to push harder. Eventually, I rolled him onto his side, slipped out from underneath his body, and then pushed him onto his back.

Half the candles surrounding us now lay extinguished on the wood floor in puddles of congealed wax. The dim light brought out the sharp angle of his jaw, the slight hollow of his cheekbones, and the depths of his eyes. He lay among the cushions, breathing rapidly through his parted lips.

"What's wrong?" I asked.

He stared up at me through glazed eyes as dark as the night's sky, blinking every few heartbeats but not making a sound. I still couldn't tell if he was drunk or stoned or if this was what happened to vampires who consumed too much blood.

Blood continued pouring down my neck, seeming to come in rapid spurts that synchronized with my pulse. I placed one hand on my wound to stem the flow and another on his warm stubbled cheek. "Talk to me."

His lips parted, but he made no sound.

My brows furrowed. If I wanted to know what was wrong with Valentine, I would have to check for myself. I glanced down at his neck for signs of injury. After finding none, I ran my hands over his broad chest, pausing at his heart, which reverberated against my palm.

Vampires had much slower heartbeats than humans or Neutrals, but his heart thudded about twice the speed of mine.

I gulped. It had to be the curse. Maybe it had turned my blood into some kind of addictive vampire amphetamine. I sat back on my heels and slid my hand to his bicep, wondering what I could do to help him.

Valentine twitched, and something on the bottom-right edge of my vision caught my attention. I swept my gaze down his arm to find his hand clenched into a fist, but something poked out from between his thumb and forefingers. It was ivory colored and small enough to fit in his entire hand.

Just like the hilt of the solid flame dagger.

The solid flame dagger Valentine told me would kill a supernatural. The solid flame dagger that I slipped into my pocket. The solid flame dagger Valentine told me to use against him to save myself.

Already knowing what I wouldn't find if I checked my pocket, I groped around in my jeans for the bulge and found nothing.

"Valentine," I whispered. "What did you do?"

The question was futile because the scene lying before me on the cushions spoke for itself. Somehow, through his haze of bloodlust, Valentine had sacrificed himself to save me. He'd sacrificed himself by taking my dagger and cutting his hand with its poisonous blade.

"Why?" I rasped.

When he didn't answer, I uncurled each of his fingers, revealing a palm soaked with blood. The dagger rolled out of his hand and landed on the cushions with a soft thud. Ignoring it, I gathered the edge of my shirt with my hand and used the fabric to wipe off the blood.

Maybe the dagger could work like snake venom. He was still alive—just dazed. If I squeezed out enough blood, I might also drain the poison.

I wrapped my hands around his wrist and kneaded, but his cut had already healed, sealing in the toxic blood. Scrambling to my feet, I glanced around the vast attic space for inspiration. Maybe Valentine just needed an antidote. Or something that could soak up the poison in his blood.

Activated charcoal worked much like a bezoar—it had a vast surface area that could draw in impurities so the body could flush them harmlessly through the digestive system. Doctors and healers used it all the time. My gaze landed on the incense table, where I had earlier seen some charcoal. Maybe if I placed it in his mouth—

"Mera," he croaked.

My heart somersaulted in my chest. "Valentine?"

He lay within the nest of cushions, his gaze clearer and his blinking more rapid. His black hair spread out like a halo against the pale fabric, and a tiny trail of blood streamed from the corner of his full lips toward his earlobe.

"Go to…" His voice was so quiet, I had to kneel at his side to hear his words. "Go to the basement."

"Is that where you keep the antidotes?" I asked.

"Mera." His voice was harsher, and the muscles of his face hardened with determination. "Leave this villa, immediately. There's a panel in the sauna that leads to a staircase—"

"No." I grabbed his arm, digging my fingers into his bicep. "How do I counter the effects of that dagger?"

"There is no cure," he rasped.

"You wouldn't have given me a weapon I could use against you." I delved beneath the cushions, looking for my phone, which must have fallen when he had tackled me to the floor.

The wards were tied to Valentine's life force. Maybe whatever was imprisoning us would ease off, now that he was hurt, and I might be able to call someone.

My fingers brushed against cool metal, and I pulled out my handset only to glance at the screen and find no signal bars.

Dread rolled through my belly like thunder. I turned my gaze toward the light streaming into the hallway and shouted, "Is anyone here?"

"We left them behind when we took that taxi." His hand brushed against mine. "Mera, listen to me."

I turned my gaze back to Valentine's shining eyes.

"The wards will fall," he said.

My breath caught. "You can't die—"

"They are tied to my life force." His voice strained as though each word was an effort.

A rush of emotions flooded my system—confusion, disbelief, and a creeping sense of helplessness, all gathering in my tightening chest and thickening throat. Valentine couldn't die. Not from a cut on the hand. Not to save me from himself.

I placed my hands on his broad chest, but my fingers wouldn't stop trembling. "Please, don't give up. There has to be something."

"My people will storm this villa when the wards fall." Valentine's dark eyes glazed over, and his expression turned slack. "They won't understand what's happened and will blame you."

I swallowed over and over, trying to digest his words, but I couldn't keep them down. This couldn't be happening. He must have made a mistake. King Valentinus Sargon de Akkad committing suicide… for me?

"My father used that dagger for years to poison others before he was finally caught. A mere scratch will kill even the strongest supernatural. There is nothing you can do for me. Go. Now." Valentine's eyes fluttered shut.

"No," I whispered.

His chest rose and fell with shallow breaths. Valentine couldn't be dying, and even if I ran downstairs and entered a secret passageway in the sauna, the wards still surrounded the house. He was just saying this to make me give up on him and save myself.

"I'm sorry for biting you," he whispered. "Despite everything that's happened, I hold you in the highest respect."

My tongue darted out to lick my lips, and I swallowed at the implication that he wasn't just interested in my blood. "But Valentine…"

"In all my eleven hundred years, I hadn't considered settling down with a woman until I met you. Please forgive my cruel words. If I had known your memories had been altered—"

"Make it up to me by surviving." I squeezed his hand.

A choking laugh rattled in the back of his throat. "I love you to the very core of my soul, but not even love can conquer death."

Heat gathered around my eyes, and my vision blurred. From the moment Valentine entered my mind in the hospital and revealed that fog, I knew that his love for me had been real. Someone out there was working from the shadows to drive Valentine and me apart, and they were too cowardly to confront us to our faces.

My heart pounded to the beat of a war drum and hot blood coursed through my veins. Now, because of them, a good man lay dying. Because of them, Valentine and I would never have the future together that we had always planned. Valentine wanted me to escape, to leave him to die alone in this attic, but it was impossible.

Furious breaths heaved in and out of my nostrils. I wouldn't run or hide or recoil because our love was stronger than a dagger, and we would find a way to be together. I wouldn't turn away from the man who paid the ultimate price to save my life. Dead or alive, we would never be apart.

My jaw tightened with determination. I had to see him through to the end… if that ever came.

"I love you." I stared into his hooded eyes, trying to memorize his features and sear this moment into my mind. "Valentine, did you hear me?"

The corners of his lips curved upward into the faintest of smiles. "The past few days with you back in my life have been my happiest."

I blinked, loosening a tear. "Even with me furious at you?"

"Just being able to look at you and have you look back at me has been a blessing."

I gulped at the implication that he had visited London and seen me from afar. All those years I had thought he had forgotten about me and moved on. While I had wrestled with my grief and anger and resentment, Valentine had also suffered.

"Mera, my time is near." His voice was so faint, I had to lean over him to hear. "Please, go downstairs and get ready to flee the moment the wards fall."

One of my tears splattered onto his cheekbone. "I can't abandon you, knowing that you never abandoned me. I can't let you die alone."

His eyelids fluttered for a heartbeat and then opened.

I sucked in a deep breath, wondering if this was the moment everything would turn around. Valentine's eyes sharpened on me, and the corners of his lips rose into a sad smile. I smiled back and waited for him to speak, but he exhaled a long, rattling breath and stilled.

"Valentine?" I shook his arm. "Valentine!"

The air splintered, and shards of invisible magic fell around my body, sending tiny slicing sensations across my skin. I clutched at my heart. That had to be the wards. The wards just fell.

My gaze dropped to Valentine's unmoving face,

and his pleas for me to save myself slammed to the forefront of my mind with a painful jolt.

I scrambled to my feet, but before I could turn around and head for the door, a large hand wrapped around my neck and pressed me against the window at the far end of the attic. Three angry faces filled my vision, each one of Valentine's bodyguards snarling at me for answers.

"Stop," I rasped.

A large man emerged from behind the trio of guards and shoved them aside. By now, the vampires' rapid movements had knocked down and extinguished all but one of the candles. When he stopped moving and glowered into my face, I flinched at features that mirrored Valentine's.

My mouth dropped open, and a breath caught in the back of my throat.

"What did you do to my brother?" the man barked.

I fell back against the wall, finally noticing his pale hair and skin. It was Sylvester, one of Valentine's four younger brothers. The vampire advanced on me with his eyes flashing and his fangs fully extended. I raised both hands and flinched.

Before he could attack, white magic filled the room, making every muscle in my body stiffen. I couldn't even inhale a deep breath to scream. Sylvester froze several inches away, his face a rictus of rage. Only his pale irises seemed able to move, and they burned with hatred. Even the vampires he had shoved aside stood around us in unnaturally still positions, looking like somebody had stopped time.

My gaze darted around the darkened room. Our surroundings had gone quiet, even though the light streaming from the window shifted, and the unextinguished single candle where Valentine lay flickered in the draft.

Soft footsteps padded toward us. I glanced at the source of the sound and found a slender outline heading toward us through the gloom. I tried to force breaths in and out of my nostrils, but the enchantment only allowed the air to graze the tops of my lungs.

A tall woman in black stepped into the light. It was Captain Zella, the enforcer who had hidden herself in the taxi.

The woman paused at the vampires crowding Valentine's body, reached into the inside pocket of her jacket, and pulled out a device the size of a remote control. Red light flashed across the space, making my insides cringe.

This was the supernatural equivalent of a forensics team taking photos and samples from a crime scene. The enchantment would record everything in the room, recording magical signatures, DNA, natural-occurring phenomena, and any lingering spells.

It would even determine the murder weapon or lead a trail to whoever last wielded it.

A tight fist of terror clutched at my already restricted chest, and the attic suddenly became too small. Would the wards register now that they had disintegrated? If Captain Zella caught a trace of Aunt Arianna's magic, they might investigate her as an accomplice.

Something glowed from Valentine's side. Captain Zella extracted a transparent bag from her pocket and shook it out, letting it expand into a plastic box with a hinged lid. She stepped around the kneeling vampires, reached between the two trying to revive Valentine with CPR, and extracted the dagger with her shadows.

She turned to me and frowned. "Miss Griffin, if I were to ask you whose energy I would find on the murder weapon, what would be your answer?"

It was a rhetorical question. Valentine might have taken it out of my pocket, but I had carried it around with me for longer. I tried to move my tongue to utter a denial but I couldn't move. Not against an enchantment strong enough to disable numerous vampires.

After placing the dagger in her evidence box, Captain Zella turned away from Valentine's body and continued toward us. A shudder ran down my spine, and I thrashed against the magical restraint, even though the effort would be futile.

She walked around the trio of bodyguards and stopped at Sylvester's side. Her gaze dropped down to the blood on my neck, and she pressed her lips into a tight line. The captain probably thought I had killed Valentine in self-defense. Because of the scandal it might cause for the vampires to have their king murdered by a lowly Neutral, she might even let his brother execute me on the spot.

Captain Zella placed the remote on my head. "Hemera Griffin, by the power of the Seven Monarchs of the Supernatural Council, you are hereby detained on suspicion of regicide and the possession of fire. Do you understand the charges?"

It wasn't like I could nod or protest or shake my head. These enchantments could last days and were often not released until a higher-up gave authorization to clear up the murder scene.

The captain withdrew the device, pulling me from the wall and away from Sylvester's flashing eyes. She turned on her heel and floated me through the attic.

As we reached the single candle, I strained my eyes to catch one last glimpse of Valentine, but the vampires surrounding him blocked my view. A dull ache spread across my heart, filling me with a grief so crushing that I could barely breathe.

Valentine's people lined the stairs, their pale faces displaying disbelief and hatred. Kain stood at the end of the procession with a look of shocked betrayal that shattered my heart. They all thought I had killed him, and they probably all wanted me dead.

They didn't need to wait long because I would soon join him. Even if the enchantment worked out that Valentine had died at his own hands, the Supernatural Council would execute me the moment the enforcers uncovered my fire magic.

When we reached the ground floor, Captain Zella turned to me, her features grave. "It's customary to render our most dangerous suspects unconscious."

I inhaled a sharp breath through my nostrils, wanting to protest, but she tapped a button on her device, and the edges of my vision turned dark.

My last thoughts were the hope that they would execute me painlessly in my sleep, and I would awaken with Valentine waiting for me in the afterlife.

CHAPTER TWENTY

The pounding of my head forced me awake, and my lips parted with a groan. Somehow, I'd survived the arrest. Light shone through my eyelids, and I cracked open my eyes, only to stare into an overly bright beam that burned my retinas. Flinching, I squeezed them shut and let out a low moan.

"You're awake," said a female voice.

"What's going on?" I asked through a throat that felt scrubbed raw with steel wool.

The speaker removed the beam from my eyes, and set it down with a clunk. I raised a hand to rub my aching throat, but a restraint held me in place. As my memories flooded back, pain radiated from my chest, a searing, burning despair that felt like acid. Poor Valentine had sacrificed himself for me. I slumped forward in my seat, choking back a sob.

"They're going to need you alert," hissed the female voice. "Don't make me inject you with a stimulant."

I leaned back and tried to blink the harsh glare from my vision.

A six-foot-tall wood-paneled dais stood thirty feet ahead of where I sat, emblazoned with the Seven Crowns insignia of Logris. I wasn't sure what to think or feel beyond the overwhelming sorrow. It crushed my lungs, and filled my eyes with an unending torrent of tears.

I would give anything to reverse what had happened, but vampires were only immortal unless killed. I glanced down at my seat, a mahogany armchair with leather straps that wound around my wrists and biceps and shoulders.

My outfit was a gray prisoner's jumpsuit, with leather straps also restraining my chest and waist with a loose one around my neck. My pulse fluttered in my throat as I glanced from side to side, taking in the rest of my surroundings.

We were in a tall, windowless chamber of about two stories in height, covered in wood panelling. It was hard to tell its exact size, because I couldn't see much beyond the tall backs and sides of my chair.

Three-tier chandeliers hung from an ornate ceiling of gold leaf depicting the seven Royal Crests of Logris. I tilted my head up to take another look at the dais to find seven golden thrones, each empty.

All the moisture left my throat. This was just like the Witch's High Court Room, only much grander. I leaned forward, trying to catch a glimpse of the woman who had spoken earlier. I had to ask her if we were in the heart of the Supernatural Council.

Captain Zella stepped into my line of sight, clad in a white version of her enforcer's uniform. Instead of the leather cap she'd worn the last time I saw her, she'd donned the white brimmed hat enforcers wore to formal events.

"What's happening?" I whispered.

Her gaze flickered up and down my form as though checking that I couldn't escape my restraints. She disappeared out of sight and emerged, holding a metallic device the size and shape of a remote control. It was a counter, which measured a person's magic.

"We've kept you unconscious for forty-eight hours," she said.

"Why?"

"After replacing over half your blood, your body was completely devoid of magical power. We needed to give your magical core enough time to convert the donated Neutral blood into your innate magic."

My throat dried. There was another feature about being a Neutral. Because our magic was devoid of character, it also made us the universal blood donor. I gulped several times in quick succession.

"What did you find out?" I rasped.

Captain Zella's eyes softened. "The results are inconclusive, and we'll probably need to wait another day or so to see if the nature of your magic changes. In the meantime, the Council has asked me to ensure you're fit to stand trial."

"For what?"

She shook her head and stepped back several paces, removing herself from sight.

I blew out a long, shuddering breath, sifting through my mind for potential wrongdoings, and a boulder of dread dropped into my stomach. This had to be about Beatrice.

Healer Dianne must have worked out what Valentine had done to her mind and remembered that Beatrice had been attacked by a wielder of fire. It wouldn't take much of a mental leap for the Council to work out that the perpetrator was the girl sitting in the hospital room.

I wanted to wrap my arms around my middle, but they were strapped to that infernal chair. Bloody hell, I was as good as dead.

A vampire herald wearing white livery marched into the middle of the courtroom and banged his official stick on the ground with seven sharp raps. Several sets of doors opened, and footsteps echoed across the vast space.

I twisted around in my seat, watching streams of supernaturals step through the doors and take their seats up in a mezzanine. Multicolored faces peered down at me as though I was a figure in a spectacle.

Anxiety roiled through my stomach and spread up to the back of my throat, making my lips tremble. They had probably waited until now to test my magic in full view of the spectators. I might even have a public execution.

"All rise for the Supernatural Council," shouted the herald.

A door within the high dais' wood paneling opened, and the Witch Queen stepped out, wearing a high-necked robe of white silk. She was tall, a white-haired woman with mahogany skin and eyes as bright as stars. I had never spoken to her directly but Aunt Arianna always described her as kind and compassionate. Today, her stare was as sharp as daggers.

Following her was the King of the Shifters and Weres, a burly man with golden skin, amber eyes and dark sideburns that took up the left and right of his face. Thick, ropey muscles bulged from his white robe, and he moved with the confident swagger of a man who had beaten every other shifter to earn his position. He bared sharp teeth at me and snarled, making my heart jump into the back of my throat.

The Fae King was next, a long-haired male whose athletic build made him look slender compared to the Shifter King. Silver hair curled around his beautiful features, highlighting his sharp cheekbones and pointed ears. Mischief danced in his quicksilver eyes, and he offered me a smile devoid of warmth. The gleeful malice in his expression said he would look forward to my execution.

Shuddering, I snatched my gaze away, only to meet the coal-black glower of the Mage King, a thin man with chiseled features and an expression as fixed and stern as a statue. He ruled all the elementals—those who manipulated forces of nature, such as water and light and shadows. Shadows danced around his hairline, reminding me of the curse that had gotten Valentine killed.

Out of all the Supernatural Monarchs, only one of them showed an ounce of compassion. That was the Angel King, a golden-haired male with iridescent wings folded behind his back. He appeared about my age with ivory skin and strong, handsome features, but he was probably the oldest of the entire group.

One friendly face wouldn't save me. Not when the Demon King trailing after him offered me a broad smile that actually reached his eyes. Terror skittered up my spine. He was the most unsettling of them all. While every supernatural on the dais looked powerful, the Demon King appeared like an averagely handsome human in his thirties and was the only one not wearing a robe. Instead, he wore a suit of white silk.

My pulse fluttered in my throat. Even though angels and demons were officially members of the

Supernatural Council, and their subjects were free to travel through Logris as they pleased, they often remained in their own realms. I'd heard a rumor that all the dead fire wielders were offered up to the Demon King as a sacrifice to keep the peace. Perhaps that was why he looked so delighted.

I stared at the door, waiting for the final Supernatural Monarch to arrive, but it clicked shut, leaving the space between the Fae King and the Mage King empty.

A tight fist of grief squeezed my heart.

The Mage King leaned forward. "Captain Zella, please introduce the prisoner."

Captain Zella stepped forth, her heels clicking against the courtroom's stone floor. I swallowed. Earlier, before the doors had opened to let in the spectators up in the mezzanine, she had moved as silently as a wraith. Was this some kind of courtroom theatrics?

My gaze wandered down to my lap, and I inhaled rapid, shallow breaths. This was my first time in the Supernatural Council courtroom. It would also probably be my last.

"Your Majesties, Lords and Ladies of the Council," she said, her voice projecting across a space even vaster than it looked from my limited vantage point. "On Sunday, I visited the Natural World, following a report of a Supernatural being contravening Subsection Two of the Supernatural Secrecy Act."

"We don't need to hear the legalese," drawled the King of the Faeries. "Tell us what you found when you caught up with the suspect."

"I found Hemera Griffin behind the secure wards of a London residence, under the protection of King Valentine of the Vampires."

Chatter spread across the courtroom, making the fine hairs on the back of my neck stand on end. My gaze darted to the dais, where the Demon King's eyes flared with what appeared to be firelight. I dropped my gaze to my lap. The man looked like he was enjoying the prospect of possessing my soul.

"I see." The Mage King rested his elbows on the arms of his golden throne. "Did Miss Griffin display any fire magic?"

Captain Zella stood in front of me with her arms behind her back. "She did not, Your Majesty."

"None at all?" The Demon King leaned forward, his features falling. "What about when you tested her in custody?"

Captain Zella shook her head. "Results were inconclusive."

"What does that mean?" snapped the Angel King. "Does Mera have fire or not?"

I sucked in a deep breath, wondering how he knew I preferred this shortened version of my name. Maybe the Angel King was friends with Valentine. Maybe angels were good and fair and truly believed all supernatural beings were equal.

Captain Zella exhaled a long breath. "All signs point toward Hemera Griffin being a Neutral."

The Demon King slumped back in his throne and turned his gaze to the ceiling with a disappointed groan. His actions just confirmed the rumor that the Council tossed souls of people like me to hell.

My chest loosened, and a breath whistled through my teeth. Captain Zella would test me again tomorrow, but at least I would survive another day. A lot could happen in twenty-four hours.

"Then Miss Griffin's execution will take place immediately?" asked the Witch Queen.

"What?" I blurted.

All six members of the Supernatural Council turned their gazes to me.

My throat dried. "If I'm still a Neutral, why would I get killed?" The words tumbled from my lips. I probably should have used correct grammar or formal English, but my brain had scrambled at the unfairness of my situation. "I haven't done anything wrong."

The entire courtroom filled with excited chatter, and the herald stepped into the middle of the marble floor, banging his ceremonial staff and shouting for order.

Moments later, the courtroom quieted.

"Did anyone explain to you the results of your trial in absentia?" asked the Witch Queen.

"Isn't this my trial?" I murmured.

The Fae King placed his hand over his mouth to suppress a chuckle. I clenched my teeth, failing to see the joke.

"Hemera." The Witch Queen leaned forward, fixing me with her shimmering eyes. "The Council found you guilty of the murder of King Valentine based on the overwhelming evidence found at the scene of the crime."

A fist of shock punched me in the heart, making me jerk forward in my restraints. All the air left my lungs, and I struggled to force out the words. "I didn't kill him. It was suicide."

Someone made a choking laugh, making my chest tighten.

"His servants found you sitting beside his dead body with puncture wounds on your neck," said the Fae King with a chuckle. "They said he gifted you the murder weapon and once heard you threaten to stab him with it."

I shook my head from side to side, trying to dislodge the memory of Valentine's heavy body pinning mine to the cushions, the pierce of his fangs on my jugular, and his excited, hot breath. For a moment, his gulping swallows filled my ears, and I could feel the rapid movement of his throat as he guzzled mouthfuls of my blood.

Then... A wave of grief washed over my senses, making me lurch forward. Then he killed himself to save my life. One of the healers who had tended to me must have dampened the memory so that I could stand trial. Now, the whole horror of Valentine nearly killing me consumed my every thought.

"He was trying to protect me," I said. "Didn't anyone check the magical forensics?"

"We will not overturn our verdict," the Mage King said. "Any further outbursts, and I will hold you in contempt of court."

The trial continued as I relived my last few memories before the wards fell, when Valentine had slumped over me, and those last tender words he uttered before succumbing to the solid flame dagger.

Somewhere on the edge of my awareness, one of the Council Monarchs admonished Captain Zella for not telling me of the verdict. Apparently, there were two trials: the first for the murder of Valentine, which they held while I was unconscious, and this was the second to decide if I was a wielder of fire.

The Demon King slammed his fist on the arm of his golden throne with a rattling bang that made everyone fall silent. He sat straighter in his seat and stared down at me with heated eyes. "She must remain alive until her blood settles."

"I fail to see the point of prolonging her suffering," said the Witch Queen. "I move for a swift execution."

He threw his head back and laughed. "Only to avoid casting shame on your citizens. I vote that we keep Miss Griffin alive and bring her in for testing at the end of the week."

"Agreed," said the Fae King.

"Agreed," snarled the Shifter King.

"Agreed," said the Mage King.

"No," said the Angel King. "Mera should be executed immediately for her own crimes. The evidence points toward the murder being carried out in self-defense."

The Fae King shook his head. "Any human entering into a relationship with a supernatural does so accepting liabilities for the risk. The Court already established that Miss Griffin was the former concubine of King Valentine, so the same rule applies to her."

A boulder of sorrow sank into my heart and settled in my stomach. I couldn't even feel outraged at the unfairness of that comment. The leather restraint around my neck tightened, forcing me to stare straight at the Council members sitting on the dais.

The Demon King hummed his approval and nodded. "Besides, it's four against two. Even if King Valentine were alive to offer the girl mercy, she would still die."

My gaze darted from side to side. I opened my mouth to ask what was happening, but no sound came out. Someone had silenced me from speaking out.

I stared at the Witch Queen, who met my gaze with sad eyes. Did she want me executed so my soul would stay out of the hands of the Demon King?

The herald crossed the courtroom and bowed in front of the dais. "The majority votes that Hemera Griffin be kept in custody for another seventy-two hours, after which she will submit herself to further magical testing. Does any member of the Council have an objection?"

The Witch Queen stood. "I do."

"What say you, Your Majesty?" said the herald.

She glanced down the row of males. "I would ask my esteemed colleagues to consider that Miss Griffin acted in self-defense, and her coven had no advance knowledge of her actions. Therefore we must hold them innocent of the murder of King Valentine."

Palpitations thudded through my heart, and my chest tightened with oncoming panic. Why on earth would anyone even consider Aunt Arianna and the rest of the coven responsible for something I supposedly did in the midst of being attacked?

The Demon King waved a dismissive hand. "Pretty words, but short-sighted. If the girl is a fire wielder as suspected, everyone who failed to report her will also face execution."

"I think we're forgetting the most important issue," drawled the Mage King. "If Miss Griffin is indeed as we suspect then King Valentine may rise as a preternatural vampire."

Shouts exploded across the courtroom, and a shocked breath whistled through my teeth. I screamed, but the sound was muffled by the enchantment someone had cast over me to stay silent. Valentine couldn't rise as a preternatural vampire. It would take an army of supernatural vampires to slay him, and—

A sob tore from my throat. What the hell had just happened?

Healer Dianne had wanted to send enforcers after Beatrice because she had been exposed to fire magic. Fire magic that would make her rise as a zombie if she were to die with it still in her system.

Valentine had drunk my blood. Lots of it. Dying with fire in his veins meant he could rise from his grave a monster that would rival the most heinous creations of Kresnik.

"Silence," roared the herald.

Nobody took notice of him. While supernatural vampires were born, preternatural ones were not only made, but they could turn others. I wasn't sure of the details, but that's what had made Kresnik so dangerous. Once he had infected one vampire, they could move around the Supernatural World, forming armies of loyal preternatural monsters for their master.

The Witch Queen raised a hand, and a burst of magic oscillated across the vast chamber, making everyone fall silent. I jerked back in my wooden seat, shuddering at the woman's sheer power.

She cleared her throat. "One in a thousand fire wielders hold the power of animation. Even if Miss Griffin tested positive for fire magic, that still wouldn't mean she transmuted King Valentine into a preternatural."

Forcing deep breaths in and out of my lungs, I concentrated all my hope on the Witch Queen and tried to stay calm. She was right. Having fire didn't mean I was in any way special. Valentine would probably just stay dead, only I would be executed for his murder, and my soul would remain out of the clutches of the Demon King.

I worried at my bottom lip with my teeth, swallowing over and over, as though I couldn't fully absorb the truth. The other Council members rejected the Witch Queen's suggestion but allowed my coven the freedom to put their affairs in order if I was found guilty of having fire.

As the herald cleared the courtroom, grief settled around my shoulders like a shroud, and the weight of my predicament sank into my soul. Valentine was not only just dead at the point of my dagger, but his tormented soul might never move on to the afterlife.

Nobody had studied the effect of turning preternatural on a person's soul, as they were more interested in finding ways to exterminate the undead, but if he turned, would he be himself? Would he suffer? What about his brothers?

The vampire throne had been empty. I didn't know if that was because his family was still mourning or if they were too disgusted at what I had done to look me in the face.

Tears stung the back of my eyes. I sent a silent prayer to whoever was listening that poor Valentine would stay dead, that my powers would remain dormant during the next testing, and that Aunt Arianna and the others would survive the wrath of the council.

CHAPTER TWENTY-ONE

The courtroom cleared, leaving me alone with Captain Zella. She advanced toward my wooden chair, releasing the leather straps encasing my torso and neck and limbs. As soon as the last of the restraints fell loose, the magic forcing me to remain silent vanished with a *pop*.

She stood back a few paces with her white cap tucked beneath her arm, and raised her hand, beckoning me to stand.

I shot the dark-haired woman a filthy glower. "Why didn't you tell me I'd been found guilty for Valentine's death?"

She raised her brows. "Would it have made a difference to your outcome?"

"Yes, it would—"

"Of course it wouldn't," she snapped. "I was at the murder scene moments after the wards fell. It was obvious to anyone who saw you both that King Valentine would have killed you if you hadn't attacked him with that solid flame dagger."

I clenched my teeth, breathing hard through flared nostrils. "He killed himself."

Captain Zella shook her head. "Even if that were true, the Council would never have allowed a scandal like that to go public."

Bitterness coated my tongue. I knew how to read between the lines. The Supernatural Council didn't want to appear weak, and they saw me as a convenient scapegoat. It was why they were so desperate to prove I could wield fire. The Vampire King murdered by a fire mage sounded more dramatic than Valentine sacrificing himself for love. Besides, it would also justify their murder of innocent children suspected of having fire.

"That doesn't explain why you kept quiet about the verdict," I said. "You should have told me before the herald arrived instead of letting me find out in a crowded Council room."

Impatience flickered across her features, and she glanced over her shoulder, huffing out a sharp breath. "The Supernatural Council deems overemotional outbursts as not showing the proper respect for their authority. I wanted to make sure you had a clean execution without dragging down innocent members of your coven for not teaching you how to act with decorum."

My shoulders sagged, and all sense of outrage drained out of me in a tired sigh. "Oh."

Captain Zella flicked her head toward a door at the base of the dais. "Get up. It's time to return to your cell."

She led the way, making me trudge after her in a jumpsuit that made my arms and legs feel like lead. Everyone knew all about these accursed garments. The cuffs and collars and seams of prisoner uniforms were imbued with a special kind of magic that weighted down the limbs, controlled the wearer's movements, and could even punish them with a lash of magic.

I'd never been in trouble with the enforcers in my life, but a group of them had visited the academy to demonstrate what happened to those who broke the law. Part of that lesson included a physical education session where we had to run from one end of the gymnasium to the other in a prisoner's jumpsuit. It was a painful experience for everyone, even those intelligent enough not to attempt to escape.

We passed through the wooden doorway, down into a darkened corridor illuminated only by the light of the courtroom. I couldn't see what was ahead of us past Captain Zella's larger body, but after several steps into the hallway, the door behind us slammed shut, encasing us both in the dark.

A shiver trickled down my spine. "I don't suppose shadow mages can move the darkness aside?"

"Feel free to illuminate the passage with a flaming fist," the captain replied with a smile in her voice.

I pressed my lips together in a tight line. This was the equivalent of death row. Worse, because if they found me guilty of wielding magic, Aunt Arianna would die. She'd sent enough nullweed-infused chocolate to convince even the most optimistic of people that she was guilty of harboring a fire-user. And if Valentine rose from the dead, every single person in my coven would face execution.

Right now, the last thing I needed was an enforcer's black humor.

"I have another question," I asked as we trudged down the dark corridor.

"Go on," she replied.

"You saw the curse on my leg, didn't you?"

She paused. "Healers took a sample of the magic, yes."

"What did they discover?"

"It's called blood lure," she replied. "It's ancient, forbidden magic used as indirect weapons against vampires."

"Because it makes them attack people?" I asked.

"That's correct," she replied. "Nobody has cast that spell in over a thousand years and all knowledge of how to cast it was erased."

One foot stumbled over the other, and I held on to the wall for balance. "Did you tell the Supernatural Council I'd been cursed?"

Captain Zella halted, and I bumped into her back. The uniform didn't blast out a shot of pain or turn hot as I had expected, but I took a few steps backward with a muttered apology.

"There's one thing you need to know," she said in a voice as heavy as stone. "If knowledge that such a curse existed was made public, everybody with a grudge against a vampire would curse people to turn that vampire feral. People would use the enchantment to assassinate their enemies via vampire. It's extremely dangerous knowledge."

My throat tightened, and the back of my eyes stung. "You withheld that information—"

"The Council deemed it inadmissible for your trial."

"But knowing that Valentine wanted to kill me—"

"Would not have made the slightest bit of difference," she said with a long sigh. "The rule still applies that anyone willing to enter into a relationship with a supernatural does so accepting the risks and consequences."

"So they made me a scapegoat," I muttered.

Captain Zella continued walking. "You're not listening," she snapped. "Everyone in the Council knew of your disastrous dalliance with King Valentine, therefore they knew you accepted the risk of him one day draining your blood—"

"Right, right, I get it."

She huffed a breath, implying that I didn't.

Captain Zella was wrong. I understood the logic behind their decision but what I didn't get was the unfairness. Never once on human television did I ever see a judge ever say that the victim of a crime knew they were associating with a criminal and therefore accepted the risk of becoming a victim. Where was the justice in that?

We continued through the dark for another ten minutes on a downward, twisting slope that became so steep I had to cling to the walls to keep from sliding on my ass.

"Where are we going?" I snarled.

"There are special cells for people like you," she replied.

"What do you mean?" I asked.

"The slaughter of a king is a threat to Supernatural security," she said.

I waited for her to mention what I had done to Beatrice, but she didn't elaborate any further. A relieved breath whooshed from my lungs. At least that meant Healer Dianne hadn't recovered her memories.

We reached flat ground, where a shard of light flooded our path, illuminating the taller woman's white uniform and grave features. She placed her hand on the wall, and a door swung open, revealing a white room and cells separated by tall, white walls.

I blinked several times, not quite believing my eyes. Had they stolen the design from a public bathroom? That's what the prison looked like to me. Captain Zella continued past a few empty cells, passing one containing a large man sitting on the floor with his legs crossed and his head in his hands.

His head snapped up, and he stared at me through wild amber eyes. Wiry hair sprouted from the sides of his face, making him look like a half-transformed ape.

"You," he snarled.

It was Mr. Masood, the creep who had sent over the expensive bottle of champagne in Souk. I staggered back, and the collar of my prison uniform delivered a sharp sting that sent sparks of pain racing across my skin.

"Ouch," I snapped.

Captain Zella turned around with her brows raised. "What do you expect for not falling into line?"

"I only..." I shook my head, remembering the lesson in the academy where the uniform punished students who failed to follow the enforcer's instructions. "Never mind."

The captain swept her hand into the empty cell next to the shifter. I stepped back, only for a nasty shock to travel up both legs.

"Alright!" I didn't dare raise a palm to ask her to stop, because the punishments came from the uniform. "Could you at least put me in a different cell?"

Captain Zella shook her head. "Each booth is

configured to counter the magic of its inhabitants, and the others are reserved for members of your coven." She swept her arm toward the empty cell. "Do I need to make the uniform march you into place? I promise it will hurt."

"Fine." I hurried into the empty booth and leaned against the wall furthest from Mr. Masood. "What happens next?"

"We'll wait until Friday to test your magic. If you're found guilty, enforcers will round up your closest family members for a trial." She raised her shoulder. "For their sakes, let's hope you remain a Neutral."

I threw back my head and stared at a ceiling of white tiles grouted with glowing lights. A thick barrier of magic slammed down on my left side with the speed and sharpness of a guillotine.

"Miss Griffin?" asked the captain.

"Yes?" I turned to meet her charcoal eyes.

"Should King Valentine rise from the dead before then, the Supernatural Council will immediately find you guilty of being a wielder of fire and guilty of raising a preternatural. In that case, every member of your coven will perish."

Tearing my gaze away from Captain Zella's, I slid down the wall, and buried my head in my hands. All those years I wished I had supernatural powers like everyone else in Logris, and I ended up becoming a supernatural with a forbidden magic that meant execution.

I finally understood the extent of the human phrase, 'be careful what you wish for'.

A low, dry chuckle drifted through the wall separating me and Mr. Masood. "Preternatural vampires?" He whistled. "My, my, have you been a busy girl."

"What are you in for?" I spat.

"You should know," he snarled. "You're the one who reported me to the enforcers."

I sniffed. "What were you doing haunting human establishments and tricking girls into drinking enchanted champagne?"

"There was nothing wrong with my booze," he roared, making me flinch. "It was the—"

"The glasses, right?" I rose off the floor, my heart thudding, and my blood boiling with righteous indignation. A supernatural like Mr. Masood deserved to be here—not me.

In a human court of law, people took self-defense seriously. Here in Logris, getting bitten was my fault for being in a relationship with a vampire. I ground my teeth. Never mind that someone threw a curse at me to make my blood irresistible. It was easier to execute me than delve into who had struck out at us both.

Mr. Masood's growl made the walls reverberate. "If you had drunk that wretched drink like a good girl, you and your coven wouldn't be facing annihilation."

"Is this your revenge?" I slammed my fist into the wall. "Did you send someone after me with a curse?"

"What are you talking about?" he said. "I only noticed you because you were sitting next to the juicy one."

My mouth fell open. All along, he'd been targeting Beatrice. It had nothing to do with me being a Neutral.

"I only worked out you were the one who reported me because I recognized your red hair," he muttered.

I leaned my head against the wall and blew out a breath. So much for Mr. Masood being the mastermind behind the curse. Captain Zella also hadn't cursed me. The woman was stern but appeared fair and more interested in exercising justice.

So who had set this up?

All the anger drained away, replaced by an onslaught of grief. Grief for Valentine, grief for having killed him, grief for the relationship we would never have. My throat swelled, and heat gathered around my eyes. I swallowed down a lump and held back a sob.

"Hey?" asked Masood.

"What?" I croaked.

"Are you crying?"

Pressing my lips together, I stepped back from the wall. "Why were you poisoning girls, anyway?"

"Not poisoning," he snapped. "The enchantment makes them relax for the feeding."

I lurched forward. "What?"

He snarled something under his breath. "My beloved is at the end of her last life. The life force of a single girl maintains her youth for a month to six weeks, depending. If you had let me take your juicy friend, I might not have needed to feed her for an entire two whole months!"

A shocked breath huffed from my lips. I was no expert on demons, but they lived forever unless deliberately killed. Even then, they went back to hell as lesser demons and spent centuries gathering the power needed to become eligible for leaving their realm and entering ours.

The thought of so many young women being sacrificed so that a single demon could cling to life made bile rise to the back of my throat. "You're killing people just so a female who's using you as her personal butler can escape death?"

"Don't act so high and mighty," he snapped. "At least the people I murder stay dead."

I flinched. "What will happen if your…" I gulped. "What happens to your beloved if she doesn't feed?"

"She will wither and die," he said with a low sob.

The tightness around my throat loosened. Thank goodness for that.

Pain spread down my right hand and up its forearm, sending with it a burst of magic that thrummed through my veins. I clutched at my wrist and lowered myself to the ground, clenching my teeth from the agony.

"Mera?" a voice whispered in my ear.

"Aunt Arianna?" I whispered back.

"Who are you talking to?" asked Masood.

"Don't speak out loud," her voice said. "This enchantment won't last long. When the enforcers came looking for a large quantity of Neutral blood, I knew something terrible had happened, and you'd been captured."

My throat dried, and I made a high-pitched cough, encouraging Aunt Arianna to continue speaking.

"Do you know Eva Storm and Natalia Watchtower from the Claymore coven?" She paused and huffed. "It doesn't matter. They volunteered to donate, and we infused their blood with this enchantment to allow you to hear my words and with large quantities of powdered firestone."

I choked on air. More of that stuff was running through my veins? Wouldn't it cause a clog, a clot or a stroke? I shook off those thoughts. Medical witches could enchant new organs into people without fear of their body rejecting them, and it was too late to worry about the state of my health when I might be executed in a few days.

Mr. Masood launched into a story about how he met his beloved, and I placed my hands over my ears to block out his rambling.

"Listen carefully," Aunt Arianna said. "The firestone bracelet I enchanted to sink into your flesh should have held back a lifetime of power, but we miscalculated the type of your flames."

"What?" I whispered.

"What?" said Masood.

"Nothing," I muttered.

"Your magic isn't the same as other wielders of fire." Her words came out in a rush. "When the ward stones I placed around the house sent back sparks of ancient magic, I realized why the firestone hadn't contained the extent of your power."

My pulse thudded between my ears, echoing the sounds of Mr. Masood. I lowered my hands to my knees and stared at the tattoo, which had turned black.

"Mera," Aunt Arianna said, her voice trembling. "You have phoenix fire. It's the highest, purest level of fire magic with the ultimate power in healing."

My mouth fell open. I had read about phoenixes in Istabelle's library. They went extinct millennia ago but were creatures of flames instead of feathers. When a phoenix died, it turned to ashes, and within hours would arise a brand new bird. Phoenixes were supposed to be immortal due to their power of regeneration, but something happened to them, making them all disappear.

I rubbed my temples and squeezed my eyes shut to process everything I'd heard. How could I have phoenix flames? Did that mean I was a shifter? Everything I had learned about them had been based on myth—stories passed down through the generations, rather than scientific or magical observation.

"You can save yourself, save King Valentine, and save the coven," she said.

My head snapped up. How?

"Find an excuse to reach King Valentine's body. Tell them you wish to make peace with him before he dies, broker a deal with them and say you know the location of other fire users and won't tell them unless they take you to his tomb."

I gulped but nodded. Right now, I was willing to listen to any plan to get out of here, no matter how outlandish.

Aunt Arianna continued, "When you get to King Valentine, you must place your hands on his body and burn it with your flames."

I parted my lips to protest. Aunt Arianna's plan hinged on three assumptions. One, that I could access my magic through the firestone. Two, that they wouldn't kill me as soon as I regained my power. Three, that they would even let me see Valentine. I shook off those thoughts. There was no need for pessimism in a situation so dire.

"Once you've burned him to ash, he will rise as a normal vampire in his prime," Aunt Arianna said. "You will have saved his life and demonstrated a rare skill that would make you worth keeping alive."

I gulped, waiting for her to tell me how to express my magic with particles of firestone floating in my blood. That part of Aunt Arianna's plan didn't make sense, but then I hadn't spent three years investigating fire magic.

"Your mother started developing symptoms around the age of eighteen." Aunt Arianna's voice filled my ears. "Our father smuggled her out of Logris to join a community of fire users. When you were born, she had to send you back because they suspected you were a Neutral and would be burned by the presence of so much fire."

My gaze rose to the grid of light between the ceiling tiles, burning their white lines in my vision. My aunt had just implied that Mom was alive and safe. Pressure built up around my chest, squeezing all the air out of my lungs.

A sour taste spread down my tongue and filled my stomach with heavy regret. Why had Aunt Arianna sent me to Istabelle instead of Mom? I squeezed my eyes shut, letting my brain form an answer. Up until recently, nobody even knew I would wield fire.

"You have three days, Mera. Three days before they return to test your blood. Find a way to express your power before then and heal King Valentine. The firestone in your blood will protect you from detection…" Her voice faded, and the magic thrumming through my veins faded.

I guess I was finally alone with only the sobbing Mr. Masood for company.

Folding my arms, I crossed my legs into the lotus position and readied myself to meditate. Valentine had interrupted my memories by breaking into the attic and launching his bloodthirsty attack.

All my troubles started on the day someone tampered with my mind. That person was also probably behind the assassin who came to the apartment and the shadow that cursed me with the blood lure.

Valentine's mind enchantment might have already done its job and uncovered our enemy, but even if it hadn't, I still needed to relive the memory of the night of the ball. It was the biggest block in my consciousness and removing it might be the key to releasing my phoenix flames.

CHAPTER TWENTY-TWO

I sat on the floor of my narrow cell with my legs crossed and leaned my back against the wall. Without the presence of a large piece of quartz or any other kind of crystal, I wasn't sure how deep I could meditate. But it wasn't like I had much of a choice. I had to unlock those memories and find out what happened to me between leaving Valentine's palace and returning to the ball.

If I didn't find a way to bring out the phoenix flames supposedly burning in my magical core, I would certainly die.

Masood sobbed from the other side of the wall. I guess it was because the demon he had kept alive would die without his tributes of young women's lives. It was either that or the comment I made about her using him as a delivery boy.

Closing my eyes, I took a long, deep breath and

shoved all thoughts of the murderous shifter aside. Cool air streamed through my nostrils, filling my lungs and pushing down my diaphragm. My shoulders rose and my spine straightened as my chest expanded.

I needed to concentrate. It wasn't just my life that depended on my fire magic—Valentine was currently dead and at the risk of rising as a preternatural creature, his soul twisted and tormented. Then there was every member of my coven who would be executed just for being associated with a fire user who had raised the dead.

Instead of taking me to the scene where someone had tampered with my memory, my mind drifted back to the steps of the palace, where Valentine's butler stood between the two footmen, staring down at me with sad eyes. I met Caiman's gaze, daring him to deny ever knowing me.

By now, a dozen servants gathered at the door, all staring at me with blank expressions. Behind me, I heard the sounds of cars pulling into the courtyard, doors opening and closing, and cars driving away. Elegantly dressed and expensive-smelling vampires in tuxedos and ballgowns now formed a crowd around me.

To my senses, it felt like standing in a room full of smoke. Not because of the vampires themselves, but my chest tightened and my lungs shrank under the scrutiny of their focused attention.

A loud neigh filled the air, and I glanced over my shoulder to find a horse-drawn carriage pulling into the courtyard, emblazoned with the seven-crowns insignia of the University of Logris.

My heart sank. Valentine had invited all the high-society vampires to our engagement ball, which probably also included some of the girls from the academy. As a Neutral, I didn't qualify for anything but an education up to the age of eighteen, but many other supernaturals with actual power went on to study at the prestigious institution of higher education.

Caiman cleared his throat. "Miss Griffin, may I suggest that you leave before your presence here causes a scene. You are holding up important guests."

My mouth dropped open, and the pulse fluttering in my throat now thrashed. "You too?" I couldn't keep the hurt out of my voice. Caiman had been one of the first people who had seen my engagement ring. The ancient vampire had beamed and congratulated me, saying something about bringing forth the next generation of Sargon heirs. "You were in the room when we organized the ball. You even took notes."

"I say," said the blond vampire male from earlier. "Do you know this young woman?"

Caiman inclined his head. "Indeed I do, my lord."

"Is there any truth in her claims?" he asked.

Chuckles broke out across the small crowd, and my skin prickled with shame. I didn't need him or anyone else to speak up for me in what was soon to be my own home. All I needed was Valentine to come out and tell these people that I was the woman he had chosen to be his wife.

An annoyed breath huffed from Caiman's nostrils. "I'm not at liberty to divulge details of His Majesty's dalliances."

Everyone—including the servants—snickered. Bloody Caiman had just implied I was a delusional fling, using this ball as an opportunity to demand more. My throat thickened, and heat formed around my eyes. Clenching my teeth, I resolved myself not to let these vampires see me cry.

I took several deep, calming breaths and tried to keep the tremble out of my voice. "Valentine and I have been together for three years—"

"Go home, blood slut," said one voice from within the crowd.

The words hit like a slap. Dignity and common sense dictated that I should make my way around these vampires, descend those stairs and walk home. Eventually, Valentine would notice I hadn't arrived and come after me.

To hell with that.

After spending a lifetime being mocked and overlooked by the supernaturals with magic, a lifetime of being told I wouldn't amount to anything, someone had finally looked into my soul and seen something worth loving. Valentine had courted me, proposed to me, made love to me. We would be married, and I would be his queen consort.

Today was my first official exposure to vampire high society. If I showed weakness and backed down now, it would be like admitting that I wasn't worthy of being at Valentine's side. They would make me the subject of little humiliations and barbs whenever Valentine's back was turned—they might even belittle our children—and I would need his protection for the rest of my life.

A rapid drumbeat of anxiety rolled through my heart. I was sure every one of the vampires surrounding me could hear it. There wasn't much I could do about the functioning of my nervous system. I'd have to show them that no matter what they did or said, I would not be intimidated.

Pulling back my shoulders, I said in my calmest, clearest voice. "Bring out King Valentine. He will tell you I'm the guest of honor."

Caiman's lips formed a thin line of disapproval. "I hardly think that's wise."

"Do as the girl says," drawled the blue-haired vampire woman from earlier. "Perhaps then, we might get a chance for a drink."

Someone snickered at the double-entendre. I was nobody's bloody snack.

Caiman inclined his head and disappeared through the palace's double doors.

"She's always been like this," said a snide voice from further down the stairs.

I turned around and placed my hands on my hips. One would think that the voice of my former academy tormentor at a time like this would make me cringe, but it was oddly comforting to deal with a familiar form of disdain.

The crowd parted, and Ellora Vandamir sashayed up the stairs, clad in a silver dress a shade darker than her quicksilver hair. With the glitter sparkles catching the moonlight, she looked like she'd been doused in the stars. Behind her were two raven-haired vampire sisters from the academy whose names I didn't care to remember.

Ellora pressed a delicate hand to her cheek and preened at the crowd's admiring glances. That was the thing about vampires. They were physically stunning creatures, regardless of whether or not their insides were as ugly as sin.

"My lady, you know this human?" asked a voice in the crowd.

"Mera Griffin was in our year at academy and was always making scenes." Ellora tossed her head and snorted. "Always so desperate to compensate for her lack of magic, always trying and failing to outsmart her betters."

"I'm a Neutral, and as you know, humans aren't allowed into the academy." I forced my lips into a smile. "And it's sad to see that you're still sore that I excelled in theory-based classes while you failed yours."

Ellora bared her teeth. "How far did that get you, blood cow?"

I forced myself not to flinch. "One would think that the girl who has everything wouldn't be so desperate for attention. You've only just arrived and already insinuated yourself in the middle of a scene."

Someone chuckled, and petty triumph flared across my chest. She was never the smartest of girls and usually tried to make up for her disappointing grades by highlighting my lack of magic.

Ellora's face twisted into the usual rictus of anger she made whenever someone failed to react to her barbs.

"Mera?" A deep voice curled around my senses.

All thoughts of Ellora and the crowd of vampires faded into the background, and I turned around to meet the owner of that voice.

Valentine stood in the doorway, wearing a black tuxedo tailored around his muscular physique. Its bowtie and silk lapels were a red so dark that they appeared black, but the effect only accentuated his masculine beauty.

As usual, he wore his black hair off his face, but the moonlight shone through its ends like tendrils of silver. It brought out the copper tones in his bronze skin, the contour of his cheekbones, and his full cupid's bow lips.

Warmth spread through my insides, melting my heart, and all notions of academy mean girls, haughty aristocrats, and rude servants evaporated into the ether. Valentine always had that effect on me. Whenever he was around, he consumed my full attention, making me less aware of my surroundings. He was everything I needed—teacher, best friend, lover, protector. We had been together so long that he had woven himself into the tapestry of my soul.

I inhaled a deep breath, my chest expanding with love. With Valentine at the door, everything would be fine. He would declare his love to me in front of the other vampires and tell them that he would make me his wife and their queen.

"I heard you were having a little difficulty," he said, his eyes softening.

"Just a little," I replied with a smile. "The footmen at the door have forgotten that this is our engagement ball."

His lips curved into a smile. "Engagement?"

Doubt crept across my skin like a wintry breeze, cooling the warmth in my chest. I exhaled a long breath. "Valentine, you proposed—"

"I proposed." His voice was flat, all traces of his smile gone.

"Yes."

The crowd's murmurs filled the edge of my awareness, seeping through the bubble of security that I always felt around Valentine.

His brows knitted into a frown. "We had an arrangement," he said in the type of even tone people used to explain things to incurable idiots. "One common among vampires who require small quantities of blood."

All sensation drained from my face, concentrating on my cooling heart. He was about to describe me as a blood cow. My throat dried, and I swallowed several times in quick succession. During the three years Valentine had courted me, he had never once asked for my blood. Even when I had offered, he had refused, saying he wanted our souls to connect before we became physical.

Without meaning to, my hand snaked up to my neck. He had only bitten me once, and that had been earlier today—the first time we'd made love.

"Why are you saying this?" My voice broke

"Mera." Valentine folded his arms, his features hardening with impatience. "We agreed I would take a small amount of your blood in exchange for a monthly stipend. We also agreed it would be for a limited time."

My hackles rose, and I felt as exposed as an injured mouse surrounded by hungry cats. Every instinct in my body told me I should leave with my tattered dignity. Leave before I humiliated myself further. The vampires standing on the steps closed in around me, their excited breaths rasping against my taut nerves.

I couldn't leave. Leaving would be an admission of defeat. Leaving would forever scar me as the blood cow who dared to think I could become the equal of a vampire king. Leaving would mean that every insult girls like Ellora Vandamir had ever hurled at me had come true.

"Then how do you explain this engagement ring?" I raised my left hand.

Valentine pinched the bridge of his nose, exhaling a weary breath. "It's a call stone enchanted to bring you to me whenever I am in need."

The crowd burst into laughter, each sound of mirth hitting me like a slap. And a huff of incredulity erupted from my throat.

Call stones were a throwback from the days before the Seven Monarchs of the Supernatural Council. Back then, the stronger beings could enslave the weaker, making them serve as cows, concubines, tributes—anything. No matter how far the slave managed to escape, the stone would transport them to their master with a single thought. They weren't tokens of love but a symbol of bondage.

I glanced from side to side, my gaze filling with a sea of mocking faces. Some of them had even exposed their fangs as though wanting to sample the Vampire King's cast-off.

Valentine appeared a foot away from me, filling my nostrils with his intoxicating masculine scent.

"Thank you for the donations, but your services are no longer required."

"Because you have an heir?" The words slipped from my lips.

He shook his head. "Mortals are like apples." The crowd quietened to hear his declaration. "Some would say they were the forbidden fruit, but there are fruits more flavorful and sweeter. The trouble with apples is that once you've taken a bite, they rot."

I flinched, my face burning with shame.

"Poor Mera Griffin," Ellora said in a mocking sing-song. "The cow with the sour milk. Twenty-one years of age and already past her prime."

Valentine tilted his head to the side and the corner of his mouth curled up. After confiding in the wretched bastard about the hardships I'd experienced at the academy, he was bloody agreeing with Ellora's taunts.

This was as much as a girl could take. I spun on my heel, picked up my skirt and descended a step.

Ellora stood in my path with a broad grin of gleaming silver eyes and dazzling teeth. I shoved past her with a snarl, but she held onto my wrist.

"Release her," said Valentine.

Ellora let go of my arm, and the crowd behind her parted. I continued down the steps, ignoring the other girls' whispered taunts. Up ahead was the car that had taken me home only hours before, and the same driver stood at the open passenger door.

"Of course, your highness," Ellora said in a loud voice. "Mera Griffin is a creature to be pitied, not mocked."

"Indeed," Valentine replied.

Anger slammed into my gut. I turned around, pulled off the engagement ring, and hurled it at Valentine's face. "Take back your call stone and stick it up your ass."

Disapproval tightened his lips, and he caught it out of the air. I turned back to the car, stepped inside, and sat with as much dignity as I could muster. Frantic breaths heaved in and out of my lungs, and I glowered at the crowd of vampire nobles disappearing through the palace's double doors.

Why? My hands clenched into fists. Why did he declare his love for me one minute and dismiss me as a blood cow the next?

"Miss Griffin?" The driver's face appeared through the gap in the door. "Are you alright?"

"Take me home," I rasped. "Please."

"As you wish." He shut the door and walked around the car.

It was only when he had fired up the engine and the car pulled out of the driveway that I raised my head again. Valentine stood at the doors with Caiman, both seeming to want to make sure that the intruder had gone. I shook my head. All these years, had he been playing some kind of sick game?

The car continued down the long driveway that

led to the twelve-foot-tall iron gates that surrounded the palace's grounds. Tears pricked the backs of my eyes, and I stared down at my lap. If Valentine had wanted me for my blood, he could have asked for an arrangement. The answer would have been no because I had always wanted more from life than selling my body.

I gulped back a sob. Even if he'd changed his mind about marrying me, why go to the effort of buying a dress, arranging a ball, and having his driver bring me here? It was almost as though he had wanted everyone to witness me brought low.

The scent of burning hair filled my nostrils. I glanced into my lap to find dark patches of charred fabric on the silk of my skirt. My shoulders slumped. Bloody Ellora Vandamir or one of her sycophantic friends must have put something on my dress.

My throat dried, and my vision turned black. The smell of burning continued, only this time, it smelled like overheated cables. I jerked back and snapped my eyes open to the sounds of alarms blaring overhead. Masood's shouts and roars to be let out rang through my ears, making my heart rate double.

Foot-long flames danced over the legs of my prison jumpsuit, and smoke rose from the fire, spreading across the white ceiling tiles like thick clouds. A shocked breath hissed through my teeth, and I scrambled to my feet to find my palms still on fire.

I'd done it.

Pressing both palms against the invisible magic encasing my booth, I concentrated my flames in an effort to burn a hole large enough to make my escape. I still didn't know what phoenix flames were good for apart from healing, but the fire of such an ancient magical creature had to be more powerful than any enchantment set up by the Council's enforcers.

Magical flames cracked and popped across the barrier, and soon spread around its surface, forming a flaming disc that spread from eye level to two feet off the ground.

My breathing quickened and I poured every ounce of anger, frustration, humiliation and confusion into the flames. That meditation had helped me tap into my power, but I was still no closer to identifying the unseen enemy who had messed with my mind.

I clenched my teeth. Because of that person, I had stayed longer than necessary on the palace steps and allowed that wretched Ellora Vandamir to get the better of me. Worse, because of that person, Valentine was now dead and at threat of becoming a monster.

"Girl," Masood roared. "That's magical fire."

Ignoring him, I pushed against the flames and stepped out into the larger room.

Masood stood in his booth with his huge body

pressed against the invisible barrier. His arms had lengthened, and a thick covering of fur spread around his face and down his neck. From the shortness of his bent legs, I guessed he was a gorilla shifter.

"Let me out," he bellowed.

I rushed past Masood to the exit and ran my flaming hands over its seal. White sparks of magic crackled under my fingertips, and the wood turned to char. The flames coating my hands fizzled, leaving them only the barest trace of smoke. Clenching my teeth, I drew back my fist and punched through the blackened wood, only to find a translucent barrier of shimmering magic, reflecting every color of the rainbow.

Behind the wall stood four figures in black. All the triumph inflating my chest turned to dread and dropped into the pit of my belly like a stone.

CHAPTER TWENTY-THREE

The door rattled and then exploded in a spray of splinters. I raised my arms above my head, stumbling back into the room, but metallic shards sliced my forearms and I fell to the ground with a heavy thud.

Four enforcers rushed at me, their arms outstretched and strings of shadow bursting from their fingers. They wrapped around my neck, my shoulders, my thighs, raising me off the ground and throwing me into the wall. Pain slammed against my spine and radiated from the back of my head. I cried out, but a shadow slipped between my lips, filled my mouth, and slithered down my throat.

Despair filled my chest with a lead weight, and everything Aunt Arianna had told me to do rolled out of my mind, replacing its contents with blank panic.

So much for managing to escape. I hadn't even gotten as far as the door.

Clicking footsteps approached, and Captain Zella strolled in from the hallway, now dressed in black, her stern features pinched. "Your powers have returned." She cast her gaze to the doorway, where a quartet of enforcers stood in the shadows with only the barest of light reflecting off the leather of their caps. "Arrest Arianna Griffin and bring the rest of the coven into custody, pending developments with King Valentine."

I screamed, but the gag of shadows muffled the sound.

"Miss Griffin." Captain Zella stood six feet away from me with her arms behind her back. "If you list all accomplices who helped conceal your fire magic from the Council's attention, I can guarantee you all painless deaths."

Behind the captain, a fully transformed Masood pounded his fists against the invisible barrier, shaking his head from side to side.

We weren't exactly allies, and it wasn't like I would admit to anyone having helped me. Valentine knew about my burgeoning power, as did Aunt Arianna. I suspected Istabelle also knew and had been keeping her eye on my magic, looking for changes. It explained why she instantly recognized the firestone and hadn't been alarmed when it had stuck to my skin.

I shook my head.

The captain sighed. "Don't condemn those who tried to protect your secret. Do you know what the Council does to the souls of those who harbor abominations like you?"

Every muscle in my body stiffened, and the fiery eyes of the Demon King filled my memory. They'd probably send Aunt Arianna to hell, so she'd become a demon's plaything. The laws protecting weaker supernaturals didn't apply in other realms, and some of the stories of what demons could do to people made my stomach churn.

Something must have shown in my face because Captain Zella told her enforcers to release my mouth. The shadows slipped out from my throat, down my tongue and out from my lips, making me cough and gasp. It had been like choking on a ghost of water—all the sensation of suffocating but still able to breathe.

"Who helped to keep you hidden all these years?" she asked.

"My magic developed on its own," I said through spluttering breaths. "Today was the first time I expressed it."

Her eyes narrowed. "Are you suggesting that the Neutral blood transfusion triggered this magical outburst of fire?"

I flinched, hoping Captain Zella wouldn't call for

the blood donors to also get arrested. "Of course not!"

She turned to a male enforcer. "Perform the tests."

He slipped his hand into a pouch he kept on a holster of his black uniform pants and pulled out a device the size of a remote control. As though something about me was infectious, he wrapped his shadows around the object and pointed it to my chest, making it beep like a Geiger counter.

I held my breath, not knowing if this was a good sign or bad.

The shadow mage moved the measuring device up my left, making the beeps slow. As he moved it to the right, they quickened. Sweat gathered on my brow, and I glanced over the enforcer's shoulders to meet Masood's wide amber eyes. His gorilla mouth gaped open as though this was the most thrilling show in Logris.

A high-pitched screech filled the air, and the shadow mage turned to the captain. "All the magic is coming from her right hand."

Captain Zella stepped forward and pulled down the sleeve of my prison jumpsuit. "Where did you get that bracelet?"

I turned to my wrist to find the tattoo gone. In its place was the row of firestone hearts. Each stone's interior burned with orange flames.

Hope filled my chest, and I sent Aunt Arianna a silent word of thanks. Somehow, during my meditation, it had worked its way out from under my flesh. Perhaps now, they would blame the stones for the fire that had set off the alarms.

"Who gave it to you?" asked the captain.

My tongue darted out to lick my lips. "There was a jewelry sale—"

"Where?" She stalked toward me, stopping six inches away from where her enforcers had pinned me against the wall with their magic.

"Outside Hyde Park." I choked out the words, hoping they would convince her of my innocence. "Some people put blankets on the floor and sell trinkets. I really liked the look of this bracelet because it reminded me of fire."

"That is firestone," she snarled.

I made my eyes go round and let my mouth drop open. "What's that? I thought it was a new form of citrine."

Annoyance tightened her features. "And you call yourself Istabelle Bonham-Sackville's apprentice?"

Pressing my lips together, I exhaled a ragged breath through my nostrils, not wanting to let her see my relief. Right now, I relished being underestimated as a stupid Neutral. Let her think I'd stumbled across a magical object and had activated it by accident.

Even though the adrenaline coursing through my veins had caused me to forget everything Aunt Arianna had suggested, this part of her plan might save us all from execution.

Captain Zella stepped back and flicked her head in my direction. The enforcer who had found the firestone bracelet wrapped his shadows around the stone and pulled them off my wrist.

"How could anyone have missed an item of such magical significance?" The captain turned her gaze to a small enforcer hovering by the door. "Didn't you inspect the girl while she was unconscious?"

"I did," the enforcer replied in a timid voice. "There wasn't any sign of a bracelet."

She was a blonde-haired woman a couple of years older than me. She didn't have the overwhelming beauty of a faerie or a vampire, and nothing about her magic said she was a shifter. Not all enforcers were shadow mages like Captain Zella and the four restraining me. Some were witches and others shifters.

Captain Zella turned her gaze back to the male enforcer, who ran his device over my skin. This time, the object didn't so much as beep.

"She's clean, Captain."

"Put her in another cell."

"And the order to arrest the aunt?" asked the young enforcer at the door.

Captain Zella rubbed her temples. "Bring her in for questioning."

The shadows around me loosened, and I dropped onto my hands and knees. One of the enforcers grabbed me by the scruff of my neck and shoved me in the cell on Masood's left. I turned around and placed my hands on the gap between its stone walls, already feeling the invisible barrier of magic.

My shoulders sagged, and I leaned against the magical barrier, watching the enforcers head toward the exit. With their dark glares now turned away from me, I could finally remember Aunt Arianna's instructions.

"Captain Zella?" I asked.

She glared at me over her shoulder. "What?"

"May I see Valentine?"

"He's dead."

"If you give me back that bracelet, I might be able to heal him."

Her brows rose, and she walked toward me with her hands curled into fists. "You admit to being in possession of firestone?"

I flinched, placing a hand over my chest. What was wrong with me today? I couldn't even keep my lies straight. Something hard pressed against my breastbone, giving me another idea.

"Sorry," I murmured. "After what happened, I'd give anything to see him once more."

Captain Zella snorted. "After your execution, you'll have all eternity to beg for his forgiveness."

She strolled out of the room, leaving me staring at her back.

"Psst," said Masood. "Was that true?"

"What?"

"Buying a firestone bracelet from a peddler?"

"Yes."

He barked a laugh. "It was a lie."

I shook my head and reached into the neckline of my prison uniform. The bracelet wasn't the only thing my magical flare had unearthed. When Valentine had returned my engagement ring and asked me to wear it around my neck, I hadn't imagined it would also soak into my body.

Wrapping my fingers around the diamond of Valentine's engagement ring, I inhaled rapid, excited breaths.

If what Valentine had said about the stone being enchanted with calling magic was true, then I might be able to use my power to find him. Powerful immortals didn't always use the stones to summon their slaves. Sometimes, the slaves could use the stone to appear before their masters.

For example, a slave sent across the Supernatural World to perform an urgent task might be able to inform their master that they had completed it, and have the master return them in an instant.

I glanced down at a cut on my arm and dipped the ring into the exposed blood. Even though I couldn't harness my own magic, Neutral blood held power, and Istabelle had spent the best part of three years teaching me how to manipulate the magic of crystals.

With the right stone and the right amount of concentration, I could access memories, protect myself from psychic attacks, attract love, and heal others. But now, all I had was a full body of blood and a gut full of determination. Instead of pushing the magic out of my body the way we had practiced at the academy with grovers, I held it inside and focused on my heart.

Valentine's face appeared in my mind's eye. Not the cruel, exasperated expressions he had pulled on the palace steps or the arrogant smirks from when he had approached me in London.

I saw the real Valentine. The man who had risked everything to smuggle out a girl with forbidden power, the king willing to give up his life so that a Neutral could continue living.

Emotion swirled in my chest, and tears stung my eyes. I focused on the love I'd held for Valentine that I couldn't suppress, even after three years of trying. It had been as futile as trying not to love myself. Valentine was in my heart, my veins, my soul. He had shaped my personality, transforming me from someone who hated being a Neutral to someone who found things to love about myself.

I loved Valentine without reservation, and I needed to be at his side. Now.

Cool air swirled through my hair, and bright light from the ceiling stopped streaming through my eyelids. I inhaled a breath, filling my nostrils with the faint scent of mildew, burned plastic, and cold, wet stone.

My eyes snapped open. I stood within what appeared to be a room within a museum with floors of gray marble, arched alcoves and dozens of raised plinths, each with lifelike statues of people lying with their arms crossed over their chests.

A breath caught in the back of my throat. I wasn't sure if it was the call stone or my fire magic or both, but I was sure as hell glad to have escaped the prison's wards.

I walked around the room's perimeter, taking in mosaics, stone statues, frescoes that belonged in places like the Sistine Chapel. Was this where they were keeping Valentine?

Flaming torches stood within iron sconces, illuminating a rectangular space of about a hundred by fifty feet. The silence in the room was so absolute that it muffled my footsteps. The diamond call stone wouldn't have taken me here for no reason, so where was he?

At the furthest corner of the room was a rectangular plinth that held the statue of a dark-skinned man whose hair seemed to meld with the shadows. Somehow, the artist had even captured his sweeping black lashes. I placed a hand on its cheek, and flesh yielded under my fingertips.

Cold shock barreled through my gut. I staggered back toward the nearest wall sconce and stared down at my fingers. That hadn't been a statue—it had been a vampire, and what I thought was stone was a layer of dust over his face.

My heartbeat accelerated, and I clenched my teeth. Recent events had addled my brain. This was no museum. It was a bloody mausoleum. All the time I spent looking for Valentine, and I'd probably walked past him.

I jogged around the plinths, giving each devastatingly beautiful vampire a glance before moving on to the next. They weren't exactly corpses—these were ancients whose souls had transcended to other realms. Former kings and queens and princes and princesses—Valentine's ancestors from the Royal House of Sargon. At any time, they could travel back to their bodies and take their positions within vampire society.

After stumbling past a dark-haired woman with Valentine's cupid's bow lips, I found him—the only body that looked like a corpse. Every molecule of air escaped my lungs in a stunned breath, and I clapped a hand over my mouth.

The color had leached from his skin, leaving a grayish pallor completely devoid of vitality. I lowered a trembling hand to his cheek, finding it cold and hard, rather than the tepid softness of his darker-skinned ancestor.

A sob caught in the back of my throat. He was really dead and not transcended. His soul had separated from his body and moved on. I swept my gaze down his form, over a tailored black jacket with a matching shirt and a tie so dark that it reflected only the barest of light.

"Valentine," I whispered. "Please, forgive me."

Aunt Arianna's voice drifted back to the forefront of my memory. I wasn't just a wielder of fire. I had phoenix flames. Flames that could burn him to ashes and make him arise alive and renewed.

"Sorry about this." I placed a hand over his heart, and my fingernails brushed against something hard and metallic. My brows deepened into a frown. "What on earth is that?"

My throat dried. If this was a plaque or a vampire equivalent of a gravestone, burning it in my fire might mingle these foreign bodies with his new, awakened form. Whispering another apology, I unfastened the buttons of his shirt, exposing his dull flesh.

A raised incision spread down his center, from his collarbone to the end of his breastbone, held together by rough stitches. Protruding from the middle of his chest was a metal stake with a flattened cap the diameter of a teacup.

"No," I cried.

I remembered something I had read in Istabelle's library—the passage I'd read about preternatural vampires and putrefying hearts. Now that I knew that a fire user like Kresnik could revive a corpse with his magic, the information I'd read seemed like superstitious garbage.

They had violated Valentine's body for nothing. They'd not only removed his heart but secured him to the stone plinth, thinking that would stop him from rising as a preternatural. I ran my fingers down his belly, his arms, his legs, searching for more of those terrible stakes and found one at each ankle.

My chest tightened, as did the muscles of my throat. My sinuses burned with a mix of grief and rage. Tears spilled down my cheeks, soaking into the fabric of his pants.

"How could they do this to you?" I sobbed. "Valentine, I'm so sorry."

A voice in my head told me that now was not the time to fall apart. Valentine needed me, and crying over his desecrated corpse wouldn't regenerate his body or bring him back from the afterlife.

With a deep breath, I pushed down those feelings into the pit of my belly and readied myself.

"This might hurt." I wrapped my fingers around one of the stakes on his ankles and pulled.

Nothing happened.

"Bloody hell," I muttered. Whoever fixed him to this lump of stone must have had the strength of a vampire.

The scraping of stone on stone echoed across the mausoleum's walls, and panic imploded through my chest. I dropped to my hands and knees and crawled away from Valentine's raised plinth.

"There's no way he is ever going to rise from the dead," said a haughty male voice. "Not after we took all those precautions."

"One can never be sure with preternaturals," muttered another voice. "It's not like anyone who fought Father lived to report back how they managed to defeat him."

"I still think we should have cremated Valentine," a third voice added. "He would rather be annihilated than rise as one of those monsters."

"Perhaps we should," said the second voice. "It's better that his soul roams free than becomes trapped in an abomination."

I held my breath, silently pleading with the men to return to the palace and leave Valentine alone. These were his brothers, who hadn't been at the Supernatural Council meeting because they'd been guarding his corpse.

The three princes continued to argue about whether it was right to keep Valentine in this terrible state, and they gathered around his body.

"You see his clothes?" said the second voice. I peered around the corner to find it belonged to Ferdinand, Valentine's red-haired brother. "He's trying to free himself."

A palpitation squeezed my heart. In a moment, they'd work out what I'd done and find me hiding on the other side of the plinth.

"No, he isn't," the first voice said. It was Constantine, Valentine's blond-haired brother. "Someone probably came inside and became curious."

"So they undressed the King of the Vampires, leaving him in this disheveled state?" asked Lazarus. He was the brother with mahogany hair several shades lighter than Valentine's. "I told you to encase him in a sarcophagus."

As the argument continued, I exhaled a long breath but not before I realized that only three of Valentine's brothers were here. What happened to the fourth? If he hadn't been at the Supernatural Council and wasn't here guarding the mausoleum, where on earth was he and what was he doing?

"You three are idiots," said the fourth voice, which belonged to Sylvester. He was the oldest of Valentine's younger brothers with hair the exact shade of silver coins. "Why on earth would you argue over the state of a corpse, in the presence of something that smells so delicious?"

Every ounce of blood trickled down from my face and settled into my frantic heart.

The curse.

The blood lure.

I was still under the influence of the curse that had caused Valentine to set upon me like a rabid leech. Now, I was trapped in a mausoleum with four vampires who not only hated me for killing their brother but likely couldn't resist my blood.

"We can smell it, too," Constantine snapped.

"Unlike you, I prefer to let my wine breathe," said Ferdinand.

Lazarus chuckled, although the sound contained more cruelty than mirth. "We wanted her to calm before we began the hunt."

CHAPTER TWENTY-FOUR

I crouched behind the stone plinth, unable to move, unable to breathe, unable to think about anything else but the four vampires who had caught my scent. Four vampires who had two compelling reasons to murder me in this mausoleum and leave my bones to rot.

Not only did they think I had killed their older brother and king, the wretched curse still snaking around my leg made my blood irresistible to their kind.

"Where are you?" Constantine whispered, his voice grating along my nerve endings.

Lazarus chuckled, the sound low and deep. "It's not exactly going to tell you its location."

"I don't know about you, but I intend to get the first bite," said Ferdinand.

Placing a hand over my mouth, I tried to muffle

my ragged breaths. Maybe if I got my fire to flare, it might deter them the way it did when I successfully fought off Valentine the first two times.

Regret washed over me like a tidal wave. All that time in the cell, I'd been so focused on getting out when I should have spared a thought for the curse. Now, I was going to die at the fangs of Valentine's brothers.

Raised voices echoed across the room as the brothers talked about my enticing scent and what they would do to me when they found where I was hiding.

My pulse pounded so loud, it muffled some of their more gruesome suggestions and gave me the courage to glance over my shoulder. Six feet away stood a statue of a woman wearing a medieval-style gown with her arms outstretched. She stood within one of the mausoleum's many arched alcoves on a four-foot-high podium.

I bit down on my lip. That would be a better hiding place than behind this stone plinth. Glancing from left to right, I found Constantine and Lazarus inspecting a sarcophagus with their backs turned to me.

With all the stealth I could muster, I crawled on my hands and knees to the statue and squeezed myself into the narrow spot behind the alcove's back wall and its stone podium.

A gust of wind swirled through the mausoleum,

skimming my hiding place. I froze, not knowing what effect it would have on the brothers hunting me.

"Did you smell that?" asked Ferdinand.

"It just scuttled out through the door," replied Constantine.

Lazarus' gleeful laugh filled the mausoleum. "Then the hunt is on."

Loud footsteps echoed across the vast space as the brothers jogged toward the exit. I clenched my teeth. They were drawing out the hunt, running slowly on purpose to give their supposed prey time to escape. If they wanted, a mature vampire could catch even the fastest cheetah.

The stone door scraped across the floor and slammed shut with a resounding thud. I leaned against the stone, exhaling the longest breath and thanking every deity imaginable for that miraculous gust of wind.

Maybe this time, I should gather my flames before stepping out of my hiding place? That gust of wind would dissipate soon, and the brothers would probably return to retrace my scent. I breathed hard, trying to get my heart to calm.

After a slow count of a hundred, I focused on channeling my magic to my hands, and a soft glow shone from my palms.

I poked my head out from behind the statue to check the mausoleum was really empty. This time, when I saw Valentine, I wouldn't speak or cry out to alert the brothers. I would focus on pushing more of my power into my hands and curing him. But first, I needed to get rid of the curse.

After spreading my glowing hands over my exposed leg, the thick, black mark on my flesh faded to gray and then disappeared. Triumph flared in my chest. I was one step closer to healing Valentine.

With tentative steps, I slipped out from behind the statue and headed back to where Valentine lay. The air was still, and fresher than it had been before the brothers had entered, and I inhaled several deep, calming breaths. After passing a few transcended vampires, I found the stone plinth that held Valentine's corpse.

He was still unmoving, still gray, and still dead.

A wave of anguish crashed through my chest, stinging the backs of my eyes. I pressed a hand to my mouth, stifling tears. No matter how many times I got to see him, it would always be disturbing—the cruel end to a man who had loved me, protected me. A man who had sacrificed his life for mine.

I shook off those thoughts, inhaled a deep breath, and placed my palm directly on the metal rod embedded in Valentine's chest. Maybe a bit of heat could melt the metal enough for me to lift it out from where it had been driven into the stone.

"What are you doing?" asked a haughty voice on my left.

Cold shock barreled into my gut. I spun to find Constantine glowering at me, his eyes a deep crimson. "What are you—"

"Isn't it bad enough that you killed my brother?" he sneered.

"It's not what you think." I took a step back and bumped into a hard body.

Strong arms wrapped around my waist. I twisted my head and glowered into the red eyes of Ferdinand, who grinned at me with his fangs extended.

"You smell delicious," he purred.

"What?" I glanced down at my leg to find the curse had returned. "This isn't really my scent. It's a curse—"

"But a blessing for us," Constantine said with a chuckle. The blond-haired vampire swaggered toward me, also baring his fangs. "Those bastards on the Supernatural Council wouldn't let us interrogate you. They cared more about suppressing a potential fire wielder than avenging the death of one of their fellow monarchs."

My throat dried, and I parted my lips to sputter out a plea for mercy, but the air shifted, and Sylvester appeared, his handsome features a mask of hatred.

Out of the four brothers, he looked the most like Valentine, with the same full lips with a deep cupid's bow, but his silver hair and eyes were in stark contrast to Valentine's. "At least we understand why Valentine was so fixated on a Neutral and why he didn't take another lover after he discarded you."

I pressed my lips together, not daring to contradict the oldest of Valentine's brothers.

Lazarus was the last to arrive, casting his gaze up and down my body with a feral grin. "What I don't understand is why our brother ever relinquished such a delicious-smelling morsel."

My pulse fluttered in my throat like a trapped moth. If I didn't flare out my fire and scare these vampires with a demonstration of my power, they would tire of frightening me and start feeding.

I pushed my magic down my arms, making my palms glow. "Wait!"

Lazarus gave me a slow, sarcastic clap. "Congratulations," he murmured. "It seems that you're something other than a Neutral."

The corner of Sylvester's lips curled into the barest trace of a smile. "What a pity you'll never get a chance to develop that power."

"Valentine wouldn't have wanted this." The words blurted from my lips as I waved my glowing palms. "He came to London to protect me—"

"More fool him," said Lazarus. "He should have drained your worthless body and left you an exsanguinated corpse."

"Which is exactly what we're going to do to you," said Constantine.

I struggled in Ferdinand's arms, but the vampire's

grip was immovable. He rubbed the tip of his nose against my neck, filling my ears with his harsh laughter.

"We will do nothing of the sort," said Sylvester.

"Don't tell me you want to hand her over to the Supernatural Council?" Ferdinand snarled.

Sylvester shook his head. "I say we keep her in the palace as a blood cow."

Lazarus snorted. "I say we drain her right here and burn her when we cremate Valentine."

The brothers continued arguing about what to do with me, Sylvester and Ferdinand wanting to keep me alive for an eternity of suffering, and Lazarus and Constantine wanting to drink me right here before the Supernatural Council discovered I'd escaped from my cell.

Ferdinand's lips grazed my neck, making all the fine hairs on the back of my neck stand on end. Right now, the brothers were clear-minded, but if any of them so much as got a taste of my accursed blood, they would all set upon me like leeches.

"I can restore Valentine," I shouted over their discussion.

The three brothers turned to me, and Ferdinand drew back from my neck.

"What did you say?" asked Lazarus.

"Valentine sent me away because he noticed I was having power flares and would probably develop into fire magic." The words tumbled out of my mouth. "I have phoenix flames. If you let me burn his corpse with my magic, a new Valentine will emerge from the ashes."

Lazarus scoffed. "Some people will say anything to stay alive."

Ferdinand's arms around my waist tightened, pulling me into his hard body. The red-haired vampire snarled, and my chest exploded with a flare of panic.

"It's true," I said in a high-pitched squeal. "Just look at my hands."

Ferdinand loosened his grip and held me with one arm. With his free hand, he grabbed my right wrist and jerked out my arm, making my palm face upward. "That's not fire."

Lazarus bent down and sniffed. "It's more like heat or light."

"So, she's a light mage, pretending to have fire," Constantine drawled. "We should definitely kill her right now for her insolence."

"No," I yelped.

Sylvester's lips thinned. "Alright then. Lay her on a stone, and we'll divide her into quarters. Two at the jugular and two at the femoral."

Ferdinand hesitated for a few seconds before lifting me into his arms and carrying me across the room toward an empty plinth. The other brothers walked behind us, speaking in low voices. Blood roared between my ears, and my pulse raced so loud and fast that the beats mingled into each other to make a continuous sound.

"Please, don't do this," I screamed.

Whatever Ferdinand replied was muffled by the sounds of my panic. He lowered me onto a cold stone plinth and pressed a gentle hand on my belly to keep me in place.

I yelled and kicked and screamed, glaring up at four handsome faces—Constantine snarling, Lazarus smiling, Ferdinand salivating, and Sylvester staring down at me with cold disdain. Each of them carried features in common with Valentine that broke my heart.

They continued staring down at me, unmoving, letting my panic heighten until it burned itself out, and my limbs slumped onto the now-warm stone. My heart thrummed a sluggish beat of exhausted resignation to match my numb defeat. I swallowed, my throat hoarse from screaming.

"Good girl," Ferdinand whispered, his voice clipped by his extended fangs. "That shot of adrenaline will make you taste all the sweeter."

"Right jugular." Sylvester moved to my right side.

Lazarus moved to my left and grabbed my leg. "Left femoral."

Constantine claimed the right femoral, and Ferdinand claimed the left jugular. I stared at the mausoleum's painted ceiling of robed beings, hoping my death would be painless. Only one vampire had ever bitten me, and I was about to be besieged by four.

"Make it quick," I murmured. "Please."

"Once we've drained you to the brink of death, we'll take you to our personal physician, who will arrange for donors to restore you to health," Constantine murmured in my ear, his warm breath fanning against my skin and making me cringe. "You'll wish you'd never murdered my brother."

"Bon appétit," said Sylvester.

A cold gust of wind whistled through the mausoleum, knocking all four brothers to the ground. I tried to raise my head, but the force of the wind kept me pinned to the stone. Fresh terror trickled down my spine. Had the enforcers tracked me down already?

Constantine's prone body spiraled into the air, his arms and legs outstretched. The wind spun him around before hurling him the width of the space and into the statue I had used as a hiding place. I sucked in a breath through my teeth. This was the work of an air mage or an extremely powerful witch.

Hope filled my chest as I clung to the edges of the stone plinth, letting my savior lift each brother one-by-one off the ground and into a wall or a pillar or the ceiling. Debris and plaster flew within the whirlwind of power, and the air shook with a low howl.

My heart thrummed hard enough to make my rib cage vibrate. Whoever was behind this magic wanted to punish Valentine's brothers. Who else could it be but Aunt Arianna? She was the only person who would know exactly where I needed to go. Long, even breaths heaved in and out of my lungs. I was safe, and best of all, this was my chance to carry out our plan to restore Valentine.

The wind stopped, and the brother at the ceiling fell to the ground in a cloud of dust. I raised myself off the plinth and dropped to the marble floor, not waiting for the air to settle.

A low voice groaned, and my heart somersaulted within my chest. That wind had only slowed the brothers. In a moment, they would rise and try to drink my blood again.

I sprinted across the mausoleum floor, passing empty plinths where the transcended vampires had been blown off their resting places. My boots crunched on broken plaster and debris from the whirlwind.

There was absolutely no way I could muster up enough power in time to burn Valentine before the brothers attacked. Only Valentine remained on his plinth, as his brothers or the Supernatural Council had secured his body to the stone with metal stakes.

As I passed Valentine's corpse, I sent him a silent apology and promised to return. My experience with his brothers just proved me incapable of generating the magic to overpower the firestone Aunt Arianna had infused in my blood.

The stone door of the crypt now gaped open, and I raced toward it. Whoever had saved me hadn't shown themselves and was either waiting for me outside or close but invisible.

Constantine appeared between me and the door. "What did you do?"

My feet skidded to a halt, and I raised my glowing palms, making him flinch. "Stay away."

"What are you, an air mage?" asked Lazarus from behind.

I spun, putting an equal amount of distance between myself and both brothers. "Do you want me to blast you again?" I injected as much conviction into my voice as I could, hoping they would mistake me for my mysterious savior. "Take one step toward me, and I'll slit your throats."

"Careful, girl," said Sylvester from the other side of the mausoleum. "You're already under a death sentence for murdering our brother."

"And I told you I could bring him to life with my magic," I shouted.

"As a preternatural vampire?" Lazarus rose from behind a plinth and stalked toward me, all traces of levity on his usually cheerful features gone. "I'll kill you—"

A blur whizzed behind Lazarus, throwing him into the ceiling. It struck out at Sylvester next, then Ferdinand, and then Constantine.

I turned to the door to make my escape, but

bumped into a cold, hard body. When I tilted my head up, it was to look into the blazing red eyes of Valentine's gray corpse.

Every muscle on my bones turned to sludge, and I collapsed onto my knees, hitting the grainy floor with a cry.

Valentine had just risen as one of the undead.

He was a dangerous preternatural vampire.

END OF BOOK ONE
READ BOOK TWO

NIGHT OF THE VAMPIRE KING

Join Bella's mailing list for a free copy of Night of the Vampire King, a Blood Fire Saga story featuring more of Mera and Valentine!

http://www.bellaklausbooks.com/

Join Bella's Facebook group for teasers of upcoming books:

http://www.bellaklaus.com/facebook/

READ BOOK TWO

Printed in Great Britain
by Amazon